D1535415

Panda Books

The Obsessed

Liu Heng was born in Beijing in 1954. In his early years he studied Russian in the middle school attached to the Beijing Foreign Languages Institute. Then he served in the Chinese Navy and upon demobilization became a worker in the Beijing Motor Factory. In 1979 he became an editor of *Beijing Literature* and began to publish stories and novels, of which *Black Snow* and *The Obsessed* have been filmed. His short story "Grain" won a prize in a national competition. His work has been translated into many foreign languages.

The Obsessed

Liu Heng

Translated by David Kwan

Panda Books

Panda Books
First Edition 1991
Second Printing 1994
Copyright 1991 by CHINESE LITERATURE PRESS
ISBN 7-5071-0072-3
ISBN 0-8351-2083-X

Published by CHINESE LITERATURE PRESS
Beijing 100037, China
Distributed by China International Book Trading Corporation
35 Chegongzhuang Xilu, Beijing 100044, China
P.O. Box 399, Beijing, China
Printed in the People's Republic of China

CONTENTS

Preface

Li Ziyun

LIU Heng is one of the outstanding young Chinese writers to emerge in the last two years. He and several other young writers have been responsible for the popularity of new realism in Chinese writing. However, his works are the most influential.

Since 1979 Chinese literature has seen a number of dramatic changes. Since the 20's modern Chinese literature with a traditional base was modelled after French and Russian critical realism of the 18th and 19th centuries. Then the Soviet Union's literature exerted a huge influence on it. After the establishment of the People's Republic, the government modified the Russian principles of socialist realism into revolutionary realism and romantic revolutionary realism. These became the tenets of creative writing. Although the word "realism" was used, this form of writing no longer magnified life or reflected the times. Over a long period it became a means of disseminating policy and clouding issues. Only a few works were able to portray life more or less factually. During this historic period, China was cut off from any cultural exchange with the West. Chinese authors were only exposed to Russian and Eastern European writers. As a consequence the only available model was again, realism. Therefore, their best works belong to that genre.

After 1979, opening to the West and reforms brought a great influx of Western writings. A great variety of modern Western literature that was barred from China became available. Stream of consciousness, the new novel, absurdism, surrealism and fantasy were a complete departure from the critical realism of 18th and 19th century, or for that matter, Russian literature. A new era had begun. China's policy in regard to literature also underwent a change. The government no longer insisted that literature must be subservient to politics, and be its mouth-piece. Nor did it insist any longer that the only acceptable means of expression had to satisfy both the needs of politics and literature. Furthermore, it no longer dictated what and how to write. Writers were given more freedom to select subjects and explore new ways of expression. They were thinking and choosing. Many schools of writing appeared.

Of course, some writers stuck to traditional realism. These were men with a social conscience, who were influenced by classical and modern Chinese literature. The axiom that writing must have universal appeal and express the cares of the masses remained. By exposing social ills they became the voice of the people. Many of these writers also adapted certain Western conventions according to their needs.

However, newer writers, impatient with traditional ways which they considered behind the times, experimented with new techniques. Their works can be grouped into two categories. The first is what is called the "root school" of writing. This is quite different from the Western notion of searching for personal roots. Instead it probed the origins of culture. More particularly, it searched for the effect of tradition on the formation of Chinese character. This school of writing is clearly influenced by Western modernism. Stylistically, it utilises symbolism and allegory, and often certain philosophies as well. It also brought about a sub-genre concerned mainly with exposing primitive customs of remote places. The first category was often too subjective, while the latter pandered to sensationalism. Readers quickly lost interest. The appearance of another form of realism followed. A number of young writers who came into contact with modern Western literature became dazzled by bold new techniques which they had never encountered before. Also, since the reform and opening to the West, changes took place in Chinese society. Traditional life styles, values and mores were questioned. Many people, particularly the young became confused. They found they could relate to certain feelings expressed in modern Western literature. Therefore they were eager to adopt them as their own. Actually they did not produce much of value, because of the basic difference between Western and Chinese society.

China is still backward socially and culturally. The lifestyle of most people, their psychology, concerns and interests are quite different from their Western counterparts. The modernist works that appeared were mostly pale imitations of Western styles of expression, thoughts and feelings. There is little that is individual and sincere. Also many writers strove for a fragmented style of narration by deliberately shattering the form and meaning of language. These works were a different fare from that which readers were used to. Although they were popular for a time, they quickly palled.

Chinese literature sank once more into the doldrums. It was during this period that new realism appeared. The school of new realism began in 1986 with the works of Chi Li and Fang Fang and came to fruition with Liu Heng. Chi Li and Fang Fang did not probe deep into the human psyche, or use the sub-conscious as their spring board. Instead their feet were firmly planted in the realities of society, and they stared unblinking at the human condition. Its main difference from traditional realism is that it does not aim to create typical characters and settings. Insteads it focuses on everyman and ordinary events. Their characters are not limned in stark black and white, but mostly in shades of grey. Plots are not developed to their logical conclusion through cause and effect. They strive for naturalism by avoiding any appearance of refinement in their language, and deliberately present life in all its triviality, as a mirror in which the reader may examine his own life. These techniques have roused the empathy of many readers.

These characteristics first appeared in Chi Li's "A Troubled Life" and Fang Fang's "View." Liu Heng has gone a step further in his novels. In "A Troubled Life" Chi Li deliberately adopted a monotonous tone in describing the day to day activities of an ordinary labourer. The narrator in Fang Fang's "View" is the spirit of a dead child. It is through the dead child's eyes that the reader sees the struggles of the parents and nine siblings , crammed into a thirteen square metre shack.

If the straight-forward narrative form of "A Troubled Life" and "View" roused the reader to ponder the value of human life, the works of Liu Heng explore that theme in greater depth. By showing what lies behind the facade, he reveals the soul of his characters as they strive for basic human rights, and self esteeem, and what precipitates their failure, or drives them to destruction.

"Damned Food" which brought recognition to Liu Heng and the top award for short fiction 1985-86, and "The Obsessed" may be cited as sister works. In them Liu Heng dispassionately examines the plight of two farmers of Floodwater Canyon as they deal with the basic problems of sustaining and propagating life. Through these stories we see that in remote areas a segment of the rural population live in near primeval conditions.

The title "Damned Food" comes from rural colloquialism, and signifies the average farmer's anxiety over a commodity so precious that it colours consideration of such emotions as love and hate. The woman, nicknamed Goitre because of her affliction, is sold to the farmer Yang Tiankuan for two hundred catties of grain. She is strong and cunning. She can do the work of a man, and she is not above stealing and conniving. Before long she is the family's main support. Even her husband defers to her. Her downfall comes when she loses the family's grain ration coupon. Suddenly the family is plunged into crisis. For without the coupon they are faced with starvation. Her position in the household plummets. Finally she is driven to suicide. Her last ironic words are, "Damned food!" The story is simply and powerfully told, and hammers home the idea that life is worth no more than two hundred catties of grain, or a lost ration coupon.

"The Obsessed" is a tragedy that evolves around the question of sex in a poor rural family. It becomes clear from the outset that it is the driving force of the narrative. Yang Jinshan who is unable to father a child proceeds to perpetrate sexual sadism on his bride Wang Judou as soon as they are married. His cruelty increases as impotence overtakes him. A third member of the household is his nephew, Tianqing, who is first shocked then angered by his uncle's obsession. In the end the two young people fall in love. Liu Heng does not treat this as an ordinary tale of illicit love. On the contrary, he shows how the restrictions of a closed society, and its mores, turn a joyful experience into pain, suffering and death. When Yang Jinshan discovers the illicit love between his wife and nephew he first attempts to kill her, and her son Tianbai, then attempts suicide. He too is a victim of circumstance. Judou and Tianqing are terrified of being discovered while Jinshan is alive. However, his death does not bring surcease. Without Jinshan's presence to shield them, their predicament deepens. The pressure on the lovers comes from within, instead of from any external forces. The guilt and fear arising from incest is deepened by Tianbai's refusal to accept his natural father. Worse still, he adopts his surrogate father's sharp, cruel and suspicious attitude which eventually drives Tianqing to suicide. His son becomes judge and executioner. In these two stories Liu Heng details the high price people in remote areas sometimes pay for the basic necessities of life; food, and the right to a normal sex life.

"Whirlpool" and "Unreliable Witness" deal with intellectuals. The protagonists, Zhou Zhaolu of "Whirlpool" and Guo Puyun of "Unreliable Witness" have satisfied the basic needs of life. Compared with Goitre and Tianqing they are well off, although Guo Puyun may have certain psychological and sexual difficulties. However, he is attractive to women and is passionately pursued. Liu Heng again questions the value and meaning of life in these works.

Zhou Zhaolu in "Whirlpool" is a success. He has a happy home. He is the epitome of the complacent intellectual. Zhou Zhaolu is a lucky man on the surface. He has pulled himself out of an impoverished rural background, went to a key university, became a researcher in an important institution, and finally rises to be its vice president. What propelled him to success? As Liu Heng describes him, Zhou Zhaolu is not only well equipped for his job, he has a keen sense for opportunity and a chameleon-like ability of adapting to his environment. He has a way with people: deferential and careful with higher-ups, and thoughtful toward subordinates. Although he is aware of the restrictions of the prevailing mores, he falls in love and strays from the straight and narrow. However, he does not allow it to get in the way of his upward mobility. The question that Liu Heng poses is how far should a man suppress personal desires and emotions to create a self image that will meet with the approval of others. The novel not only bares the soul of a hypocrite, but more importantly, asks whether people such as Zhou Zhaolu are successful human beings.

This theme is extended through "Unreliable Witness", which probes the causes of the suicide of an intellectual dis-satisfied with his circumstances. The life of Guo Puyun is not as unlucky as he thinks it. The things that Zhou Zhaolu strove for do not interest him. He craves things he cannot have. He laments not being a professional dancer; he envies his friend's success as a painter; he wants to write poetry. On closer examination, all these things are pipe-dreams. He does not have the necessary talents, nor does he have the tenacity for success, and a firm goal. In fact he does not know what he wants. His inability to find the meaning and value of life is due to his lack of direction. Instead he sees himself as cursed. He missed being admitted to a key university because of six marks; his painting did not bring success; an accident scarred his face. Most of all he was cursed with impotence. Each was a blow that weakened his will to live, until it drove him over the brink. In fact the curse that dogged him was an excuse to avoid realities. He needed a crutch to prop himself up, which he was too weak to find. The purpose of life eluded him to the end.

The unifying theme of these works by Liu Heng is the value and meaning of life. These themes expressed in terms of modernism and new realism, are quite different from the social concerns found in the traditional realism. Stylistically Liu Heng is constantly changing. In "Whirlpool" and "Unreliable Witness" there is a tendency toward repetition, and convoluted sentence structures. Structurally they are less successful than "Damned Food" and "The Obsessed". But in these defects we can see that as a writer, Liu Heng is not standing still. There is evidence that he was influenced by the styles of the investigative and psycoanalytic novel. By using a third person to probe the death of Guo Puyun, and telling the story in fragmented flash backs he has moved away from the investigative novel which requires proof at the end. Instead through an objective sifting of motives he has produced a fascinating if inconclusive testament of a blighted life. This treatment has brought the character's psyche and the central theme of the piece to vivid life. Liu Heng and his new realism can be expected to rise to new heights in the future.

The Obsessed

YANG Jinshan's wedding day was late in the autumn of 1944, before the first frost heralded the onset of winter. The date had been fixed by a necromancer after much judicious head-shaking. Indeed the day had dawned gloriously. Yang Jinshan climbed on his black mule, and accompanied by his sixteen year old nephew Yang Tianqing riding a borrowed donkey, headed up the mountain track to Shijia Village to fetch the bride. Yang Jinshan swayed with the plodding gait of the mule, his wide-brimmed hat sat on his head like an overturned lampshade. The Nephew's head had been carefully shaved for the occasion, and gleamed white and vigorous with the joy of youth in the brisk wind of autumn. By the time they gained the jagged ridge of the mountain, clouds began to drift in. The golden disc of the sun swam through the ragged shreds of morning cloud like egg swirling in pumpkin soup. As men and beasts disappeared beyond the ridge, the sun vanished behind dark clouds. The wind was dank. At noon it began to rain. Tentatively at first, as an old man's piss; then gathering force, and finally pelting down. The valley was filled with the sound of rain. The wedding guests scattered for shelter to their own homes. Only a few die-hards remained huddled under the eaves puffing on their pipes. The talk turned to the bride. It was rumoured that the second daughter of Pock-mark Wang of Shijia Village was a beauty. Though no one had actually seen her, the gossips quickly made a juicy morsel of her. They pronounced, sourly, that she was too good to be wasted on Yang Jinshan who was just a shade short of fifty. Not that he was unworthy, mind you. It was his good luck they resented. For without his thirty *mu* of land on the hill he would not have rated a backward glance from a mangy ewe. For it was generally thought that Yang Jinshan was lacking in manhood. And the best proof of it was that he had thrashed about on the *kang* with a wife for nearly thirty years and produced nothing. However, the Japanese ended that problem for him. The day they swept through Floodwater Canyon, Yang's first wife was cutting hay in the sesame fields on Loma Ridge. A Japanese bullet ended the life of the sweaty, baren woman whom some thought was a Communist guerrilla. Since then the small land-owner, Yang Jinshan was obsessed with making a child. That explained his fascination with young women.

Wang Judou was a pretty woman of twenty. She had a small oval face, and her long slender body was as straight and supple as a poplar tree. She guided the donkey down the steep mountain track with the pressure of her firm long thighs. Her red jacket glowed like a non-extinguishable flame in the pelting rain. Her wet, glossy black hair shone like the embers of a charcoal fire.

Yang Jinshan was impatient to begin his enterprise. Had his young nephew not been in the way, he would have risen from his mule like a great eagle, seized the woman and accomplished his purpose there and then.

"Tianqing, take good care of your Aunt!"

Tianqing stumbled along, slipping in the mud between the donkey and the mule. He stroked the donkey's rear with a tree branch, not so much to urge it on, as out of a deep and mysterious boredom. And the donkey flicked its tail at the touch of the branch. The fleeting sight of the animal's elementary organs was strangely disturbing yet fascinating. Tianqing was numb; mired in reverie; beset by emotions he did not understand.

The track took a sharp downward turn. The donkey stumbled, and Yang Jinshan became concerned.

"Tianqing, guide the donkey by the reins."

Yang Jinshan was annoyed that the Nephew was completely unaware of possible hazard. Little did he know that the Nephew harboured the same interest in the woman as he.

Tianqing moved ahead and seized the donkey's short leather rein with one hand and its bit with the other. His hand grazed the donkey's mouth and the warm, moist touch startled him. He looked back. The face that loomed out of the rain was no longer touched with a blush of rouge as he had glimpsed it in Shijia Village. The rouge had streaked in the rain. Now it looked like a ripe pumpkin. He had the inexplicable longing to dry it with a cloth, and to cradle it tenderly in his arms. He guided the donkey blindly through the mud. Tianqing felt a great emptiness. He had become as insubstantial as a breath of cold air. The autumn rain had not only destroyed his Uncle's wedding day, it destroyed his tender, care-free heart.

"Shall we stop a while at the shrine?"

"We're already wet. Might as well press on."

"Tianqing drape my jacket over your Aunt...."

"No, don't. I'm already wet...."

The Aunt's voice was low and melodious. The Uncle fell silent. Tianqing did not look back. He was painfully aware of the sound of eight hooves and his own feet squishing through the mud, and the breath of the donkey warm on the back of his hand. The donkey's warm breath and the woman's presence made his scalp and the nape of his neck tingle.

The rain became a steady down-pour. Three miles from the stone quarry at the head of the canyon, there was a shrine that sat facing the mountain track like a huge toad with its mouth wide open. The Uncle got off the mule grumbling and lifted the woman off the donkey as carefully as a jug of oil. The Aunt dashed into the shelter of the toad's mouth and the Uncle squeezed himself in after her. Tianqing realized there was barely space left for him. The expressions on the two faces inside contradicted one another. But the Uncle's was more commanding.

"Go find some shelter in the woods. And see that the animals are properly tethered. Don't let the mule take fright."

Tianqing was not wanted. As he turned away, the Uncle came after him, tossed him a towel and clapped his felt hat on Tianqing's head. The shrine was a black pit, from which Tianqing fancied he felt the warmth of the Aunt's gaze follow him. He tethered the animals in a grove of trees a short distance away, and squatted under a tree for a while. But he was restless. Finally he found an out-crop of rocks and took shelter in a grassy hollow beneath it.

The plaintive murmur of the rain mixed with other undefined sounds held Tianqing in thrall. He thought he caught a sharp cry from the Aunt, whether of joy or anger, he could not tell. He strained to hear more, but there were no more sounds from the shadowy shrine. The cold rain drummed on.

The gods were aiding his Uncle in his mysterious enterprise. The rain had delayed the wedding ceremony but not its consummation. The evidence was quite plain to the sixteen year old Yang Tianqing when the three resumed their journey. The Aunt seemed languid. There were mud stains on the shoulders and back of her red jacket. Her rouge was smudged. Some of it had rubbed off on his Uncle's cheeks and forehead, and even the rim of his ear.

The Uncle rode complacently looking this way and that, coughing and spitting. The Aunt's hooded eyes reflected neither joy nor pain. A strange aura surrounded her. An overwhelming weariness descended upon Tianqing's strong, young body. Every foot fall of the donkey seemed to land on the back of his head and shoulders, trampling him into the slush. The donkey ambling along under the weight of the woman was better off than he.

"Damned beast, are you blind!" and "lazy good-for-nothing," Tianqing roared at the animal, his neck stiffened like an angry monkey's. The Uncle chuckled.

"Tianqing, we're late as it is. Might as well take our time...."

"Nephew, stop and rest a while...."

The Aunt's voice calmed him. He hung his head and walked on as doggedly as the animal. The Uncle had no idea what went through the younger man 's mind.

Tianqing himself did not recognize what was in his heart. He had entered Pock-mark Wang's home as happy and carefree as his Uncle. He emerged from it burdened with strange emotions he could not control. He was bewitched by the Aunt's tiny mouth, and her willowy body. In this state of mind the Uncle's words and deeds grated upon him. He vented his frustration on the donkey. It was only when he tired of bawling at the animal that he realized with a start that his venom was really directed toward the Uncle. The Uncle's uncomprehending chuckle washed over him. But he suspected that the Aunt knew his secret. Her response rippled through the donkey to the hand that held the bridle and he fell silent. Pent-up tears stung his eyes. He felt a silent bond between himself and the woman. Her glance cut into him; tiny cuts that tingled between pleasure and pain, like the cuts inflicted by the serrated leaves of the corn as he worked the fields bare-chested. Without looking back he could conjure up her red rouged cheeks. A tremour rippled through him. His thoughts made his flesh squirm like a serpent inside his clothes. In his mind he was licking the rouge from the woman 's face. He was sinking inexorably into a quagmire of desire and confusion. The sudden surge of emotion gradually dissipated. But the little donkey unwittingly roused him again. He cursed the donkey again, but this time he was really cursing himself and all the half understood things that roiled within him.

Because the mountain track was treacherous, and they had stopped to take shelter on the way, and because an important event had taken place, it was dusk before they returned to Floodwater Canyon.

The women of the neighborhood who had come to help, hurriedly laid out the food they had prepared. The guests stood or squatted on the *kang*, in the courtyard or at the edge of the fields, shovelled some cold food into their stomachs and left. A second marriage does not entail much ceremony. There was no high-spirited joshing in the wedding chamber, and a few grumbled at not being able to take advantage of the jollity to take a few liberties with the pretty bride. However, the proper niceties were observed. Usually it seldom rains in the autumn. That it rained so heavily was seen as a sign that the gods did not favour this marriage. Although many people who were there felt it, none gave voice to their sentiments. The gossips said although the bride had a pretty face, it was not a lucky one. They complained that she ate vermicelli as she would noodles. The loud slurping sounds she made were a sure sign of stupidity. It never occurred to them that she was hungry.

However, Yang Jinshan was content. The woman had spunk and a firm, strong body, quite different from the tired sack that was his first wife. His only concern was that she might drain him.

After a confusing day, Yang Tianqing crawled into his tiny side room and fell into an exhausted sleep. He slept so heavily that he was not wakened by the mule gnashing its teeth waiting to be fed, or the tumult of the old man's heavy breathing and phlegmy coughing in the next room that lasted late into the night.

A pretty young woman had ridden into Floodwater

Canyon that rainy autumn day and changed several lives. The Japanese were withdrawing from the surrounding mountains, and the Communists advancing in their wake were reducing rents and interest rates wherever they went. Yang Jinshan had been a small landowner. However, he had relinquished twenty out of his thirty *mu* of hilly land in exchange of a woman, and thus divested himself of a burden. Now he was free to concentrate on the pressing business of making a child. That day also marked the awakening of Yang Tianqing. He had fallen in love with his Aunt at first sight. Although lust flared hot and urgent he was still able to keep a rein on his emotions, and his behaviour was no different from that of any other youngster in love.

Trouble came afterwards.

Yang Tianqing had a family once. The summer when he was eleven, his father Yang Jinhe took his family up the south slope of Jade Creek to scoop out a cave dwelling and to clear some land for themselves. One evening his father sent Tianqing to borrow some grain from his Uncle Jinshan. A furious storm blew up, and he was forced to spend the night at his Uncle's. The next day, when he returned with five measures of corn meal the whole mountainside had changed. A landslide had carried the newly cleared land into the ravine. The cave dwelling had collapsed burying all within it. He was left with not so much as a tooth or a shard.

Yang Jinshan wanted to adopt the orphaned boy as his own. But the young ingrate would not accept the Uncle as father. The boy harboured a deep resentment against the man. For had the Uncle given his Father a small corner of his holding, the Father would not have been forced to court disaster seeking his own at Jade Creek. Yang Jinshan perceived this, and did not force the issue. Instead he kept the boy as a hired hand, but treated him well, only giving him tasks which he could manage without difficulty. Actually Yang Jinshan had plans for his Nephew.

Yang Jinshan did not believe that the Nephew was his only hope. He firmly believed in his own virility. He was willing to stake his entire fortune on begetting a son. And to that end he was willing to give all he had in exchange for the pert second daughter of Pockmark Wang. If necessary he would swallow her alive. After all she was only a woman. A woman was his land, to plough and scatter seed in as he chose. She was his chattel, as much as the black mule, to ride and whip and use as he pleased. She was his meat patty to seize and bite and masticate when he was hungry or greedy. He had exchanged twenty *mu* of land for a juicy morsel of female flesh and he would use her as he saw fit. Time and again he threw her on her back, and leaped on her as though he were collecting his dues. There was no need for niceties. A creditor's demands are fierce and unrelenting. He gave her countless nights of violence. There was seldom any serenity or tenderness. Even the young Nephew could see the woman was wilting rapidly. Six months passed and the woman's belly remained flat, and empty. Yang Jinshan was driven to the point of exhaustion. His body could no longer stand up to the demands to which it was put. At the climax he went limp. Spasms of coughing shook him and left him breathless. In despair he strove even harder, thrusting and grinding as though he were determined to destroy both the woman and himself.

In the eyes of the woman he had become a wild beast. But in his own mind no cruelty was excessive so long as it accomplished his purpose. His cruelty did not end on the *kang*. The woman was unpaid labour, no better than Tianqing.

Tianqing was wracked with confusion watching his young Aunt weeding the corn fields. There was genuine concern and pity, for in a sense they were birds of a feather. But at the same time the wild clamouring of a vigorous young body thundered through his veins. Behind the Uncle's back his eyes raked the young Aunt's body, fondling and caressing her hips, and thighs and seeking her secret places. The fields became a tutorless classroom in which he sought the knowledge of life. And the woman, unaware of the young man's fascination, became the book whose pages the Nephew thumbed tirelessly.

"Auntie, rest a while. I'll hoe the rest for you."

The woman smiled and stopped to rest. Tianqing felt a rush of joy. He put his back into hoing, showing off his strong young body. And the Aunt rewarded him by mopping the sweat off his brow, and holding a jug of water while he drank. At such moments Tianqing was wafted away in such a burst of joy that the monotony of the day vanished. Life was good; his Aunt and even his Uncle was good. Yang Jinshan had no inkling of what was happening. All he saw was that the Nephew was working harder than ever during the day, and did not have to be roused to feed the mule during the night. He was genuinely proud of the youngster and went about telling everyone how responsible and mature the Nephew had become. But Tianqing was pitched on the horns of dilemma, precariously balanced between joy and misery. He wanted more. Yet the confusing signals of awakening manhood were not yet fully understood. Through the long, steamy summer nights his naked body flipped as restlessly as a pancake on a hot griddle. His fingers brought fleeting relief to his swollen flesh while his brain filled with impossible fantasies day and night; fantasies that he despaired of ever becoming reality. Yet he clung to them in spite of the utter hopelessness of his situation. Despair added poignancy to his misery. He was convinced he must abandon all hope of the events and person he desired, for he dared not believe they would ever be fulfilled. The passionate fantasies of the night vanished in the light of day leaving him listless and spent. He could not meet the woman's eyes. She was enveloped in a mysterious aura that filled him with reverence and self-loathing. He discovered a small mole, like a tiny spider nestled on the nape of her neck behind her ear and was fascinated by it for half a year. Then he became obsessed with the way she turned her head when she spoke or looked at something. It had nothing to do with her anatomy. It was the way she moved, the way her slender neck curved and the slant of her shoulders one higher than the other that sent the blood rushing through him.

The mere thought of her sent a shiver through his frame as delicious as a caress, and drew from him a shuddering groan. No one recognized the changes in Yang Tianqing. He was still the loyal and gallant young fellow he had ever been. The old men of the village, lounging in the sun-light would remark that

Tianqing had put on weight one day, and comment on how tall and thin he had become the next. Only Tianqing felt himself sliding inexorably into an abyss.

Another autumn began. The Uncle ordered Tianqing to clear the smoke ducts of the *kang* in the side room. The duct had been blocked in many places and both the *kang* and the ducts had to be dug up. The digging caused the smoke chamber to collapse, leaving a hole in the wall the size of a fist. Tianqing was so intent on clearing the ash and debris out of the smoke ducts that he did not notice the hole until a sound on the other side of the wall sent the blood rushing to his head, and the muscles in his calves knotted painfully. A breathless moment passed. A solemn determination dawned in his brain. He moved with cat-like swiftness across the caved-in *kang*, and pressed a tense, white cheek against the hole in the wall like a thief about to leap on his prey. He crouched in a corner of the *kang*, motionless, hardly breathing. He felt no shame. He had to see what he craved and had been denied.

On the other side of the wall was the pig pen which also served as latrine.

The spot where one stood or squatted was beside the gate. Although the sound continued for several moments Tianqing could see nothing. It was a question of angles. The hole in the wall was in a dead corner. Only the part of the pen where the pigs were was visible. Nevertheless Tianqing stuck to his post. He twisted his body this way and that trying to gain a vantage point. Ashes and cinders fell from the broken chimney onto his face and head, turning him into a wild looking demon. The splashing sound beyond the wall finally stopped. He heard movement, then the sound of clothes being adjusted. The gate of the pen opened and light footsteps receded across the flagstones of the courtyard toward the kitchen shed. After a moment's silence, the same light, tripping footsteps came toward the side room. The woman stood on the threshold, and gazed at the dusty figure crouched in the corner of the *kang* like an idol in an abandoned temple. Tianqing had his back pressed against the wall. One leg was tucked under his buttocks. The other was stretched out at an awkward angle. The woman gave a throaty chuckle.

"What a mess this place is!"

"Auntie ... have you finished in the hemp fields?"

"No. The vines are thick and hard to cut.... Your Uncle's staying out there and wants food taken to him.... But there's no water in the urn.... Can you take a breather and fill it?"

"I'll fetch the water...."

"Rest a while first...."

"I'll fetch it now...."

"And wash while you're by the stream.   You're filthy...."

"I will...."

Tianqing did not move. Although the stiffness had gone out of his body, the wall seemed to hold him fast. The woman looked at him curiously, wondering if he was over tired. She smiled and left.   Tianqing crawled off the *kang* after carefully blocking the hole with a stone. He found a pail and ambled down to the stream. He suspected the Aunt's smile had to do with the hole in the wall, and he was choked with shame. He comforted himself with the thought that it was a universal secret not worthy of reproach. By the time he could hear the splashing of the stream the pangs of guilt and terror had left him. His mind had already reverted to splashing of another sort.

The spring bubbled through the crevices of rocks, collected in a pool the size of a millstone, and cascaded down a deep gorge. Tianqing filled the bucket then ducked his head under the mouth of the spring. The icy water made him tingle from the top of his head to the soles of his feet. He arched his head back and let out a primal scream. The water ran down his neck wetting the front and collar of his shirt. He lifted a sleeve to wipe his face, and the patch that the Aunt made, which he hardly noticed before, leaped out at him like an intricate piece of embroidery.

It was afternoon before he finally had the smoke ducts cleared. There was no time to do any other work. The repairs to the smokestack and the wall had to be left for the following day. There was still some tidying-up to do in the hemp field, and the trough for soaking the hemp needed to be dredged as well.

The Uncle and his wife left the house at first light. That day Tianqing was left alone to mend the wall. The work was not difficult but time consuming. The rocks did not fit, and the thin mud would not seal the crevices. The trowel shook so much in his trembling hand, that he very nearly sliced his hand several times. Tianqing could not keep his mind on his work. But the task was completed somehow, and he even added an individual touch to his handiwork. Inside the pig pen he fixed five wooden pegs of date wood, gathered up the rusty hoe, and a few dilapidated baskets and hung them from the pegs in a neat row. The Uncle did not find fault when he came home, but seemed well pleased with the innovation.

"Not bad at all! We ought to put up a few more pegs and hang the rest of the rubbish out to dry!"

Tianqing ducked his head. Yang Jinshan and Wang Judou both thought he was embarrassed by the praise. Little did they know it was his way of atonement.

He had deceived them both. In Tianqing's mind he had the upper hand for the time being.

Three days later, under cover of the darkness before dawn, and spurred on by a hunger he could no longer control, Yang Tianqing shifted a sack of grain that sat in the corner of the *kang* a few feet to the left. Then he shifted an identical sack a few feet to the right. He carefully tapped the adobe wall between the sacks till he found a stopper-shaped stone that was loosely wedged in the hole. The execution of his plot required great care. He did not pull the stone out at once. Besides his hunger still terrified him. The pig grunted in its pen. The cock crowed for the third time. The Aunt had not yet risen.

There was still time to reconsider. He cursed himself even as he hesitated.

Finally he worked the stopper-shaped stone loose.

A gust of autumn wind and the stench of the pig pen struck him in the face. He crawled under the covers again and lay with his arms hugging his head, thinking.

He had carefully worked out the angle of vision. That was not the problem.

Nor was he concerned about being discovered. The sacks of grain inside concealed the peep-hole. On the outside a tattered basket hid the opening.

The line of vision was framed by the ragged outline of the basket. He was quite safe. What frightened him was the conflict within himself. Was he degrading the beautiful Aunt? Would a glimpse of her nakedness bring surcease, or would it aggravate his distress? Was he permitted only to gaze on the face of the beloved, and nowhere else? Why could he not get her out of his mind? Were they bound to each other by some terrible destiny?

Tianqing questioned himself mercilessly, and excused himself eagerly.

He heard the bolt on the door of the north chamber withdrawn. There was no coughing. Clearly it was not the Uncle. Tianqing's body tensed. Breathlessly he followed her footsteps across the courtyard; listened as she unlatched the chicken coop; followed her to the kitchen shed. He heard a bunch of kindling dropped on the ground. She was moving toward the pig pen now. In a moment he heard the gate open. Finally she was at the place where one stands or squats.

Yang Tianqing could barely breathe. He felt that he was dying and his soul was seeping out of him through the soles of his feet. He dragged a quilt into the corner, and huddling under it, pressed an eye shakily to the peep-hole.

His gaze darted through the hole, passed the ragged edges of the basket, tore through the wisps of morning mist and plunged into a strange new world. He was lost in a welter of strange sensations; of light and shade, colour and texture. What could not be, was. It was destiny. Tianqing had finally opened the last and most secret chapter in the book of life. He was dazed with excitement. He sought swift release, which left him more confused than ever at his turbid body.

In the days that followed Tianqing was like a drunkard who had tossed off a jug of strong wine. His face was flushed. He dropped his eyes when anyone approached. He wandered about like a wraith, with hardly a word to anyone.

However, he worked doubly hard and seemed tireless and infinitely patient. In the day that it took Jinshan and his wife to clear a field of autumn cabbage, Tianqing had ploughed one *mu* of yams, and gathered up the stalks and leaves for the compost heap. When Jinshan drove the mule to Clear Water town with a load of autumn grain for the market, Tianqing followed with a load on his back. Jinshan and the mule arrived late in the morning, and Tianqing arrived shortly after noon. When the load he carried was weighed, it was not much less than the one the mule had carried. The Uncle bought pancakes for the Nephew. The young man's appetite was amazing. Jinshan realized with a start that the boy had become a young man who was half a head taller than himself.

He was pleased that the younger man had become gentler, more quiet, but seemed to brood. Jinshan often caught him gazing wistfully at the mountains and the sky, and concluded he was a bit daft. But as long as it did not interfere with his work, the Uncle let it go. He had no way of knowing the price the Nephew was exacting for his ignorance. Nor was he aware of the secret lurking in the side room, or the danger that stalked his most precious possession.

Tianqing drove himself to exhaustion. He slept heavily, and in his sleep ground his teeth, snored, tossed and turned, and smacked his lips. But still he seized every opportunity of renewing the secret encounters through the peep-hole. Wang Judou unwittingly obliged his fantasy with her lithe and slender body. Like the old men who went to pray at the shrine of the Mountain God, Tianqing had found a shrine at which to worship with all the fervour of his being. He had plunged into a new world of sensations. His spirit rose to new heights of awareness through the sense of sight. Hunger had led to wantoness. However, passion had in turn become a strange reverence. He finally recognized that love went beyond the clothes that draped the form of the beloved. It touched every inch of skin and every strand of hair. Tianqing's love for his Aunt had reached an intensity that was beyond the pale. It had reached a point where the existence of the Uncle was scarcely noticed.

The Japanese were defeated. Great events were happening beyond the mountains, but nothing disturbed the tranquility of Floodwater Canyon. It was a peaceful time. The Eighth Army rolling across the north ridge headed south, did not even stop at the village. The militia who came in the vanguard asked the people for food and water. Yang Jinshan told Tianqing to carry out a couple of buckets of boiled water, but he stopped the woman from supplying pancakes.

"What's the matter with you, showing off as though you were rich!"

Yang Jinshan stood by the roadside watching the strong young soldiers file passed. Finally he approached a young soldier who had stopped for a drink of water and asked, "Are the Japs really finished?"

"They're finished...."

"Are they gone?"

"They're gone...."

"Then who's coming?"

"What?"

"I asked who's coming?"

"Us."

The soldier wiped the drops from his chin, hefted his rifle and went his way.

He was a handsome lad, Jinshan thought. Had his first wife given him a son, he would have been about the same age. The pity of it was that she had been a useless thing. Had the sturdy lad been his son, he would never have permitted him to join the army. But the soldier was not his son. He had no son. He had nothing, Yang Jinshan thought sourly. He turned around just as Wang Judou reached out to touch a woman soldier's sleeve, and anger blazed from the pit of his stomach. Was that not a craven look on the woman's face? Was she not another piece of useless trash?

"Get home!" he roared. "If the food is burnt I'll have your hide."

Judou paled and scurried home. The woman soldier wondered whether she was a daughter-in-law or a daughter. It occurred to her that the man's savageness and the woman's timidness cast them in quite different roles. Theirs had to be a relationship between man and woman that was timeless and nothing could change in this primitive place.

Tianqing glared at his Uncle from the middle of the crowd. He had lost interest in the weapons of the soldiers.

The Aunt's humiliation hurt him to the quick. She was his goddess, and in his heart he railed at the Uncle for his boorishness. The seventeen year old Yang Tianqing, with his shiny bald pate was ready to leap upon the Aunt's tormentor.

"We'll see who gets whose hide," he muttered ominously.

The peaceful days ended with the land reforms. Yang Jinshan was one of those fortunate souls who benefited from disaster. He had sold off twenty *mu* of land for a second chance at marriage. Although he regretted the transaction at first, it proved to be a blessing in disguise. By divesting himself of the land, he could no longer be classified a land-owner. Then too his preoccupation with the woman, and more particularly with the son that he failed to beget caused him to neglect the small holding he had left. The farm was gradually going to seed. Now he could only be classified an upper middle class farmer. That rare stroke of luck was due to the woman. On the other hand, his father-in-law at Shijia Village reaped the wild wind. Pockmark Wang took the bundle of silver from Yang Jinshan and bought land. He put everything into the land. He lived simply; he ate simply; he watched his pennies. Just as he was prospering, he found himself turned into a vicious criminal. According to rumours from Shijia Village, the old land-owner went out of his mind the day they came to divide his land. He grabbed a shovel and attempted to guard his property. In the end he was trussed up like a chicken, hung from the chestnut tree and walloped with a carrying pole within a gasp from death. It was said that his eyes rolled so far back into his head that only the whites showed and that not a whole bone remained in his leg. The story was exaggerated, of course. Nevertheless Pock-mark Wang was soundly thrashed. Days later Wang Judou quietly went home to visit him. The old man was on the mend, and having regained his wits, raged and ranted at the middle class farmer Yang Jinshan.

"Damn it, who have I cheated? I'm the one that's been wronged ... look what you've done to me...."

Wang Judou went home, eyes red rimmed from weeping. Sensitive souls in the village heard her muffled sobs the next few nights. The first night Yang Jinshan did his best to comfort her. On the second night his patience began to wear thin. But on the third night he howled like an angry wolf.

"Useless thing, what have you to cry about! When your father kicks the bucket I'll bury him and you can howl as much as you like!"

The one most affected by her grief was the young man in the next room. Lying on his *kang* Tianqing absorbed the Uncle's curses and chewed it like cud. He did not understand his Uncle's fury at first. But as he ruminated on the angry words, he began to perceive their deeper meaning. It was indeed strange that such a beautiful body could not produce a child. It seemed even stranger that the Uncle who enjoyed all that beauty should revile her so.

There was a tearing sound and a resounding slap. Tianqing sat bolt upright. His Aunt groaned. He was sure the Uncle had struck her. In the silence that followed he imagined the Uncle was stubbornly perpetrating something vile.

"His uncle, pity me! Let me off tonight."

"Shut up ... or I'll slit you...."

"His uncle...."

"Alright! Alright! I should've known the blood line of the Yangs would end in your hands, vile monster! Had I known, I would've exchanged that twenty *mu* of land for a dog ... a mule or a goat ... and been better off!"

"His uncle...."

"Damn it, are you determined to end my bloodline? Even though I'm almost buried up to my neck I can still destroy you. Dearest ... give me some peace...."

There was a furious thrashing about. Finally it was quiet. There was not a sound from the Aunt. Crouched on the threshold Tianqing heard his Uncle coughing, and then he thought he heard him sobbing as though his heart would break.

At last there was silence. The north room was as silent as a tomb, and the night, lit by ghostly fox fire was a gigantic grave yard. Tianqing slipped between covers that enclosed him like a coffin. The smell of filth and decay from the pig pen that seeped in through the secret peep-hole was all around him. He was on the verge of tears. But the pig slept in peace on the other side of the wall. The sound of its contented snoring lulled him. He swallowed his tears, and gritted his teeth to regain some of his lost pride. Gradually he sank into fretful dreams.

He became more taciturn. He ignored both his elders and his peers. People remarked that the lad had been so ill-used by his Uncle that he was becoming silent and anti-social. A few remembered that the lad had been a pensive child. Perhaps some part of his soul had been swept into the depths of Jade Creek with the rest of his family. They concluded Tianqing was not a youngster to mess with, and gave him a wide berth. But the old people who thought they saw things more clearly opined that the Uncle lacked compassion. They felt Jinshan did not treat his Nephew fairly; that he worked him too hard. Even an animal would break under those conditions. What nobody understood was that Tianqing was only happy when he was working. The harder the better. For work obliterated his worries and fantasies. The black mule who had food brought to him did not have a bad life. Tianqing was one of Yang Jinshan's draught animals too. So was the daughter of Pock-mark Wang. They were all of a kind. These things became clear to him as he worked. He waited for the inevitable, quiet and content.

When the long, dreary winter set in, Tianqing drove the Uncle's mule to Clearwater Town to earn some money making deliveries. The Uncle sipped a bowl of potato wine as he counted out some coins for Tianqing. It was not the first time. Tianqing knew the ropes and the Uncle was content that the mule would come to no harm. He watched his Nephew tuck the coins into his belt. Yang Jinshan was impatient for the younger man to be gone. Although Jinshan had aged rapidly, his mind was still clear. With Tianqing gone the house would be quieter. All the better to pursue his enterprise. He had consulted the witch doctor and got a prescription for himself and the woman. Even before he swallowed the potion, he could feel a stirring in his loins. He was impatient to deal with the hot *kang* and the icy woman in it even in broad daylight.

The Aunt was going down to the creek for water and accompanied Tianqing to the end of the lane. She gave his coat-tail a playful tug. Tianqing leaned against the mule trying to be nonchalant. His gaze swam dizzily from her lips, to the row of small uneven teeth that were slightly parted as if ready to bite. There was no one else in the street. He wanted to touch her. Every time he parted from her this urge became stronger. He did not know what to do. Vaguely he wondered if she knew that he was familiar with every line of her body, would she still treat him with the kindness of a mother? Tianqing's legs quaked. He gave the bridle a savage jerk.

"Your jacket is much too thin," she said touching his sleeve. "I'll ask your Uncle for some money and make you a thicker one in the new year. We mustn't let you catch cold...."

"I'm strong. I won't catch cold."

"If there isn't enough business, come home. There's no place like home."

"I will...."

"Feed yourself properly. Your Uncle's greedy. Even if you bring home a sack of money it won't satisfy him. So eat well. Remember...."

"I will.... The creek is icy. Mind you don't fall and hurt yourself." "Take care of yourself. Watch out for hustlers, and don't worry about your Uncle. I'm here."

"I will.... I will...."

The flame that lit Tianqing's eyes made her duck her head. It was the same tiny flame that she had seen before. A mere flicker that spluttered on damp kindling and quickly died. It was a flame that would never light up the hidden things in their hearts. He was the thoughtful Nephew. She was the kindly Aunt. That was all. The bonfire he yearned for could never be lit. A chill gripped Tianqing's heart. The mule trotted merrily ahead. Tianqing followed with the whip slung carelessly across his shoulder, and the mule led the man away from winter-bound Floodwater Canyon, along the frozen mountain track that meandered into infinity.

Tianqing transported coal for the smithy, grain for the warehouse, dowries for wedding parties. They were big spenders, who pressed large tips on him that both embarrassed and delighted him. In the end it was all money when he toted it up. During the day he trudged after the mule along the mountain tracks. At night he fed the fleas on the *kang* of a wayside inn. There should not have been room for fantasies in such an existence, yet he was still haunted by her face and her body. Her body beckoned like an exotic flower, a promise of spring that came out of the cold, lonely blast of winter.

While Tianqing struggled through the blizzards of December, his Uncle was drifting into madness. No one remembers exactly when it began. One night some-one heard a howl that resembled the baying of a wolf. Yet it was not a wolf. After a while it stopped. The next day when Judou went to the stream one eye was black-ened and swollen the size of an egg. She limped as she carried water. Either her leg or her foot was injured. All was peaceful for the next few nights, then the howling from the north chamber of Jinshan's house was heard again.

The villagers were distressed. Finally a member of the women's league stopped Jinshan in the street.

"Are you trying to kill Judou?" she demanded, spit flying in all directions.

"I can do what I like. The woman is mine."

"Not in this society. Unless you want to be criticized."

"It's still none of your business...."

"You've got no balls, and you call yourself a man!"

The woman's wit was no match for Jinshan's tongue. His eyes narrowed into little slits.

"Who was dragged through the streets by the roots of her hair? Settle your man first, before you meddle in other people's affairs. You hear?"

"You beast...."

The village elders came to talk to him after the women's league ran into a brick wall. Jinshan pulled a long face, and whined.

"You have grandsons. Your women whelp as easily as falling off a log. But my bloodline's about to end. What'd you do if you had a useless woman?"

"Are you going to beat a child out of her then?"

"We'll see. If I poke a live one out of her, I'll slave for her the rest of my life. If not, I'm still entitled to some fun, aren't I?"

"You hurt her bad, and you'll pay for it!"

"Why not kill me. I've lived long enough...."

Jinshan squeezed out a few crocodile tears which took the elders by surprise. Being childless was indeed a tragedy, and in their misplaced pity they made allowances for him.

Toward the end of December Yang Jinshan was preparing to slaughter the pig. All the good baskets he had were already in use. He thought of the dilapidated one hanging from a peg over the pig pen. It would do to hold the hog's head and innards. He picked up a hoe and hooked it off the peg, and discovered a hole in the wall. He did not see the hole as an opening for deception or invasion.

It was merely a bit of loose plaster and a stone that had worked itself loose. Not a shred of suspicion was aroused. Which shows how unimaginative he was and how unnecessary was Tianqing's fear of discovery. Yang Jinshan climbed on the *kang* to fix the hole from inside. He did not remember noticing a hole in the wall when he stacked the sacks of grain with Tianqing. Nor did it ever occur to him that Tianqing might have deliberately concealed it and why. It was a mystery his dull wit was incapable of unravelling. He pulled out the stone stopper and peered into the hole. A nest of pink, hairless, new-born mice writhed in the cavity. His gorge rose. With a flick of the wrist he brushed them into the pig pen below. It seemed he was even jealous of the fertility of rats. Had Judou been squatting on the other side of the wall, his suspicion might have been roused. But there was no one on the other side of the wall, and Jinshan was convinced rats had made the hole.

Tianqing returned on the twenty-eighth of December. The creek had frozen. As he guided the mule gingerly across the ice, a pair of eyes followed his slithering progress from the opposite bank. He loosened his grip on the bridle and slowly made his way up the icy steps toward her. Judou threw a flowered jacket into the eye of the stream, and dried her plump reddened hands on the legs of her pants. She gave him a tremulous smile. He stopped. His eyes widened with disbelief. Her smile was different. There were several gaps where teeth were missing. There was also a greenish bruise on her temple, and a purplish patch on one cheek where the blood had collected under the translucent skin. Her sad smile told him something untoward had happened while he was gone.

"Tianqing, why didn't you send a message that you were coming home?"

"All the business was on the other bank. I didn't meet a single familiar face. What happened ?"

"I'm going home on the fifth next month and these clothes haven't been washed all winter. I'll be laughed at if I go as I am...."

"What happened to your face?"

"I slipped on the ice carrying water. Go on ahead. I'll be there in a while. Your Uncle's slaughtering the hog."

"But he said he'd wait till next year...."

"He changed his mind. What difference does it make...."

"Did you break your teeth too?"

"I swallowed them...."

Tianqing could think of nothing more to say. The Aunt tried to smile. Instead her eyes moistened, but the frozen tears refused to fall. He bent to help her pull the clothes out of the icy water. She pushed him aside and his hand brushed against her cold arm. His eyes brimmed. Pain gripped his heart like a vice. He could not tear his eyes from her ravaged face.

"You're so thin. But we'll have lots of meat to eat. Do you hear the pig squealing?"

The Aunt turned away. Her tears finally fell like tiny pellets of ice into the stream.

The pig's squeals rose and fell. Tianqing found the animal trussed to the *kang* table. Only its long snout moved sounding its death rattle. The Uncle stood beside the pig's head, lazily rubbing the blade of his knife on his sleeve. He was content to let the animal squeal, prolonging its terror. Tianqing saw a sickening viciousness and savagery in his Uncle that he had not seen before. He had knocked out his wife's teeth and damaged her pretty face. But that had not assuaged his fury. He lusted for blood.

Tianqing tethered the mule, and handed over the money he earned to his Uncle. Jinshan took the wad of bills without a word.

"How much?"

"Count it. It's all there."

"Rest a while, and come help me finish this fellow...."

"The animal hasn't been fattened yet...."

"People need to be fattened too. And people come first...."

"It's a pity to kill it now..."

"Don't you want to eat well? Someone from Damo Village said there were bandits on the west bank. You didn't run into any trouble did you? And the mule looks thinner...."

It was true. The mule was thinner; the pig was lean. Even the people were thin. His Uncle was as thin as a rail. The angles of his face were as sharp as a hatchet. Heaven knows what drove him so that the warmth of a winter *kang* failed to add an ounce of fat to his bones.

"What kept you so long, wasting time on those miserable rags. Where's the basin I need for the pig's blood? Fetch it! And stop the snivelling, or I'll fetch a cane to you. Look at the time. Half the day's gone!"

Tianqing couldn't believe it was his Uncle speaking to his wife. The veins in Tianqing's neck twitched. Something had definitely happened while he was away. The Aunt's body had not thickened. Clearly it was the same problem that plagued the Uncle. Only there was a note of hatred in the Uncle's voice now, that threatened violence any moment.

The Uncle slapped the pig's belly as he bellowed at the woman, oblivious of the animal's renewed cries. The knife rose in a wide arc and plunged into the animal's throat. The pig gurgled, and blood gushed from the wound and splashed into a basin. Tianqing held the pig's head, and out of the corner of his eye saw the Aunt crumple onto the threshold. Her face was ashen. The blood fanned out in a dark red puddle. The pig let out a final scream which trailed into stillness. The beast was at peace.

Tianqing held the pig's severed head in both his hands. The eyes and the mouth were open, and a pinkish foam dribbled onto his hand, warm and sticky. He threw it into the broken basket as if it scalded his hands. He stared at the basket, and slowly the reason for the killing became clear. He watched the Uncle wielding the knife, warily following its every move. His own knife plunged into the carcass with a violence that outdid that of the Uncle. One leg was almost torn clean off in one stroke. He moved to the head of the animal, and quickly hacked off the front trotters.

"You're strong," the Uncle exclaimed.

"Tianqing, be careful...."

Tianqing shrugged off his jacket and plunged a hand into the pig's gaping belly and pulled out a slimy mess of bowels that snaked around his arm. It was a violent gesture, and cruel, but he was suddenly at peace. He realized the Uncle's show of violence was not directed at him. But an invisible hand had seized the Aunt, shaking and tearing at her, until her very soul seemed to have flown with that of the dead pig.

Slabs of pink and white meat were hung out under the eaves. The courtyard was again cloaked in silence.

On new years' eve the meat was served. Tianqing rolled the wobbly bits of white fat into his belly, and watched the other two ranged around the short-legged *kang* table. The Aunt ate slowly, gnawing the meat, slowly forcing it down. The Uncle ate with noisy slurping sounds as if he were eating noodles. When he lifted the wine cup to his lips, he made curious squeaking sounds of a creaky door hinge. When the meal was almost over, the Uncle suddenly started mumbling.

"Oh, my dear mother!"

When the Aunt removed his cup, he snatched it back.

"Oh my dear, loving mother!" he went on, his beady little eyes fixed on the rafters.

He slapped his thighs with the palm of a large calloused hand as if he were searching for a rhythm which escaped him.

"Oh, my loving, scolding, dead mother ... look at your childless son ... oh, mother...." It was the same complaint, repeated again and again.

The flame in the lamp flickered in rhythm with the slapping sound. Tianqing suddenly lost his appetite. The food churned in his stomach.

In the middle of the night Tianqing was wakened by

a howl. He lay clutching his pillow, wondering whether it was a wolf. When it came again, he realized it was his Aunt. Behind that wail was the grunts of his Uncle's despairing, and violent efforts.

Tianqing crept silently from the room, and crouched under the window of the north room like a wild beast ready to pounce. In the dark he groped for the axe that was used to chop off the pig's feet. He knew it was under the doorstep but he could not locate it in the dark. However, his bare foot struck the handle of a scythe, and he seized it.

"His Uncle, you're choking me...."

"I curse you to the eighteenth generation! Are you satisfied!"

"... I can't take it any more...."

"I swear I'll soften you yet, you worthless heap of trash! I'll fix your screaming!"

The woman's scream was stifled by something soft thrust into her mouth. Over the woman's muffled protest came the Uncle's laboured breathing. Something thumped against the *kang*, like a head being slammed against a hard surface in rhythm with the Uncle's triumphant rasping. Something was hauled up and slammed down like a sack of grain.

Tianqing stood frozen to the ground. When he heard the smuck of a broomstick or was it a stick of firewood, against flesh he could stand it no longer. Anger raced through his frame. The muscles in his arm bunched up. His body arched upward. The scythe caught a slab of meat hanging under the eaves and sent it flying into the courtyard. The scythe flew in a shining arc and bit into the wooden post of the north room. Instantly the sounds of violence ceased.

"Who's there?"

Tianqing did not answer. The cold of the flagstones penetrated him through the soles of his feet, and he was numb.

"Who's there?"

"Me...."

"Is that you, Tianqing?"

"Yes...."

"Have you fed the mule?"

"I have...."

Tianqing rubbed his bare feet, suddenly wary.

"Is Auntie ill?"

"It's nothing ... just a bit of indigestion...."

"Shall I fetch the witch-doctor?"

"No ... I'm better now...."

"Shall I go back to bed?"

"... Go back to bed. What was that noise just now?"

"I don't know. It's so dark I can't see anything."

Tianqing went back to his room. It was impossible to get back to sleep. He sat cross legged on the *kang* pondering. He had deliberately left the scythe embedded in the post as a warning. Let the miscreant consider whether his head is as hard as a post before he visits more violence on the woman. But as anger subsided be began to question the soundness of his action. Perhaps he had exceeded the bounds of a dutiful nephew. That might give the Uncle the idea that the woman had been unfaithful, and make her life even more miserable. He crept out of his room again before dawn, replaced the scythe and threw the slab of meat into the ruins of the neighbour's house.

The year a co-operative was established at Floodwater Canyon was the beginning of an eventful period.

Yang Tianqing still tossed restlessly on his cold *kang* till day break, clutching the woman who lay on the other side of the wall in his fantasy.

A red hot sun heaved itself over the horizon.

At the age of fifty-five, Yang Jinshan was wallowing in despair. For the first time since he reached adulthood, carrying a basket of a hundred *jin* into the fields left him breathless. His back ached and his knees turned to jelly after a few swings of the hoe. With growing horror he realized his body would no longer respond to the demands he placed on it. However the most unbearable weakness was when he climbed on the *kang*. His frenzied activities were an attempt to ward off the fear of impotence. He sought relief in violence, working himself up to a fever pitch of excitement by inflicting pain, and thus hanging onto a little of the hope and joy that was slipping from his grasp. But even that failed. He was left with the strange yearning to weep, to die. When he tore at her flesh, and kicked her from one end of the *kang* to the other, he was punishing his own flagging flesh. Her cries echoed his own cries against unrelenting fate. The woman was wedded to his despair. He enjoyed punishing her. He sought unguarded moments to beat her; to attack her in ways she could not expect. She became furtive. She walked in constant fear of him, and that made him strong. For a fleeting moment he forgot his shame and uselessness. The woman was no longer human. She had become a sexless hulk that absorbed his abuse. He treated the mule better. He was even kinder to

Tianqing. The loyal Nephew worked from dawn till dusk, and was even less trouble than the mule.

One day in the spring the three were weeding the corn field. A warm breeze blowing off the ridge of the mountain made them drowsy. At mid-morning Judou went home to prepare the midday meal leaving Uncle and Nephew to work by themselves. The two squatted in the field side by side, pulling up weeds and separating the seedlings which stood in neat straight rows. By noon the Uncle was too tired to continue. He lay in the grass beside the field and turned his face to the sun. Tianqing worked on alone. The Uncle spoke to him from a distance, drowning the ants in the grass with spit.

"Tianqing, do you know the big footed woman at Mulberry Canyon?"

"Isn't her name Zhang?"

"Old widow Zhang is a marriage broker...."

"I know."

"I met her at old Jiao's the other day."

"Oh...."

"She wants to find you a woman...."

"Who...."

"I shut her up."

"Oh...."

"You've been with me all these years, so you must know my problems. It doesn't matter whose son you are, or whose son-in-law you become, you're still my brother's seed. When things get easier in this family, you can do as you please. What do you say?"

"I haven't thought about it."

"Let it go another year. Maybe next year the village will give us separate plots. It would be better for

you to be on your own then…. I'll give you some
money to do as you please … as much as I can afford…. Your Uncle has wasted a lifetime. It's no
good holding on to it. Sooner or later all I have will
be yours…."

"I'll make my own living. Keep it for Auntie."

"I'd sooner give it to an animal. The minute I'm
gone, she'll find another. You mark my word. I'd
sooner end my blood-line myself. I'd never lie in peace
otherwise. Damn it! where's the food. Has the woman
stuck her legs in the stove with the kindling?"

Jinshan scrambled to his feet and searched the path
that snaked around the knoll. There was no sign of
movement. The dappled shadows of the trees had
shifted. It was past noon when Judou's blue blouse
flashed around a cluster of boulders. Jinshan let out a
roar and leaped on her as she came up the path
knocking her into a ditch. Tianqing was not quick
enough to stop him. He stood on high ground to see
what would happen next. He was too far to make out
what his Uncle was saying, but the Aunt was backing
away from him fearfully. Then Tianqing saw the basket
of food rolling down the hillside, and the Aunt rolling
after it. The Uncle ran after her, kicking and yelling.
He planted one final kick on the small of the woman's
back and hurried toward the village like a black whirlwind. The woman sat in the grass with her head
down, slowly rubbing her back. Finally she stumbled
down the slope to look for the food basket. Tianqing
quieted the wild beating of his heart. He willed himself
to put all that he had just seen behind him. When the
woman brought the food, silently dashing aside her
tears, he was squatted in the field calmly weeding the

rows of corn. His back was turned to her and for a long while he would not look at her. She gazed at him through her tears.

"Tianqing have some food...."

"You eat first."

"I'm not hungry."

Suddenly the woman was shaken by racking sobs. Tianqing kept his eyes on the ground, resolved not to notice.

"What's the matter, Auntie...."

"Tianqing ... listen to me. Your Uncle will kill me one day! I can't take it any longer. Whatever you see or hear, go and tell them at Shijia Village. But don't try to stop him. Let the old thing kill me ... I'm tired of living...."

"My Uncle has a bad temper."

"Your Uncle isn't a man. I have to bear it, but do you? Dear nephew, tell them what my life's been. Sooner or later he'll kill me. I can't stand it much longer."

The woman wept bitterly. Tianqing buried his head in his arms, groping for words of comfort that would not come. He wanted to gather her in his arms and let her pour out all her misery. It was the first time she had ever turned to him for comfort and he was plunged into helpless confusion. He had only to turn and reach out for her but he could not. He was a nephew and he could not tell what lay ahead.

The yellow earth before him was spattered with moisture. He could not turn to her. A flame licked his back where her eyes touched him.

"Tianqing, eat while the food's still warm...."

"I'll eat ... in a moment...."

He hurried across the corn field, pretending to be in need of relieving himself. He squatted down beneath a birch tree behind a boulder, and the pent-up tears flowed uncontrolled. He struck his head against the tree, and bit off a strip of bark. He chewed it angrily until the flood of tears subsided. She must not see him weep. In that moment he had plumbed the depths of her despair and his.

Yang Jinshan did not come back. His original excuse for beating the woman was that she was late with the food. But when she said the mule was lying in its stall, and would not get to its feet or eat, that added fuel to the fire, and spurred him to greater savagery. The woman's hip was injured. She half crouched and half knelt as she worked. Tianqing did not offer to help. All he did was urge her to rest. There was a coldness in his voice that was his only means of holding himself together. All afternoon he wanted to gather the woman into his arms and carry her beyond the corn field. A hundred times he resolved to do it, and a hundred times his resolve melted to nothing. But the woman drew comfort from his words despite the coldness of his tone. The wetness of his eyes was proof of the secret in his heart.

The mule was indeed ill. Jinshan felt its belly and found a soft lump that could be the beginning of dry cholera. He did not wait for the woman and his Nephew to return, but hastily latched the gate, and dragged the reluctant mule out of the village. In the evening old Jiao sent word that the Uncle had taken the mule to Damo Village for treatment. If they could not help the animal he would go on to Mulberry Canyon. He might be gone several days. He told them to get the fields weeded while the weather held. But keep an eye on the vegetable garden too, lest the pigs root in it and so forth. The messenger chuckled as he recalled how solicitously Jinshan had felt the mule's belly, and how he was close to tears. If the mule were to die, the messenger feared Jinshan would also expire. Judou shrugged. Tianqing did not respond, but went on slurping his cornmeal gruel. He was left alone with the Aunt for the first time. It had happened so suddenly that he could not decide whether he hoped for it, or feared it more. After the meal, he watched the woman moving about and the fear became greater. In his heart he knew he had rehearsed this scene countless times on countless nights.

"Sleep well. You won't have to feed the mule tonight."

"Auntie wake me early so I can water the vegetable patch...."

"Have a good sleep. He isn't around, so why worry."

"I'll water the garden early, otherwise he'll complain when he gets home. Besides I'm used to it. Work is work."

"You're a block-head."

The Aunt tidied the chicken coop. She stood in the moonlit courtyard, a faint smile full of mysterious tenderness lit her face. Tianqing could not tell whether the tenderness was meant for him. When she called him a block-head was she teasing or complaining? What did she want from him? She bade him goodnight went into her room and bolted the door. He went into his room, barred the door with a pole, and laid down on the *kang*. The lamp in the north room went out.

The lamp in his room had never been lit. He lay there for a long while thinking of crossing the short distance to the north room, of standing under the eaves; of opening the door. Step followed logical step until he crossed the threshold. Then everything became muddled. He shrank. He did not get off the *kang*, or go into the courtyard, or do anything. His fingers stroked his belly till the flesh leaped and his pounding fist released his frustration and shame. A tremor rippled through him. He wrapped himself tightly in his thin quilt, and pulled it over his head.

The block of wood had fused itself to the mat and the quilt, and drifted into sleep. In his dreams he seemed to be rehearsing all his old schemes. The exotic flower of a body drifted, became a thing that had nothing to do with him. A stranger was huddled against the mule weeping. No matter how he kicked and shoved she would not go away. He took an axe to strike her but it was too heavy to raise. The world was filled with the sound of weeping, of lips sucking up tears.

Tianqing woke with a start. He groped groggily under the covers for his axe but it was not there. The sound of weeping persisted outside the window. He was wide awake now. As he struggled free from the quilt, the weeping stopped. The door to the north room creaked softly and there was silence. Moonlight flooded the courtyard. The flagstones glimmered like the surface of a pond. Tianqing crouched beside the window for a long while. Finally he flung himself on the pillow again, and lay staring up at the ceiling. Had he imagined it, or was he still dreaming. What he heard was real, and what was in his heart was also real. But he trusted neither. It could not happen this way, though he wanted it. It was because he desired so much that he was confused. He had dreamed so much, and perceived so much because he was losing his mind. A madman sees many things. Hadn't his Uncle seen his grandfather in the yard dragging something? Then the ghostly figure went into the kitchen shed, grabbed a handful of black beans which it tossed to the mule and vanished. Uncle had seen him quite plainly, but he was too frightened to speak to him. His looking for the axe and seeing the Aunt outside the window was no different. He was seeing things because he too was going mad, Tianqing told himself. Though he scarcely slept that night he rose early to water the vegetable patch. The first thing he saw was the pole barring the door. He used it at night to keep out the wind or animals. He wondered why he could not have been careless just once in his life. But he was not used to questioning himself, and went off to work vaguely annoyed at himself. He dragged his weary body into the vegetable garden while the Aunt was still asleep. He wanted to avoid her. It struck him that she might feel the same way. If they started avoiding one another, it would be impossible to go on living in the same house. By the time he had finished watering the garden, his brain had cleared. Just then the Aunt's clear voice calling him home for the morning meal cut across his reveries. He sighed. She called him the same way every morning. But there was a subtle difference in her voice today. His pulse quickened. He turned his face toward the mountains that rose in unbroken undulations on the far side of the creek, fold upon fold of green towering toward a clear blue sky. He wanted to call out in answer. Her voice had lifted him like a giant bird into the morning wind that blew across the valley.

It was an exceptionally clear day. The sunlight was glorious and a gentle breeze was blowing. The creek babbled gaily as it wound in a gleaming ribbon of white light to the bottom of Floodwater Canyon. As Yang Jinshan's Nephew and his wife went into the cornfields near Loma Ridge, he was dragging his sick mule up the tortuous trail from Damo Village to Gentle Canyon. Each was wrapped in their secret hopes. At the moment the mule occupied all of Yang Jinshan's thoughts. He was oblivious of the abyss his kin were about to slide into.

The woman who was about to betray him laughed. And with that reckless laughter she tossed her pain and misfortune to the wind. The shackles that held the young man for so long were also loosed. He followed the woman he had secretly loved for so long into the field, rushing eagerly to a wondrous destiny.

They worked side by side, happily through the morning, chatting, but not saying much of any importance. They sat on a grassy knoll facing each other as they ate their midday meal. They drank from the same gourd. There was only one pickled carrot. They each took one end, leaving different teeth marks. In a while they became confused which end was which. He took a bit of her end and she, his. The woman took the pickle and sucked on it, filling her mouth with its salty tang. Suddenly they lost interest in the food. Tianqing stared at the trampled grass beneath his feet. How stubbornly they slowly pushed themselves upright again, green sap oozing from their wounds. And just as they stood upright again, he tramped them down. The grass pricked the sole of his foot, like tiny embroidery needles. The woman with a mouthful of food, narrowed her eyes against the wind. The sunlight danced across her smooth skin. Her red lips were speckled with crumbs. A tireless insect buzzed around her head.

Tianqing's throat constricted, his tongue cleaved to the roof of his mouth.

"Auntie...."

"What?"

"I had a frightening dream last night."

"Did you dream of your parents?"

"I dreamt that you were crying...."

"Why was I crying?"

The woman blushed and smiled. He concentrated on parts of her face, unable to meet her eyes. The woman being more worldly, had the advantage.

"What are you afraid of Tianqing?"

"Afraid?"

"You're a man now."

"I'm not afraid of anything."

"Then why did you bar your door?

"To keep out the wind ... and wolves...."

"Am I a wolf?"

"Auntie...."

"Take a good look at your poor Auntie and tell me, is she a wolf?"

Tianqing's weakness egged her on. Her words slashed at him like a knife but the smile remained. A faint smile that quivered between self-pity and resentment that Tianqing could not grasp. The events of the night before were not a dream. Of that he was quite certain. Tianqing bowed his head. It was so heavy he thought he would never lift it again. A weight pressed so tightly against his chest he could hardly breathe. Something landed on the top of his head. Perhaps a leaf that he could neither shake off nor the breeze blow away. Dreamily he realized it was the woman's hand. He shut his eyes, and clenched his teeth against the trembling that rippled through him. When that failed,he let it spread outward through his limbs.

"Auntie … my Uncle…."

"Forget him. Let the old thing die."

"Auntie there's a shepherd on the hill."

"The herd has gone to the other side of the hill."

"…. What are you doing?"

"Am I a wolf?"

"Auntie don't tease…."

"Tianqing, you can deny it with your mouth, but you can't deny it with your eyes."

"Were you crying under my window?"

"Yes. Your Uncle wants me dead, but I won't die. Heaven can watch how I intend to live. I want to be happy…. I want to share it with you. I want to curse that old thing that's destroyed half my life!"

Her fingers clutched at his hair but it was too short,and the hand slid to his collar and fastened on to his neck, where a thick vein throbbed.

"You love me Tianqing!"

"Careful! You'll break the water jug…."

"Is there room for me in your heart? I'm yours."

"Auntie … you're tearing me apart … My heart is cracking … Don't tease…."

"I'll swallow you alive, before I let you go!"

She would not let him go nor did he wish her to.

There was nothing more to say. Her head drooped against his chest, shoving his stubbly chin backward. Her arms snaked around his neck and shoulders, finally tightening around the small of his back. Tianqing shut his eyes. Her soft and fragrant mouth glided across his face leaving a damp trail. His lips blindly sought hers. His mouth ground against hers teeth. His breath became short and painful. The sun burst into a thousand flaming fragments. Hands and bodies sought each other in a frenzied dance. His hardness and her softness melted into one. Above them the sky was a sheet of gold shot through with light. Beneath them the mountains heaved and rolled like ripples on the water. He was anchored in her, as sky and mountain pressed together in a seamless unity. The sky was crumbling around him, as he slipped over the edge into the chasm, a wave of exhilaration swept over him. He was lifted up by a thunder bolt and a whirlwind. A fearful spasm shook him. The sun exploded. Everything became black like the charred remains of a yam dropped in the fire, or the hide of sow hanging under the eaves to dry. It was very dark. Tianqing who had been fearful and confused was liberated at last.

They did what they had to do, until they fell swooning into each other's arms. From noon till dusk their love making continued sporadically. Thus began a relationship that would last several decades. That noon was a milestone in their lives. They had also began digging their graves.

Fifty *li* away, Liang, the witch-doctor of Mulberry Creek, quickly diagnosed the mule's ailment. The tip of his knife glided lightly across the animal's belly searching for the right spot to make an incision. Yang Jinshan could not bear to watch. He waited outside the witch-doctor's house leaning dejectedly against the wall. His eyes wandered across the landscape while jumbled thoughts raced through his mind. The mule was inextricably bound to his past and his future. Of all the living creatures he had encountered in life, it had been the most faithful and reliable. And it was also the dumb animal that he cherished the most. However, his compassion for the mule was not untainted with self-pity. He found himself often pondering death. He did not wonder whether his parents who had long since vanished into the netherworld, were content. Rather he was trying to probe the mystery of his own future. It was his unborn sons and grandsons that occupied his thoughts. Somehow the life that his parents had passed on to him had to be preserved and passed on in turn. Yet the fulfillment of that desire continued to elude him. He suspected that he was atoning for some irreparable sin in another life. How else could he explain being driven to the brink of despair by two barren women.

Basking in the warm sunlight of spring, Yang Jinshan's thoughts turned dully on his home, and even more dully on his wife and Nephew. They were no more to him than pieces of furniture. He could not imagine that on the other side of the mountain his strong young Nephew was labouring as he had never done, ploughing the same field Yang Jinshan was determined to break, and sowing seed more effectively than he ever could.

Yang Jinshan heard the mule's piteous neighing. The sound of the knife cutting into living flesh was like window paper tearing. The sound brought a flood of tears he could not hold back.

At that moment Yang Tianqing was also crying out in a paroxysm of pain and ecstasy. It was the triumphant cry of the killer as he plunged in the knife. It was also the dying sigh of the victim.

"Auntie! Auntie!"

It was the final outburst that rose from the depths of his manhood at the end of an arduous battle. A medley of words that barely made sense.

"Judou! My darling Judou!"

He had finally reached a safe haven. Perched on the pinnacle of sensation, everything was finally clear.

"My darling little dove! Oh, my dove ... my dove...."

The sunlight splashed down the mountainside, and across the golden field of corn where two bodies twined, clashed and separated, crying out, dazed and shaken,rising like two large white birds flying into the sunlight.

"Oh, my darling little dove! My dove ... my dove...."

The woman was twenty-six and Yang Tianqing was twenty-two. In the months and years that followed they would snatch moments together fraught with guilt and ecstasy. Yang Tianqing would renew his vows of love again and again, and the woman would clutch them hungrily to her bossom exalting in his cries and groans. It was the unchanging litany of their secret ritual, primitive and beautiful, to be repeated into eternity.

The co-operative system was being established in Floodwater Canyon. The last of the reluctant land holders had finally capitulated. Yang Jinshan stubbornly resisted. He felt he worked hard and well enough on his own. Besides he was self-sufficient and he was not about to share the fruits of his labour with strangers. After the early harvest the county government organized reading classes in an attempt to wipe out illiteracy. At dusk the youths and women of the village gathered beneath the old chestnut tree, laboriously picking out characters: man, mouth, hand, horse, cow, goat, sky, earth, water and so on. Yang Jinshan would not permit his young wife and Nephew to learn to read. Sitting under the chestnut tree evening after evening, feeding mosquitoes was a waste of time. Besides the endless buzzing of the readers was laughable. There were more pressing things to accomplish at home.

Just what tasks he had in mind was unclear. He often sent his wife and Nephew scurrying about with contradictory orders. The water jugs were full but he ordered them to be filled again. The mule had been exercised, but he demanded it be taken up the mountain one more time. The other two quietly did as they were told, clutching their guilty secret to their bosoms. They could see the older man was becoming feeble minded. Ever since the mule took ill, something went awry with its master. Perhaps it was fate. The two young people took advantage of the situation. They became bolder as time went by, though their stolen moments were fraught with ecstasy and pain.

Even in his confusion Yang Jinshan noticed a subtle change in the woman. When a fit of violence came over him, he could still elicit a tremor of fear from her, but he could no longer induce the animal screams that excited him. Although he left bruises on her white flesh and twisted her limbs more viciously than ever, she clenched her teeth and remained silent. She no longer refused any demands, however repulsive and degrading. At times she seemed to welcome them. He suspected that in a twisted way she was taunting him for his impotence. During the day he noticed the woman hurrying behind the bushes. He thought she had gone to relieve herself. He did not see her struggling to quiet her retching and bringing up mouthfuls of bile. During the rest periods, his husky young Nephew wandered off into the woods looking for wild mushrooms and quail eggs. He did not suspect it was the small sour, wild apricots that Tianqing was after. Nor did the old man notice the Nephew surreptitiously popping them into the woman's parched mouth. To all appearances the wife and Nephew were working hard, the crop was coming along nicely, and the harvest ought to be good. He could find no fault with the two. But he was indefinably jealous of them. His limbs were weakening at an alarming rate. He could no longer swing a five foot hoe and make it sing through the air. It was not only the land that filled him with sadness. A seedling was growing in his field. One day he would become its surrogate father without knowing it. It was a role that could only be played by one who was lost in a dream.

Yang Jinshan learned of his wife's pregnancy three months later. One night in a fit of violence he struck her in the face. To his surprise she did not try to ward off the blow, but hugged her belly instead. He gripped her by the arms and searched her with his eyes. She lifted her gaze to meet his and tears spilled down her face. She rubbed her belly gently. He questioned her, and her answer almost sent him reeling off the *kang*.

He let out a strange piercing laugh, and cupping the woman's white belly between his palms, he began to sob. His face crumbled. His whole body sagged.

"Damn it! How long have you known?"

In the side room Yang Tianqing's eyes snapped open at the sound of the strange laugh. When he heard the sound of sharp slaps, his body coiled in a tight spring, ready to leap at the first sign of danger. His breathing came easier when he realized the deliriously happy man was slapping himself.

"Heaven has eyes!"

"Judou, I've treated you badly!"

"Father of my child, you have been blessed...."

Confused sounds came from the north room until the small hours. Then there was silence. Three people lay wrapped in their separate concerns. Yang Tianqing was certain the child was his. The woman had told him her husband was impotent. His childlessness was proof of that. But the Uncle's half-crazed laughter also told Yang Tianqing he had not only deceived his Uncle, but dishonoured his parents as well. He had committed a sin that put him beyond the pale. How to face life from this day forward became an insoluble riddle that loomed before him like an unscalable mountain. He lay on his *kang* like a cornered beast with nowhere to turn. He lay awake a long while, chewing the reeds of the *kang* mat that filled his mouth with bitterness and grated against his teeth. Gradually fear dissipated and he slept.

Yang Jinshan awoke the next morning a changed man. In his happiness he roused Tianqing early to light the fire and prepare the morning meal. When that was done, Tianqing was ordered to feed the chickens and the pig. Before he had any food, he was told to split firewood, and water the mule. Yang Jinshan stood in the courtyard while his orders were carried out, at last the master of all he surveyed. Wang Judou sat cross-legged on the *kang*. Following her husband's strange and stubborn orders, she must henceforth protect the new life in her body every minute of the day, though it meant the loss of the freedom of movement. Through a tear in the window paper she watched Tianqing doing her chores. He was clumsy but determined, and she was sorry for him. Yang Jinshan carried a breakfast of gruel and pickles to her. He thought the dampness in her eyes was an acknowledgement of his solicitude, and his eyes brimmed too. To cover his embarrassment he put a few extra drops of sesame oil on the pickles. He tasted it, and added some more. Then, satisfied, he noisily licked the bottle, as if to congratulate himself for his generosity.

"Eat up!" he said.

Judou obediently lifted the bowl.

"Don't move around.... Take care of the child, or I'll have your hide. Tianqing will do all the heavy work from now on. You rest."

Yang Jinshan felt a rush of tenderness toward the woman. For the first time he laid a big, calloused hand on her shoulder not to injure but to comfort. The woman's tears dropped silently into the bowl. He was satisfied. Silently he vowed to be good to her from now on, completely unaware of the curious rush of events around him. The woman's sudden burst of tears was not brought on by the sound of the chickens pecking at their feed, and the two pigs rooting in their trough. They were brought on by the sound of the young man hurrying back and forth, and his heavy breathing. These sounds were the harbingers of her husband's plans for the future. The strands of both their lives were held in another's hand. With the child in her womb, she was pardoned but that grip would become tighter. Her burden had been shifted onto the shoulders of the young man. Sooner or later the pressure would become unbearable. She did not know what to do. Nor did he. Footsteps in the courtyard became a jumble of sound without pattern or purpose. The joy and the strength on the mountainside in the spring was gone. She was listening to the footsteps of one waiting for the axe to fall.

Judou kept to her *kang*. Yang Jinshan scarcely gave the crops a thought. He lived in a dream world, wandering through the village, telling the news to everyone he met. It was important to his ego that everyone should know and marvel at the feat of a sixty year old man begetting a child. After all the striving, it was an accomplishment not to be ignored. Indeed everyone in the village seemed genuinely pleased. Or at least as interested as they could be in a gravid animal.

There is man, and there is woman; male and female. Birth is a part of life. Most people pitied Yang Jinshan, and felt he was making a mountain out of a mole hill. Gradually, in the bits of old wife's tales that pass for advice he was getting, Yang Jinshan got the notion the villagers did not share his sense of wonder. That dampened his spirits. However, he still went about with a smile on his face, and a spring in his step. He felt young again and he was content.

By the time the crops stood tall in the fields of August, Yang Jinshan could no longer last out the day till sun-down. On the other hand Yang Tianqing had become more calm and collected. When they irrigated the corn fields, Yang Jinshan spent a good part of the day clearing the ditches, and ended in letting the water flow into the neighbour's field. It was Tianqing who took things in hand and corrected the mistake. Had the error been his, the Uncle would have had a temper tantrum. Tianqing noticed that the Uncle had become more and more critical of late. After the child was born, he would probably be unbearable. But he did not mind. The Uncle's erratic behavior gave him courage. Tianqing no longer felt any remorse. Nor did he fear the man any longer. In fact he despised him. Tianqing was at peace thinking of the child the woman carried, and remembering the ecstasy of its making. He marvelled at his own strength, and the woman's too. When the Uncle bawled him out as master to servant, he was not angered. His shield was a sense of joy and confidence. He knew he could be whatever he set out to be, including a real husband and father. He felt he had finally evened the score for the debt that was made more than ten years ago on a rainy autumn night. She was his. His! He had nothing but contempt for the surrogate father.

That summer and autumn Yang Tianqing did the work of three. He worked like a man possessed while Yang Jinshan was seldom seen in his own fields. The gossips of Floodwater Canyon commiserated with the poor dumb Nephew who was so loyal and so terribly alone.

"Tianqing, I'm going home. Tidy up the corn by the edge of the cliff, will you. Don't worry about the evening meal. It can wait till you're finished."

Often it was late at night when he finally finished, and he dragged his weary bones home along the winding star-lit path. But once he crossed the threshold he was a different person. His movements became brisk. He made a great clatter, lighting the fire, and cooking the meal. He slurped his food noisily in the courtyard. All this was to tell the shadow in the window of the north room that he was still the strong, vigorous young man she desired, and there was no cause for her head to droop so low. Every movement of that shadowy figure made him shuck off a layer of weariness, and slip inexplicably into another kind of lassitude. Lying in the side room, weary and dejected, he tried to recapture the past. But all he could conjure up were fragments of blissful moments. He longed for her touch. His flesh swelled, burst, and melted in sticky, alien puddles. Then he thought of the child, and the hot urgency in his blood, became an all-embracing tenderness. He was reminded of duty, and of patience for the days ahead.

Wang Judou's belly swelled rapidly. When there was no one in the house, she would sometimes slip into the lane to sit in the sun. The villagers sometimes stopped to pass the time of day, and to enquire when the child was due.

"Perhaps some time in December," she said vaguely.

If she was questioned too closely, she would resort to asking advice from the questioner. The women who had many children found her ingenuousness charming and somewhat laughable. She had answered Yang Jinshan's questions in the same vague manner. In such matters he was as ignorant as she, and so he accepted her reply very solemnly. He tried to count on his fingers when the child was conceived. He seemed to remember succeeding once or twice, but he could not remember the details. The woman, blushing furiously, reminded him how it had been one time, and how it had been another time. Yang Jinshan nodded agreement. In truth he was still not sure which time it could have been. The line between success and failure had been so indistinct that it was hard to distinguish one from the other. Nevertheless, he had filled the woman's belly and that's what counts. Besides he had always been a rough man. Yang Jinshan took the woman's meekness as proof that he did indeed have the power to turn stone into gold. In fact he was already planning new successes. If he could have one, he could have two. One was definitely not enough. He misread the fear in the woman's eyes. He thought it was the memory of his strange demands that brought a pink flush to her cheeks. He found fear in a woman titillating, and he was pleased. It gave him greater authority in the role of husband and father. He would show all those who scoffed at him, that Yang Jinshan was indeed about to be a father.

January 16th of the following year was a day of bustle in Yang Jinshan's courtyard. The woman had been in labour since the middle of the night, and her cries were heard till almost dawn. The lamp in the north room suddenly went out. The midwife tottered out and solemnly extended a bloody finger at the ashen Yang Jinshan symbolizing a part of the new-born's anatomy. Yang Jinshan understood at once. The child's lusty cry was the most joyous sound he could hope to hear. It confirmed everything he needed to know. His son was strong, content, and demanding his father.

"Damn it, that's my son!"

Yang Jinshan plunged headlong into the north room, tripped and fell beside the *kang*.

The guests in the courtyard chuckled.

Yang Tianqing was not at home. He had left with the mule on the 5th to haul goods on the west bank. He wanted to avoid the birth, and stayed away for nearly a month. He returned ten days later. At the edge of the village he met the second son of old Jiao who told him that Judou had a son. The child had already been named according to family tradition. Its name was Tianbai (meaning white sky), in contrast with his cousin Tianqing (meaning blue sky.)

"Better hurry and have a look at your fat little cousin."

"How is my.... Aunt...."

"They say she lost half a basin of blood. But your Uncle is treating her like a Buddha. Quite a change from the days when he used to beat her."

Tianqing sighed and hesitated. He was not ready to go home. He led the mule onto a knoll, and stretched out on the stubbly grass. The grass scratched his face. Overhead clouds scudded quickly across the sky. The wind moaned in the trees.

The child was called Tianbai. That made him Tianqing's cousin. It had been done according to the Yangs' family tree. Up to now he had not given the naming of the child much thought. He intended to be the child's father. In fact he was the father, thus the naming ought to be up to him. The ancient family tree was the work of some besotted ancestor, drunk on potato wine. He could not leave things as they were.

He could not understand why the little beast had to bear a name which had not been given by him. He would not allow his life to be dictated by whim. But it was not that simple. Now and forever he was the child's cousin, just as he would always be the woman's Nephew. Nothing could ever change that either. The shared passion on Loma Ridge had become the meaningless clash of bodies. He could not bear the injustice of it. He would howl and scream and demand the return of what was his. He would steal, or rob, or kill to get it back. But whom would he kill? Perhaps himself.

When Yang Tianqing stepped across the threshold, he was his usual loyal and reliable self. He tethered the mule to the trough, then he handed a wad of warm bills to his Uncle. The Uncle smiled smugly. His eyes swept Tianqing up and down. Tianqing dropped his gaze, embarrassed by the appraisal.

"Is the mule alright?"

"As good as ever."

"What've you been feeding it?"

"Black beans just as you said. I was afraid oats might make him weak."

"You did well. I see a bit of fat on him."

Although Tianqing's eyes were elsewhere, he was straining for some sound from the north room. There was a faint rustling within, but the woman did not call a greeting.

"And Auntie...."

"She's had the baby."

"What is it?"

"A boy!"

"Healthy?"

"As fat as a hog."

"And strong?"

"As sturdy as a rock."

Tianqing licked his lips and waited. The Uncle yawned, deliberately ignoring him. It was clear he had no intention of inviting the Nephew into the north room where the new-born was.

"Have a rest. Try to be quiet. The baby needs his sleep."

"Is Auntie alright?"

"She has lots of milk. Too much in fact."

"Everything's fine then...."

"That's right.... Are you going to fetch water? Why not rest a while..."

"This barrel ... is empty...."

"Well, please yourself."

Tianqing squatted on a slab of frozen stone beside the stream for a long while. A shepherd passing by saw him gnawing an icicle as if it were an ear of corn. Finally he staggered back with two pails of water, swaying from side to side like a clown in a country play, and humming under his breath. Now and then he stopped to wipe his face with his sleeve. It was not clear whether his face was cold or whether he was dashing away tears.

On an afternoon in March, Yang Jinshan went to the west end of the village on business. Tianqing climbed on the wood pile against the wall and watched him out of sight, then he ran to the north room. As he lifted the filthy cotton door curtain the woman was holding one white breast for the infant to suck. There were no words. Their glances met and held and travelled together to the small face nestled against the woman's breast. The tiny mouth was firmly wrapped around the nipple, but a pair of shiny eyes moved from one to the other. Tianqing reached out to touch the child.

"Gently, my love...."

"I missed you!"

"Does he look like you?"

"What do I look like?"

"Just look at him...."

Tianqing laughed softly. The woman leaned her head against his chest, snuggling against the hollow of his shoulder, breathing in his musky maleness. His hand sought her other breast, kneading and caressing. The woman whimpered softly. Suddenly she stiffened, startled by a sound. But it was only the lazy scratching of a foraging hen.

"Go now. He mustn't find you here."

"I don't care."

"If he finds out it will be the end."

"I wish he would find out!"

"He'll kill you!"

"He'll have to kill all three of us."

"That's crazy talk, and you know it."

"Alright. Let it go ... just this once."

Tianqing withdrew his hand from the enclosing warmth beneath the woman's belly. Tianbai had fallen asleep, and released the nipple. His nostrils moved softly and the tip of a small pink tongue showed between his parted lips. The woman took a bare breast in her hand and held a bowl under it with the other. She gently kneaded and squeezed. A jet of milk shot into the bowl. Tianqing's eyes widened with the fascination of a child.

"Want some?"

"I...."

"Then have some...."

"Will it hurt?"

"Oh, my silly love...."

Tianqing's wide mouth encompassed the warm fleshy mound, and the warm sweet liquid shot to the back of his throat. He knew then how much she loved him. She was his eternal enchantress. In his fantasy he had swallowed her whole.

When Yang Jinshan came home, Tianqing was sitting on a basket in the courtyard knotting cloth flowers into the mule's halter, and humming to himself. As he passed the Nephew without a word, Jinshan gave him a sidelong glance, wondering why the Nephew was so happy. He recalled that the villagers thought the young fellow was not quite right in the head.

Jinshan wondered whether the young man was really a bit dim witted. However, he sensed there was something deeper lurking behind Tianqing's placidness that he did not understand. He had just rejected a marriage proposal for Tianqing because the settlement demanded was too high. Even if it had been less, the Uncle would have rejected it, for he could not manage without the Nephew. Would Tianqing be humming a tune if he knew, Jinshan wondered uneasily. If he were still humming, then his show of happiness would be a cloak for malice. Yang Jinshan comforted himself that the Nephew had a full bowl and a warm *kang*, and really wanted for nothing, and he brushed the worrisome thoughts aside.

Tianbai passed his hundredth day in June. The next day Yang Jinshan went alone to Shijia Village with gifts for his in-laws. At dusk he had still not returned.

Just before the evening meal, the riderless mule trotted into the courtyard and stopped in front of its trough but refused to eat. Tianqing thought his Uncle had stopped to chat with a neighbour. They waited a while longer but still he did not appear.

"Could he have taken a fall?"

"Nonsense. He's ridden all his life."

"If he didn't take a fall, why isn't he here...."

"If he isn't here, he isn't here. Why worry."

"I'll go up the South Cliff trail and see...."

"Wait a while...."

Judou tried to stop him with her eyes, but Tianqing would not look at her. He hurriedly shovelled the rest of his food into his mouth and left. He borrowed a lantern from Old Jiao and headed up the South Cliff trail.

It was only then he understood the look in the woman's eyes, and cold sweat popped out all over him. He looked back at the village. The house was wrapped in an ill wind. Two points of light pierced the dark like a pair of beckoning eyes. He could not bear to think on.

In a bend on the dark trail, Tianqing's foot struck something in the dark. In the faint light of the lantern it looked like a rock, and his footfall gave off no sound. He lowered the lantern for a closer look, and the muscles in his legs tensed. It was a face he had stepped on. He wanted to smash his foot into it. The body lay in a clump of grass close to the edge of the cliff. All he had to do was give it a little push, and it would be dashed to pieces and all his misery would be over. But his parents were watching coldly from beyond the grave. And so Tianqing heaved Tianbai's surrogate father on his back, and staggered home through the menacing dark.

At first they thought Jinshan had had too much to drink. They threw him on the *kang*, and he lay there with his mouth open, spewing garlic breath. Judou cowered in a corner. The stillness oppressed her, and she pinched the child's bottom making him cry. Any noise was better than the silence. Jinshan was completely at peace and slept like a log. In the side room Tianqing also slept well, his snoring seemed to make up for his anger and disappointment. When Yang Jinshan did not wake at day break the other two sensed that something was wrong. The neighbours were call in, and together they pinched and prodded; shook him and bent his limbs this way and that until they roused a glimmer of life. Yang Jinshan opened one eye. One hand moved, but he did not speak. He drooled from the corner of his twisted mouth, making strange unintelligible sounds all the while. Judou stood back frowning, not knowing how to react. As soon as the neighbours were gone, Tianqing leaned up against the door jamb and grinned. The man on the *kang* who tried to move but could not, and tried to speak but only made feeble noises was comical indeed. There was no pity in him or the woman. Tianbai broke the silence with his wailing which the woman stopped by shoving her breast into his mouth.

"What's the matter with him?'

"You tell me."

They went into the kitchen shed. Neither had an answer. Tianqing crowded the woman onto a stack of kindling. His mouth and hands sought her greedily.

"It's noon ... time to make pancakes...." she tried to struggle free, laughing. He held her fast. He was her master now. The other one in the north room was rubbish; neither man nor beast.

The witch-doctor from Yellow Pagoda concluded that Yang Jinshan had suffered a stroke and that he would be paralysed for the rest of his life. There was no cure. However, if he was properly cared for he might live,and if he had been in reasonably good health, he might even regain a little movement, and speech. But for all intents and purposes he was an invalid. They dosed him with herbs. But as expected, it did not help. And so they ended by feeding him rice and water. Yang Jinshan reverted to the helplessness of an infant, and like Tianbai, the woman had to feed and clean him. The upper-middle class farmer Yang Jinshan who strove to be a man among men, or at least one who never bent his back, was no more than an empty shell.

Six days later, in the middle of the night, a shadow crept into the side room. The mat on the *kang* rustled and groaned for hours. The moonlight was filled with whirling motes and a hundred darting moths. The moutains heaved and fell in shuddering weariness.

"Oh, my dove ... my dove...."

A bright shaft sped through the night wind into the boundless sky, and burst in a shower of bright sparks. A long sigh froze in eternity. Rasping breath subsided into nothingness,and silence rippled outward further and further.

Yang Jinshan was completely helpless for thirty days. Suddenly one morning he began to speak. Judou was holding him by the hip, cleaning the waste stuck to his buttocks. Jinshan was making protesting sounds which particularly irritated her that morning. She was deliberately heavy handed. Suddenly he said quite clearly, "... sore...."

Judou thought she was hearing things. She pressed the handful of corn husks hard against the tender flesh between the cheeks.

"... tearing ... me...."

The words were barely intelligible. Deep rooted fear flashed across the woman's mind, and her movements became gentler. Afterwards she told Tianqing and the two tried to talk with Jinshan. But the old man's mouth seemed fill with mush, and all he could manage were a few animal sounds. The other two were relieved, convinced that the old man was useless and nothing stood in the way of their happiness.

Yang Jinshan only became aware of his tragedy several nights later. He had wakened from a light sleep, and found his son peacefully sleeping in the far corner of the *kang*, but the rest of the space seemed empty. The full, round shape of the woman was missing. His eyes slowly probed the corners of the *kang* until he was sure she was gone. His dull brain mulled her absence over with painful slowness. Little by little understanding seeped through the fog, and exploded with a great flash.

Before dawn the door of the side room creaked. Yang Jinshan who had waited so long for this moment was determined to confront the woman on his feet. Frantically he pushed himself toward the edge of the *kang*. The woman stole into the room to find Jinshan hanging head first over the edge of the *kang*, desperately tugging at his useless leg. He slipped and crashed to the ground. The woman bent to lift him, and the fingers of his one good hand seized her by the hair and tugged with all his might. The woman lost her balance and pitched forward, striking her head against the side of the *kang*. For a moment she was too dazed to fight back. The fire guard had been knocked aside, and two faces, one coarse and the other tender were lit by the lurid glow.

"… kill you…."

"His Uncle…."

"… kill…."

"You're mad!"

"…. Kill…."

"See if you dare!"

"… bitch…."

Jinshan tightened his grip. Judou gritted her teeth and refused to cry out. Vaguely she sensed a crackling at the ends of her hair. She felt her face being pressed closer and closer to the flame. The heat revived her and she fought back with blind desperation. Jinshan's burst of strength suddenly ebbed and the struggle was over.

"You're paralysed. There's nothing more you can do to me."

Judou climbed onto the *kang* and sat cross-legged rubbing her throbbing scalp. Recalling all the hellish nights, the pathetic creature slumped against the clothes chest had subjected her to, she could weep.

"There's only shit between your legs," she spat at him. "I'll tell you everything. You could have killed me many times. But I refused to die. The gods gave me a real man. It's Tianqing. Now turn that over in your head, you god forsaken old thing!"

Yang Jingshan lay shivering on the cold ground, his face pressed to the earth as if waiting for it to open and swallow him. The woman on the *kang* went to sleep, leaving him where he lay. It was the longest and most enlightening night of Yang Jinshan's life. In the morning the room was filled with the acrid smell of scorched flesh. During the night he had tried to push his head through the opening into the fiery heart of the *kang*. But a stronger force held him back. The skin on one side of his face was singed. The eyebrows had been burnt off, but the eyelids still fluttered. He would not die. When Tianqing lifted him onto the *kang* and the pressure of the pillow against his face burst the blisters he did not make a sound. It was only when he was alone that he turned his face to the wall and tired old tears trickled down his face. The world had become a prison.

Yang Jinshan turned the keys of his money-box over to the woman, and gave her a handful of money for medicine for his burns.

Now there was one more ghost at Floodwater Canyon.

Yang Tianqing's explanation that Jinshan had fallen off the *kang* and burnt himself was generally accepted, but many sensed a deepening mystery surrounding Yang Jinshan's house. Visitors remarked that Yang Jinshan was terrible to look at. Yet he clung to life, demanding more than two bowls of gruel a meal. Yang Jinshan stared at the infant sleeping in the far corner of the *kang* for hours on end, with such avarice that the villagers wondered what was behind that strange look. They believed Yang Jinshan doted upon the son of his old age, and that Tianqing was a dutiful Nephew. The one they mistrusted was the pretty young wife. They began to watch her every move. But she was a paragon of decorum, and they were easily duped. The tide of passion that ran high behind shut doors was beyond their ken.

It was mid-summer and the mosquitoes were buzzing. One evening Yang Jinshan did not eat, but sat in his corner of the *kang* gaping at Tianbai. Judou had grown careless. She thought he was suffering from the heat and left a bowl of cold water for him beside his gruel. As usual she put the infant to sleep as soon as it was dark, and calmly went to the side room, not even bothering to wait till Jinshan was asleep. Yang Jinshan was buffeted by the heat of passion that penetrated the thin walls, and glared balefully at the sleeping child.

Two drifters lost in a star speckled summer's night were oblivious of the storm gathering around them. The *kang* and the walls of the rude dwelling were buckling. Their striving was suddenly halted by a half strangled cry and a muffled roar. Yang Tianqing rolled off the woman and ran naked to the next room. The woman struggled into her under things, but her legs gave under her and she slumped onto the threshold.

Yang Jinshan had laboriously hooked his can to the child's diapers and pulled him within grasp. His good hand was clutched around Tianbai's throat. His mouth was split in a mirthless laugh. He would eliminate this wild seed or he would not die in peace.

He almost succeeded.

Tianqing seized Yang Jinshan by the throat and was choking the life out of him with the same force and determination. Jingshan let go the child. For a moment he lay dazed, gasping for air, almost expecting to die. In the flickering light of the lamp he became aware of another man's naked body bending over him; of another's rigid manhood thrust before his eyes, and his despair was complete.

"Kill the cursed thing!"

It was the woman's voice. In it he heard, a strength that derived from what she had stolen and what he had never given her. It seemed fitting. Perhaps marrying her had been an offence against the gods, just as the village elders had predicted. Even dying by his Nephew's hand seemed preordained by fate. Yang Jinshan struggled for breath. Urine slowly flooded across the *kang* in a warm puddle that seemed to carry him upward.

"What are you waiting for? Kill him!"

"Put out the light!"

The vice-like grip around his throat slackened. Dimly Yang Jinshan heard the child wail, and stop. A breast had been thrust into its mouth. He thought he had exerted all his strength, but it was clearly not enough. Yang Jinshan was engulfed by shame. If he had not been betrayed by weakness, the woman would not be standing so contemptuously over him now. At the thought of his lost manhood, all he longed for was death.

Tianqing laid a heavy hand beside his head.

"Are you tired of living?"

Jinshan waited without a word.

"I'm not going to end it for you. So long as you breathe, I'll look after you."

Jinshan did not believe him. He waited.

"But hurt a finger nail of my son, and we'll see...."

He withdrew the hand. The woman sighed. The shadows of the man and the woman on the wall, merged and separated again.

"Let me know when you're tired of living. Judou put the child to sleep. He won't try it again...."

They talked in urgent whispers for a while. Finally, Tianqing went back to the side room alone, leaving Judou to sit cuddling the child for the rest of the night. But Yang Jinshan slept soundly. In the morning Yang Tianqing was seen carrying his Uncle on his back, heading out of the village. The villagers asked where he was going. He smiled without answering. Jinshan kept his eyes shut feigning sleep. When they came to the stream. Yang Tianqing slipped behind a boulder and shucked off his clothes. He got into the water to test it, then came back for Jinshan. Jinshan struggled and mumbled as the Nephew pulled off his clothes.

"What's the matter? Afraid of drowning?"

Tianqing carried his scrawny Uncle into the water and sat him on a rock. The water rose to Jinshan's chin. The old man clutched at the Nephew's leg with his good arm, his gummy eyes blinking fearfully. Tianqing laughed. He had brought along a cake of soap that he bought for Judou. He examined it curiously and showed it to the Uncle. He wet it and rubbed it against the old man's head and body as vigorously as if he were polishing stone . It was the first time he had used soap, and the bubbles delighted both men. Yang Jinshan's fear slowly ebbed. He enjoyed having his back rubbed, and a secret smile touched his face. Tianqing carried his thoroughly cleansed Uncle onto a flat rock and laid him where the warm sun of mid morning would warm him, and went back into the water. Uncle and Nephew presented such a picture of peace and harmony that no one would ever suspect any conflict between them.

Jinshan understood that his Nephew sincerely meant to look after him, but he was equally ready to attack him. There was nothing he could do to stop him and the woman, nor was he able to refuse any kindness that would prolong his life. All he could do was ignore Tianbai: to turn away from the wild seed. But that was almost as painful as death. Since he must go on living somehow, this seeing yet not seeing was unbearable. He discovered that he was afraid of dying. He was especially afraid of dying violently. His death would mean nothing to anyone. But he really did not want to die. Even living in shame was better. In his dreams he saw himself strong and virile as he used to be. Believing in the prophetic nature of dreams, he secretly prayed for that day. Then he would show them. But in the meantime, he had to go on living.

Yang Jinshan lived in a triumphant fantasy. The unfaithful wife who crept from his *kang* into that of another in the dead of night no longer aroused any grief or anger. He toted up the sum of their sins, and gloated at the final reckoning.

The only weapon left to Yang Jinshan were the cauldrons of hell. In his fantasies, wife and Nephew were already fried to a crisp. Day and night he ground them between his teeth, feeling righteous, listening to their piteous screams.

"My dove ... my dove ... my darling little dove!"

They were slipping inexorably into a chasm as bottomless as death. Each time they climbed out of it, they rushed toward it again as eagerly as before. Caution was tossed to the wind.

It was Wang Judou who first sensed danger. Her period was three days late. The rush of joy, quickly turned to fear. Wang Judou blanched. A cloud gathered over the side room. Yang Tianqing knotted his brow not knowing what to do. However, the period eventually came. It was a reprieve, but fear dogged them from then on. Their love-making was fraught with fear and regret. They were slowly drifting apart.

In October there was peace.

One day in autumn, Wang Judou covered her head with a flowered kerchief and left the village, telling everyone she passed that she was going to the fair. But her destination was actually the Nunnery of Two Purities a few *li* away. She lit a bundle of eight josssticks, and banged her head on the ground countless times before an image, then meekly followed an old nun to a quiet corner behind the great hall. She threw herself on her knees before the old woman. The old nun smiled knowingly and asked a few questions. She explained the difference between the deities for begetting and for not begetting. Wang Judou had prayed to the wrong one, said she. The old nun led Wang Judou into a side chapel. She knelt at the foot of a clay image who grimaced at them out of the gloom like an ancient witch. The old crone mumbled prayers, and the woman joined her palms and mumbled along with her, eyes shut tight. At length the old nun produced a packet of medicine from the folds of her robe and handed it to Wang Judou. She cautioned the woman not to open it until it was needed. But she would not say how it was to be used until they had found a secluded corner away from the chapel. Judou was blushing before the old woman spoke. She turned bright red afterwards. The medicine was not to be taken orally.

"But how is it applied?"

"The man must do it for you."

"But won't it slip off?"

"A little water will do the trick."

Although the nun spoke with great patience, nothing she said penetrated Wang Judou's dull wits. She left the nunnery, and turned her burning face to the autumn wind as she trudged homeward along the mountain path. It dawned on her that the nun had been deliberately obscure. Actually it was as simple as eating a sprig of scallion dipped in beanpaste.

It was painful the first time they used the remedy. It was excruciating the second time.

Once again Wang Judou went to the fair. This time she sought out the old nun, made a sizeable donation and timidly suggested that the miraculous potion did not work. The nun's eyes raked the woman.

"So you couldn't stand it," she sneered.

"It burnt something fierce! The man was in so much agony he bit me...."

"Did you hurt?"

"Yes."

"If you didn't hurt, would you stop doing it?"

The nun's eyes devoured Judou's pretty face. The woman dropped her eyes in confusion. The nun produced another packet which she pressed into Judou's hand. Judou did not dare refuse it.

"Are you sure you've had six children?"

"Yes".

"If you're not tired of frolicking, have some more."

"The man wants it...."

"And you don't?"

"I...."

"Use this ten times, and I guarantee you'll be sick of it."

"I'll try it."

That night the two unwrapped the packet and examined the mysterious powder under the lamplight. They hesitated,unwilling to use it yet not daring to take a chance. Once again Tianqing was in agony, sinking his teeth into her shoulder as he writhed. The woman too was in excruciating pain.

Yang Tianqing dashed the packet on the ground, and thought he caught a whiff of black pepper as its contents scattered. They had been duped by the malicious old crone. The mysterious powder was nothing more than a mixture of pepper and incense ashes. They soaked themselves in clear water, and tenderly caressed each other's smarting flesh. That night neither slept.

Like all the neighbouring villages, Floodwater Canyon was establishing a primary commune. One day the cadres in charge came to Yang Jinshan demanding he turn over the last ten *mu* of land he held. Yang Jinshan leaned into a corner of the *kang*, and pretended to be deaf and mute. In exasperation they called on Tianqing to act on his Uncle's behalf. But Tianqing only grinned like a fool and spread the fingers of his big clumsy hands in a gesture of helplessness.

"It's fine as long as we get enough food."

The cadres thought they were getting somewhere.

Then Tianqing added, "My Uncle is a stubborn man. If he gets excited it might kill him." He chuckled pleasantly and continued, "There's not much left in him now. I work the fields for him. Once he goes, I'll have my Aunt turn the land over to you, I'm single. I'll be one of you sooner or later. Without you I wouldn't even have a place to beg."

The cadres were taken by surprise.

"Your Aunt comes from a family of land owners. Are you sure your Uncle won't persuade her to hold on to the land?"

"My Aunt's family may be land owners, but she isn't. Why she's constantly praising the government's generosity."

"You promise to talk to her when your Uncle dies?"

"I do."

"And you'll give up the mule too?"

"It's as you say."

"But when will your Uncle die? Seems to me he could go on forever, paralyzed or no. Some people have all the luck. Better fix your thumb mark here … so you won't renege later on."

"I won't renege. I swear."

Yang Jinshan was allowed to keep his land for the time being.

It was one of those unforeseeable events in the early history of Floodwater Canyon that became obscured by the passage of time.

Yang Tianbai began to walk and then to utter his first words. The first word he learned was mother, and the next was father. In the beginning "father" was every man he encountered, and sometimes even the mule. But in the end it settled on the man with the shock of grey hair and the horribly scarred face. It took the child longer to learn how to address the younger man. The word cousin did not trip off his tongue quite as easily, though the look of perpetual misery on the man's face was quickly etched on his young mind.

Yang Tianbai had the same large head and high cheek bones as Yang Tianqing. But no one noticed. The fact is no one remembered Yang Tianqing as a child. Besides Tianbai had also inherited his mother's fine features.

He was a fine boy. Finer than both Yang Jinshan or Yang Tianqing. He had intelligent eyes and a firm jaw that did not grow slack when he was deep in thought. Nor had he inherited any of the other less desirable traits of the race. He laughed and cried while his elders coped with the calamities of life. His parents were mired in the practical problems of their lives, for which there seemed no possible solution.

Yang Tianqing experimented with different movements and positions but he sought something foolproof. The old nun had sown a grain of thought that slowly took root in his mind. He thought of wormwood leaves and vinegar and finally of soap.

Yang Tianqing pinned his hopes on soap because it could remove greasy stains, and make the eyes smart. So he reasoned it must also kill sperm. And even if it did not work, anything would be better than the old nun's pepper powder.

Yang Tianqing shaved bits of soap into a bowl. He sniffed the waxy yellow grains the size of hazelnuts, and then tested them gingerly with the tip of his tongue. The nights in the side room were no longer blissful. Two naked bodies faced each other hesitantly. The bowl of soap pellets between their legs glistened like an offering for some sacred ritual.

Judou spat into the bowl and Tianqing pressed a trembling finger tip on a pellet and slowly ground it against the side of the bowl. The slippery object eluded him. He caught it and ground it until a bubbly foam appeared. He lifted his head and sighed. All the strength drained from him. She spread herself, pleading with her eyes. Carefully he inserted three pellets.

Afterwards Yang Tianqing was miserable. He was passionate and virile, and she was beautiful, but the unaccustomed slipperiness of the soap reduced their act of love to the gyrations of a mechanical device. Their passion had become a sham.

The fires of youth had come against an insurmountable obstacle, which hemmed them in and turned them into strangers. For a while they practised self denial with fierce determination. They still slept together, expressing their passion with mouths and tongues, and seeking gratification with work-roughened hands. When they held each other shuddering and whimpering Tianqing recalled the secret of the peep-hole years before. He thought it would amuse her, but she only snuggled against him more miserable than ever and buried her teeth into his shoulder to stop from crying out.

"Lover!"

"Darling...."

"Lets die together."

"No. You live and I'll die."

"I can't live without you."

"My love ... my love...."

They pulled the bedclothes over their heads and wept.

There were also moments of cool headed calculation. At such times the woman's tongue was as venomous as a snake's.

"I'll put a spell on him and make him die."

"And then what?"

"Whatever you say."

"There's nothing we can do."

"So we have another child. Let them gossip all they like."

"Let them say what they like...."

"So what if they blacken us...."

"... we'd be better off dead...."

"Lover, lets run away."

"Where can we go?"

"We could go out to the frontier and herd sheep for the Mongols."

"Who are we going to leave the land to? If we lose the land we might as well be dead. Do you remember the time when there was famine, and how many starved on the frontier?"

"I can't go on like this. If I don't properly marry you, I'll drown myself."

"Don't talk nonsense. Just give me some time. Let me...."

"I'm sick of waiting."

"You won't be satisfied till you worry me to death!"

"Are you angry? you devil!"

They were not husband and wife, yet they quarrelled as if they were. Yang Tianqing was experiencing none of the joy of having a woman but all the exasperation.

Still he did not consider her redundant for then he too would have become un-necessary.

The unfaithful wife and Nephew were slowly sinking into despair. They were listless. The joy of life had gone out of them while Yang Jinshan grew stronger day by day. When the child was running about in the village, the old man finally learnt to shift himself from one place to another, sitting on an overturned basket and propelling himself forward with his one good arm and one good leg. He loved to sit in the sunlight leaning against the north wall of the village, though it took two hours to push himself that far. The child gambolled about him. It amused him to have the child, piping "Father! Father!" for all to hear. Though the child was not his, it was no one else's. Yang Jinshan, shut his eyes against the sunlight. The childish prattling of Tianbai added to his content. The other two could dig their own graves, he thought maliciously. The devil had them in his clutches already. Once he thought Tianqing had stolen from him. In fact he had stolen from Tianqing. And no one could take away what he had seized, for he was a father in Floodwater Canyon, and not Tianqing. He was the victor in the end. When the day's work was over, the Nephew came and carried him home. The younger man was thoroughly beaten. Nothing could mar Yang Jinshan's triumph except the smell of soap that Judou carried back to his *kang* in the hours before dawn. He was jealous of her fastidiousness, nor could he understand her inability to face up to the things she had done.

The years passed. Yang Tianqing lost count of the cakes of soap they used up until the general belt tightening came, and he had to make the pellets smaller to stretch the supply. Finally he could no longer afford soap at all. For the sake of his ambiguous reputation, he resorted to a five-cent bottle of watery vinegar, which he spooned into the woman. At least it did not sting, or have an unpleasant slippery sensation. Although it was better than the nun's concoction or his own earlier invention, he was heart sore. Their passionate encounters become few and far between. One day Yang Tianqing noticed that his flesh had turned white. The woman had also began to rot. The devil had them in his clutches indeed, and they were at their wit's end. Finally Judou collapsed complaining of a sharp pain in the chest. Tianqing put her on the mule and rushed her to the hospital. When they had passed Jade Creek, beyond the prying eyes of the village, Judou sat up in the saddle. Tianqing was also grimacing with pain. They turned and headed for the hospital in the next county instead like beasts being led to slaughter.

The doctor questioned Judou closely. She almost let slip the word, "vinegar" but caught herself in time. The doctor could get nothing out of her. Her reticence only raised more questions. Outside, Tianqing heard the doctor pronounce that the beautiful body of his beloved was a stupid and corrupt thing. Helpless anger flared. Judou was given a thorough cleansing. She came away dazed and humiliated, clutching a bottle of medicine. Tianqing surrepticiously took her hand. He wanted to hold and protect the woman he had dragged through hell.

Soon after the government's itinerant medical team arrived in the village. At dusk men, woman and children gathered under the chestnut tree, while the nurse stuck a coloured stick in a volunteer's mouth and poked about until it frothed. After the demonstration of dental hygiene, the nurse produced a pair of clippers to cut finger nails. The parings as fine as fish scales, fascinated the rough village men. During the last part of the meeting the elders herded the men and the children away, leaving only the women of various ages to hear a woman doctor speak. Tianqing caught a glimpse of a diagram of buttocks that had been sliced open hanging in the lamp light.

Lying on the *kang* that night Judou carefully repeated what she heard, counting off each item on her fingers. Tianqing listened fascinated. Although most of the women had paid scant attention to the talk, Judou hung on the doctor's every word. It had been the wickedest talk ever given in the village of Floodwater Canyon. It dealt with how to avoid pregnancy.

Their love-making did not become more satisfactory. The so-called safe days were days of fear and danger. That the woman did not become pregnant was the will of god.

"Oh, my dove ... my dove ... my little dove...."

That ecstatic murmur had lost its fervour, and become mechanical from counting and from desperate measures to escape the inevitable. Years later stringent measures of birth control would rouse the villagers to an unprecedented pitch of anger. Little did they know that a lone pioneer, stubborn but cunning had gone before them.

At the age of thirty Yang Tianqing was showing signs of aging.

The year before Yang Tianbai started school, on the

eighth of June according to lunar reckoning, the greedy old landowner, pock-mark Wang of Shijia Village swallowed arsenic and died. Someone came to break the news to Wang Judou. She was told that her father had been a restorationist bent on disturbing the social order. She was warned not to follow in his misguided ways, or she would come to the same sticky end as her father. There would be poor, and lower-middle class farmers keeping an eye on her. Tianqing was also warned to keep out of the family affairs of his Aunt. As long as he devoted himself to caring for his Uncle everything would be fine. It was several days later that Wang Judou went home. By then her father was already cold in his grave. Tianqing accompanied her as far as the South Ridge. At home her sorrowing old mother who stoically stifled her tears, pressed a snuff-bottle into Judou's hand and told her to throw it over the edge of the South Ridge. Then she would be at peace. The old woman impressed it upon Judou that she must make certain nobody saw her. Pock-mark Wang had bought the snuffbottle and the poison years ago when he went to the city to trade. At first he said it was for everyone he hated. But in the end he swallowed it himself. He was probably the only one fit for it anyway. Wang Judou was pale and drawn when she returned to Floodwater Canyon, drooping like a withered leaf caught in the frost. Some thought she too had taken something. Yang Jinshan lying on the *kang*, mumbled. She turned her back on him. She stopped having anything to say to the old thing long ago.

In the middle of the night, Wang Judou quietly lifted the latch of the broken door through which a gale blew. A ghostly blast filled the room. Tianqing lit a match and touched it to the wick of the lamp, and shifted the pillow for the woman. She did not undress or lie down beside him, but stared fixedly at the sputtering lamp. A chill ran through Tianqing. He reached for her hand and found she was clutching a tiny delicately wrought snuff bottle.

"What have you got?"

"Nothing."

"What's the matter?"

"Nothing's the matter. Shall I put out the light?"

"Leave it on. I don't feel good."

"What's bothering you? .... There's something the matter...."

The woman took no notice. She moved the lamp over to the window sill, and tapped the snuff-bottle against the grey brick. Grains of shiny crystals like coarse salt spilled onto the grey bricks. Tianqing was terrified.

"Judou! Don't be silly...."

"If I had the guts I would have taken it on South Ridge."

"That's stupid. Why do you want to die?"

"I'm better off dead."

"You can leave me, but what about Tianbai?"

"I can leave the both of you. I can't stand it any more. The old thing just hangs on. Every day it gets worse. I can't be your woman. I can't look anybody in the face any more. I think I've lived too long!"

Tianqing snatched the bottle from her and tucked in under the pillow. He undressed her, dried her tears, stroked and petted her until she was calm, then he heaved a sigh of relief.

"We've been through a lot already, and there's more to come. If it's not our time taking this stuff is not going to make any difference. There'll be a day for the three of us yet. Just wait and see."

"If I don't take it, then he must."

"Who?"

"Who else?"

"Listen, if he dies, we all die."

"Tianqing, lets take Tianbai and get away from here. I'll work like a beast for you. I promise you won't regret it.... Tianqing, listen to me.... Take us out of here...."

"It's not that simple."

"Oh, my love, why can't you see it my way?"

Yang Tianqing could no longer hold on to her. The little dove had become a hawk.

Wang Judou stole back into the north room. In the deep indigo of the hours before dawn she could make out Tianbai's bare legs dangled over the edge of the *kang*. The boy was barely seven years old, but his young-old eyes were fixed balefully on her. Judou shuddered and slumped against the side of the *kang*. From the corner where the old man lay came a chuckle, cold, muffled but infinitely malicious. Her heart that was aflame moments ago, turned to a lump of ice. The cold coursed slowly through her body. The child silently slid between the covers, and pulled his small pillow aside. She reached out a mother's hand and stroked him. She was still stroking him when the sun rose turgid and dull, and the chill had gone from her fingers. The morning mist that rose laden with the stench of Jinshan's waste was a silent reproach. Somewhere a cock crowed.

Winds of change were sweeping the nation. Floodwater Canyon was being collectivized. The price of livestock plummeted. It was rumoured that a strong ox would fetch no more than twenty *yuan*, and a small donkey was worth nothing. Yang Tianqing was worried about the old black mule. He went to his Uncle and tried to explain the situation as simply and clearly as he could, hoping to get some reaction from him. The old man ate and slept as usual. But he had aged. Yang Tianqing marvelled at the invalid's tenacity; his refusal to die. Nevertheless he wondered whether the shock of losing his property so abruptly would be too much for him. But to his surprise the Uncle was neither annoyed nor agitated. He gazed at the Nephew with his dull yellowish eyes, and his scarred face broke into a beatific smile. It was a smile so full of hidden nuances that it chilled Tianqing to the marrow. It flashed across his mind that perhaps Judou was right and fate was conspiring against them. Life had become a burden. Sooner or later they too would become as helpless as the paralytic, shamelessly soiling themselves, their humiliation exhibited for all the world to see. He did not know how he could go on living. Could he eliminate this burden and give himself a breathing space? He waited for a sign from heaven, but the gods were silent. Tianqing's breathing became laboured. He trembled all over. Once more he was the dutiful Nephew.

"I am afraid we have to let go of the land on Loma Ridge."

The smile went awry.

"The mule will be confiscated, and we won't be able to transport goods for money anymore."

The smile congealed into a grotesque lump on the

old man's face.

"I'll take it out and sell it for what I can get. What do you say...."

The smile became a sound and the sound became a knife that stabbed at his breast.

".... Heaven ... curse you ... wastrel.... Devil ... take you...."

Tianqing was petrified. Blood rushed toward his heart. His limbs became jelly and he reeled against the *kang*. Only he could make out the curse uttered by the tongue that cleaved to the old man's palate.

Even without the words Tianqing could grasp their meaning from the quivering of the snake-like tongue. The air of the room was heavy with the stench of human waste. A withered hand fluttered like a tattered battle-flag. The terrible smile exploded. Tianqing reeled out of the room. Fragments of the smile followed him all the way to West River where he haggled and finally sold the old mule. Still the memory of the smile lingered in the valleys and the ravines like an evil omen dancing around him.

Late in the afternoon of an ordinary autumn day, Yang Jinshan quietly died. He had led an extraordinary life. That noon he had two bowls of gruel. Afterwards he dragged himself on his basket to his favorite spot along the north wall and sat in the sun which was already low in the sky. He was feeling fine. Yang Jinshan leaned against the wall and never moved again. His face was turned to the sun. There was a look of contentment on his face, as though he was drunk from too much sun and wind. He did not respond to Tianbai's shouted greeting as he raced by waving a willow switch. Nor did he acknowledge the greeting of old Jiao's woman. The hens foraged around his feet, pecking at the dried scabs of gruel and caked spit on his shoes. Judou passed him on her way home from the field with an armful of autumn cabbage, and glanced at him from the corner of her eye. He smiled fixedly, the light of the setting sun glinting in his eyes like tiny pearls. She lit the kitchen fire, washed her hands and face in the stale water at the bottom of the urn, and went to fetch him, a tiny frown furrowing her brow. She touched him, and he toppled to the ground like a wall collapsing. He was still smiling, his eyes fixed on a greenish puddle of chicken droppings. One side of his face lay in another puddle.

A keening wail sounded along the lanes; a sound that had not been heard for many years. Young and old came running from their houses. Two figures writhed on the ground: one moving the other still; one wailed and the other, silent. One of them was clearly dead. The woman was dishevelled. She hammered herself with her fists, and pummelled the corpse. She beat her fists against the walls, and the ground. She tore at the dead man's clothes with her teeth, and tugged at the hair that fell in her face. Her gurgling cries shattered the peaceful sunset of Floodwater Canyon. She was beautiful even in her grief. As in days gone by, the woman was once more battered beyond endurance, and her cries sent shock waves through all those who came to watch. The husband continued to smile mysteriously though he had vanished into the underworld forever. Did she really grieve for the useless paralytic? Did she not hate the man who had treated her so badly? Perhaps she really was a soft-hearted creature who had carefully tended the old thing. How else could he have managed such a pleasant end? They decided she was a good woman after all. The old man smiled, content even in death. And he should be, for no one in Floodwater Canyon had slept with a finer figure of a woman. He had had a good life, and was probably worrying beyond the grave who would come along to pick this rare flower. Several pairs of hands lifted her by the waist and buttocks and carried her to the house. The hands that picked up the dead man were less gentle. They carried him like the carcass of a dead goat ready for slaughter, his head lolloping from side to side.

"Damn it, take care!" An angry voice rang from the back of the throng.

The clumsy men carrying the corpse took no notice. The dead man was heaved unceremoniously onto the damp and stinking *kang*. The crowd parted. Yang Tianbai stood on the threshold his small mouth trembling, on the verge of tears. Earlier when he saw his mother weeping he shrank to the back of the crowd, and no matter how he was pushed and pulled, would not go forward. But now he was angered by the rough treatment his poor old father was getting. He pushed the grown-ups aside and slipped a pillow under his father's grey head. Still there were no tears. The dead man faced the wall. Tianbai took the head between his hands and righted it, so that he faced the ceiling. But the head plopped to one side again as soon as he let go. The child tried again and again, but the head had a will of its own. Yang Tianbai burst into tears clutching his father's stubborn head. The storm of tears was so sudden and heart-rending that many eyes reddened. Judou had calmed down, but the child's grief stirred a fresh outburst. The neighbours took down a door and propped it between a stool and a basket for a bier. Matches were struck and the spirit lamp sputtered to life.

Yang Tianqing heard the sounds of grief when he reached the old chestnut tree at the edge of the village. Over the din he could make out his son's shrillings and Judou's hoarse wails that hovered in the stillness of the gathering dusk. When he came through the door with two hundred *yuan* he got for the mule, his Uncle was already laid out on the bier. He faced the door. Beside his shoulder a spirit lamp lit his way to the underworld. Everything became clear.

Yang Tianqing pushed his way through the crowd, his face expressionless. He looked about him as he slipped the knapsack off his shoulder. The weeping suddenly stopped. Judou sitting on the *kang* with Tianbai beside her searched his face. Tianqing foraged in his knapsack for a pencil box, eraser, ruler and exercise book which he handed to Tianbai. Then he took out a felt hat and a bag of sweets. He was going to take out something else, but caught himself in time, and handed the knapsack to the woman instead. She quickly tucked it under her seat. In the knapsack was a wad of money and a flowered kerchief. Yang Tianqing paced the room restlessly, and the women in the crowd were overcome with grief for the young man who had lost the only living relative he had.

It took Yang Tianqing a while to figure out what was expected of him. He drew close to the dead man and touched his paralysed leg. His hand slid down until he gripped the ankle. The body was still warm, and its heat shot through him. His gaze moved timidly to his Uncle's smiling face. The dead eyes gleamed maliciously through half open lids. He squatted down, breathing heavily.

Someone caught him by the arm and helped him to his feet. He took the hat and slipped it on the dead man's head, then he took the bag of sweets outside and called the children in the crowd.

"Taste some ... taste some...."

"The apple candy is very tasty...."

"Do try some. Everyone ... please...."

"Try some. All of you...."

But no one would come near. He squatted down again and hugged his head. He did not weep, but muttered under his breath. The others listening were worried.

Suddenly he began to sob, softly and without hope. The others tried to comfort him. As the sobbing stopped, the crowd drifted away, leaving the courtyard to the sad pale light of the new risen moon.

Behind locked doors, Aunt and Nephew kept vigil over their dead. The child had been put to bed in the side room. The man and the woman's gaze grappled unhindered. The man that lay between them was already hurrying along the road to the underworld, no longer concerned with the activities of the living.

"Did you do it?"

"What are you talking about?"

"Don't lie to me."

"What do you think I've done?"

"Don't pretend. Aren't you afraid lightning might strike you?"

"Devil! Your Uncle's time was up, and he went. Look at him. Is that the face of someone who was pois oned? And you blame me. I guess it's just my fate."

"Quit acting! If you did it, we're in it together. Do you think I'd give you away."

"What can I do to make you believe I didn't do anything!"

"I'm worried and confused...."

"The lamp's gone out.... Better light it again...."

Yang Tianqing took a stick and adjusted the wick of the lamp. The flame flickered, setting off a shower of sparks that flew into the darkness and disappeared.

He sighed.

They did not notice a figure sitting on the threshold of the side room. In the dark the silent figure of Tianbai loomed large and menacing. The autumn wind moaned. The courtyard was filled with secrets that threatened to burst its seams.

The glances of father and son, cousin and cousin, clashed and separated again in the dark. The one who held the strands of secrets together, coughed nonchalantly and said, "Cousin, it's cold. Get to bed...."

"Your cousin will sit with your father. Go to bed."

"You don't want to fall asleep at the funeral tomorrow...."

"You won't be allowed to carry the banner, if you don't do as you're told...."

The child hung his head and went inside. Tianqing approached Yang Jinshan's dead smile, and tried to shut his eyes. But the lids would not move though he pressed down hard. Finally he retreated to the safety of the *kang*, and sucked noisily on his pipe.

He was weary. Too weary to go on living. He wondered who was the lucky one: the living or the dead. Everything was a muddle. He could not think.

"Where's the snuff-bottle? Did you get rid of it?"

"Would I get rid of the evidence?"

He did not understand why the woman was so angry. When she took out the snuff bottle, he felt the blood rush to his head, and he gritted his teeth.

"Did you keep it to feed to me? It was all my fault in the first place, and I'm tired of living...."

"Tianqing, you're forcing me to take this stuff...."

"Take it if you like! I will too!"

The snuff-bottle flew across the room, struck a corner of the bier and rolled into a corner. When he was calm, Tianqing found it, took it into the pig pen and buried it under three feet of pig droppings. At dawn the woman started wailing again. A funeral is a festival and everyone in the village rose early.

Soon after Yang Jinshan was committed to the earth, his son began school. By the time he had been in the ground a year, Tianbai was at the top of his second grade class. Tianbai and his cousin did not get along. Often Tianqing would try to talk to him. But the boy would glare at him and stalk away before he finished what he had to say. But the boy loved his mother. However, Judou was often unhappy. As a matter of fact no one in the house was happy. The face that Tianqing showed in the village was care-worn. He seemed older than a man in his thirties. He was a man in his prime and still a bachelor. He needed a mate.

After Yang Jinshan died, Tianqing decided that Judou and her child should live as a separate household. Each would work their own plot of land, and earn their own points. However, their food was still cooked in a common pot, but Tianqing would eat his in the side room or out in the lane. Judou was now a widow and she had to be careful of every move. He too had to be doubly cautious. One false step and the fabric of their lives would unravel. They had already committed an unforgivable sin. Now the two must tread extra carefully not only for their own sakes, but for Tianbai's as well.

But how long could they go on that way?

Yang Tianqing became a bachelor indeed. The wide *kang* became wider and colder. His son watched him night and day. He watched her too. The boy stood between them. Whenever Yang Tianqing wanted to take advantage of a moment, or a place, his son appeared in the nick of time, cold and relentless. Even if he did not appear, his presence dogged them. The boy's cold, unrelenting eyes hovered all around Yang Tianqing. Through his son Yang Jinshan was reaching for him from beyond the grave. Yang Tianqing burned in an unquenchable fire. He began to hate the boy. He wanted to strangle the little beast. Then in a fit of remorse, wanted to kill himself. The woman's body thickened and lost its litheness. But still she was the torch that could burn him to a cinder. He was still the flame that warmed her. He wanted to take her in his arms and press his lips to every inch of her body. She was the only woman he desired. No one existed beside her. He treasured every inch of her, loved every hair, worshipped even the accumulated dirt of winter behind her knees. No one could stand in his way except his son. His seed was growing into a huge tree that threatened to block out the sun.

Somehow they weathered the hungry sixties, Judou developed the habit of going to her family once every season. Each time she would be gone a fortnight. She came home looking radiant and happy. Three days after she left, Tianqing would go up the South Ridge to gather firewood or wild herbs. He would be gone three days at a time till the Aunt returned from Shijia Village. Wang Judou followed the same schedule when she was home. She too went to the South Ridge on similar errands. The old land-owner's woman sighed and muttered about her daughter's hard life, and her diligence.

On the South Ridge between Floodwater Canyon and Shijia Village there is a place known as Badger's Rock. Off the beaten path and hidden by clumps of tall grass is a shallow cave. The cave was the width of two *kangs*, but too low to stand in. This became their trysting place. They were ill-fed and the distance was long. By the time they reached the cave, both were too exhausted for love making. Still they went there. It was the only place they could be man and woman.

Tianqing built a small fire and took off his jacket. The woman picked lice for him. Her fingers worked quickly, deftly squeezing the lice between her finger nails and making them pop. He lay on a pile of straw watching her silhouetted against the sky and sighed. He sighed again, and she came to him, planted a hasty kiss on his face and went back into the light to work. Contentment washed over him, filling the cave.

"Yesterday Tianbai won another prize."

"As good as the last one?"

Tianqing had to think before answering.

"Well it was the same yellow paper with a fancy border."

"What was it for?"

"He got a first for arithmetic and a second for calligraphy."

"I suppose he was careless and wrote the wrong characters."

"Who knows. I asked, but the little devil won't speak to me."

"Why not ask the teacher?"

"How can I? He's not my son. If I ask too many questions they might get suspicious.... Let it go. If he won't speak to me, let him be...."

Tianqing's throat constricted and he fell silent. Judou helped him into his jacket and lay beside him. They held each other, sighing and whispering about nothing in particular. Tianqing said she was the best woman in the world, and he had dragged her down. Judou said it was she that ruined his life. They wept together like a pair of motherless children.

In the warm weather they hurried to the cave beneath Badger's Rock and rekindled a little of their lost passion. They recognized their need and the inevitability of their actions. Once they accepted the price that was exacted for the fleeting moments of release, they became resigned. It was the only way of finding peace. At times they felt constrained. The nakedness in which they delighted, was embarrassing. Now that they had become like animals of the field they had lost their natural freedom. They became awkward, and melancholy settled on them.

"My dove ... my dove ... my darling little dove...."

The whispered words seem to seep out of the dampness of the cave, bringing with it a breath of another world. The two bodies twined, parted. They gazed at each other with misty eyes.

"Did it happen?"

"It's not the time."

"If we don't, we'll shrivel up."

"We'll shrivel up anyway."

They spoke desultorily as if they were discussing the crops. The veins in Tianqing's neck and legs were thick as ropes, glistening and smooth as external bones. Judou's firm round breasts had grown slack as half empty sacks of grain. When she went out of the cave, and into the sunlight, he noticed the grey mixed in her jet black hair. Where had the time gone. Tianqing gave her half his firewood. She hoisted the bundle on her back. He watched the square patch on her shoulder and the round one on her rump as she moved down the path. He followed a few steps, and a few steps more.

"Judou, take care of yourself."

The weight of the firewood bore down on her. She could not turn so she waved. He stood and waved back until she was gone from sight. He looked about him then. For a moment he did not know where he was. The path snaked away into the distance, becoming narrower and narrower until it disappeared.

The widow of Pock-mark Wang of Shijia Village died several years later. Her death also demolished the precarious bridge her daughter had built for love. Without an excuse to go home, the lovers returned their trysting place to the foxes and badgers who were more adept at wandering the wilderness which was theirs. They shied from the scent of humans. They looked to the wind to drive away that evil scent and never let it return.

That same year Wang Judou got rheumatism and could no longer work in the fields. Now and then when she did, she would be confined to her *kang* for the next few days. Yang Tianbai graduated from primary school, and abandoned the idea of going on to high school. He became a full fledged commune member and joined the work force. The strong young worker who was good with his hands was well liked. Yang Jinshan had sown good seed, and everyone thought the widow would be well cared for in her old age.

Yang Tianqing remained single. He seemed to be shrouded in clouds that obscured the future. He waited patiently for the clouds to disperse when fate would dash him into the abyss below, or lift him into the void, and so end his nightmarish existence.

Floodwater Canyon was caught up in a tumultuous new era. The literate took the lead demanding sheets of white, pink and green paper from the brigade and carrying them home to be turned into big character posters. Not to be outdone the illiterate followed suit. Everyone was enthralled by a new mission to attack and destroy. The attacks came from all sides. The guerrilla assaults on their own were far more vicious than any waged against the Japanese invaders.

The first big character poster accused a certain brigade leader of striking a worker six times on a certain day. Although the brigade leader had apologized afterwards, the poster demanded a more practical apology: money to compensate the worker for a toothache.

Another poster accused a certain person for keeping a fevered pig, spreading sickness, and causing the destruction of half the pigs in the village. The heads of eighteen families signed the poster. Clearly the accusers meant to bankrupt the offender.

The latest poster accused the mild mannered brigade secretary of pinching a certain part of the anatomy of a worker's wife. The part of her anatomy that had been so rudely interfered with was never specified. The woman concerned did not attempt suicide or make a fuss at the time. She claimed she had been intimidated. But she was over her fear. Now she was bent on vengeance. See if he dares do it again!

Turmoil was everywhere. Criticism was the court of last resort. It was a strange, confusing time.

One day a poster appeared about Judou. The writing was childish. The author was Tianguo, the village idiot. The idiot could not remember the exact date. Though the scribe who had a conscience, did not embellish the story, he did render a vivid account. It happened in a clump of bushes beside the path up the South Ridge. At first the idiot thought it was some animal; a deer or perhaps a fox. But it was a woman. He was sure it was Judou, astride a man. Because he was hidden by the bushes the idiot could not see who the man was. The horrified villagers turned away from the poster. But the rowdies seized the idiot and made him read the poster out loud. The idiot stuttered fearfully for he could not read. Then someone offered him a cigarette and he brightened.

"Who was underneath?"

Tianguo frowned, clamped his cigarette firmly between his teeth as if someone might snatch it from him, and puffed furiously.

"Did she move as though she was washing clothes?"

Tianguo got down on hands and knees and demonstrated what he had seen. The others laughed. As long as he had free smokes, he was content to go on gyrating indefinitely. The members of the Yang family gave the lewd exhibition a wide berth.

Yang Tianbai noticed the whispers and the peculiar expressions on people's faces before he read the poster. When he saw the idiot's grotesque performance and the laughing crowd egging him on, he knew what he had to do. He slipped into the woodwork shop beside the brigade headquarters. His handsome face was expressionless. When he came out of the shop he was armed with an axe. Tianbai moved purposefully through the laughing throng as if he was about to split kindling. Fear rippled through the mob and laughter petered out. The axe whistling past his head took the idiot by surprise. He shot to his feet and made a dash for it, the butt of a cigarette still clenched between his teeth. The banked up fury in Tianbai exploded. He loped after the idiot waving the ax. The idiot ran pell mell toward the South Ridge, screaming, "Save me! Save me!"

The idiot slid off the edge of a terraced field, splashed across a stream and plunged headlong into the woods. The tangled branches of the underbrush rustled for a long time.

Yang Tianbai threw the ax into the woodworking shop and went home.

"Good on you, Tianbai!"

"Your father was an upper middle class farmer. You've nothing to fear."

The villagers tried to engage him in conversation, but Tianbai would take no notice. He went home grim faced. His mother was preparing a meal and his cousin was digging up the dung in the pig pen. Something inside had shattered. He tried to calm himself by fixing the handle of a hoe. But wild thoughts kept racing through his head and he could not concentrate. He vented his fury on a pickle jar, and throwing the shards over the wall into the field.

The three of them did not exchange a word the next few days.

Tianguo's old father bought half a catty of biscuits and came to apologize to Judou. He cursed his son roundly. Then he praised Tianbai for his filial piety; and Tianqing for his loyalty. He even praised the dead, saying that Yang Jinshan was indeed the epitome of a wise and prosperous farmer.

"Why, look how fat those chickens are!"

Before he started in on the finer points of the pig, Judou hustled him from the house. He went down the street, bowing and muttering, as though his son had offended the mountains, and the trees and the grass and all had to be appeased.

Yang Tianqing turned forty amid the turmoil in Floodwater Canyon. His foot had been injured while he was constructing a terraced field for the production brigade. While he was convalescing on his *kang* he had time to think. Bits of his life flashed through his mind. He forgave others and himself, and in so doing found peace. Fate was fair, and the heavens had granted him all that he had. He had no complaints.

When Judou came to change his bandages and found him calmly gazing at the smoke blackened rafters, her eyes brimmed.

"Tianbai is forever grumbling. I suppose the only

thing's to ignore him.''

"He's a good son. Let him be.''

"One of these days I'll have to tell him the truth.''

"You'll kill him, if you do. Leave it alone.''

"But it's unfair to you....''

Tianqing took her hand and pressed it against his chest. They embraced. Tianbai's unblinking eyes seemed to hover over his head, but he was beyond caring. He pressed his lips to her eyes. She had been cold so long, she trembled with fear. He trembled too. He pulled her down beside him forcefully. She struggled free.

"We've been cold for years. It's over.''

"Tianbai's ploughing. He won't be back.''

"But he does come home at odd times.''

"If he does we'll tell him...We're getting old, Judou ... my Judou....''

"There's got to be a right moment....''

Wang Judou was still beautiful. Her cheeks were flushed when she left the side room to cook and wash. She was happier than she had been for a long time. It was like the old days. Her man had not forgotten, and she was proud and at peace.

One winter's day while they were building a wall on a terraced field with the work brigade, Yang Tianbai stopped for a break. That day he did not drink his bowl of pea soup the brigade provided. Instead he asked leave to go home for some solid food. All the way he thought about his mother's changed appearance, and his cousin's suspicious silence. He whistled and cleared his throat loudly as he went down the lane, deliberately making his footsteps click on the hard surface.

The courtyard and the house were deserted. There was no one in the kitchen, or near the stacks of hay and firewood, or in the pig pen. His hair stood on end. He snatched up a cleaver lying on the chopping board in the kitchen and rushed into the north room. He lifted the mat on the *kang*, and looked under the mat in the side room too. He was not sure what he was looking for, except that it was something to sink the cleaver into. If he caught his cousin, he would split him like a melon.

He thought of killing his mother too.

He remembered the vegetable cellar behind the wall of the north room, and his brain seemed to press outward against his skull. The lid was shut so tight that there couldn't be anyone down there. Nevertheless a hen had been accidentally shut in there and suffocated by the gases given off by the fermenting cabbage. Remembering the dead chicken his grip on the cleaver slackened. He lifted the lid and looked down. There was the ladder, and bunches of carrots, and black shadows. He exchanged the cleaver for a flash light and climbed down the ladder.

He had only gone down three rungs of the ladder when he stopped. The yellow beam of light picked out the sacks of potatoes and a few empty sacks. His mother and his cousin lay with their heads together, their bodies twined in dark defiance. They were both unconscious. However, he could hear their calm, blended breathing.

With a heavy heart Yang Tianbai did something he had never done before. He pulled a pair of pants on his forty-four year old mother and carried her back to the north room, and left the other, where he lay.

He bolted the gate to the courtyard and contemplated the opening of the cellar. He thought of sealing it. But it was too much trouble. All the strength had suddenly drained from him. He grinned stupidly at the cleaver, vaguely thinking of trying the blade on his own neck.

The clean air revived Wang Judou. Her eyes fluttered open and shut again. She was not fully conscious. Her lips formed words that tumbled out uncontrolled with a stream of saliva.

"Tianqing, I can't breathe.... I'm dying...."

Those words smote Tianbai's heart.

A cobweb from the vegetable cellar was tangled in his mother's hair like a white decoration. His mother's hand clawed helplessly at the tattered *kang* mat, the reeds crackled like splitting bones. Tianbai was horrified.

Tianbai wet a towel and carefully wiped his mother's face. Her hand still clawed blindly at the pillow, clutching it convulsively, squeezing it as if it were a heart from which she meant to take every drop of blood.

"Tianqing ... my poor ... luckless ... love...."

"Be quiet, mother! Be quiet!"

Yang Tianbai could stand it no longer. He ran down the cellar, and carried Yang Tianqing back to the side room and threw him on the *kang*. Tianqing lay there like a dead fish. A thousand words and a few moans were lodged in his gaping mouth. There was fear and surprise too. He wondered why the fates always struck him down just as he was reaching for the moments of joy in his life. He had thought of cutting himself and the woman off from the bright light of day. He did not think that the fates left him no place to hide. The carbon monoxide would obliterate the shame that had gone on so long. He let out a primitive and silent scream of protest. Only when Tianbai had thrown a couple of ladles of cold water over him and cursed him was he finally able to shut his mouth and grit his teeth.

"You dirty bastard!"

His son's voice came from a great distance. The potatoes that had shifted under his elbows and knees were gone. The belt that held up his pants was very tight and knotted in an unaccustomed way. He was slipping into unconsciousness again. He wished never to open his eyes again. He had no wish to see the things around him. The warmth of Judou was nestled beneath his ribs. He wanted nothing more.

Tianbai did not go back to work. He managed to put together a meal and carried the food in for his mother and himself. Judou was too ashamed to eat. But she pointed pitifully at the side room. Tianbai ignored her. Again she glanced pleadingly at the side room though the look in Tianbai's eyes made her tremble .

"Better think of yourself. There's no room for the both of us in this family."

There was no sound from the darkened side room.

The next day when Yang Tianbai came home from work, his animal of a cousin was just coming from the kitchen, a bowl of gruel clutched shakily in his hand. Tianbai brushed passed him and spat on the ground. He threw down his tools viciously, and faced the animal who stood woodenly.

"Are you tired, Tianbai?"

"Tiredness never killed anybody."

"My foot's better. I'll be going back to work in the morning...."

"Nobody's stopping you."

"Cousin...."

"Damn it! Haven't you any decency!"

Yang Tianqing quietly returned his bowl to the kitchen shed. He wandered to the pig pen and then to the chicken coop, then as if suddenly waking from a bad dream, rushed into the side room and crashed onto the *kang*. In the silence that followed, the only sound was the woman's muffled sobs that sounded like hungry rats grinding their teeth in the dark. Her lover's sad smile and her son's triumphant grin cut her to the quick. She was too ashamed to speak. Yang Tianbai would brook no compromise. They could no longer eat together. Yang Tianqing took a water jar, and a small iron pot, two old bowls and some odds and ends, and began a life on his own. He built a stove which smoked when the fire was strong. The villagers could hear him coughing and gagging all the way down the lane. They pitied him. He struck the villagers as such a loyal and dependable person that they wondered what he had done to alienate the family. However, everyone agreed that it was probably for the best that the bachelor should take care of himself. After all one of the joys of being unattached was freedom. The hard muscled man had changed. His work was sloppy and his mind seemed to wander. During rest periods he would go off to a quiet corner and gaze fixedly at the mountains. The villagers whispered that the single life was finally too much for the man, and he was going out of his mind.

The clean and pretty widow had also become strange. She was seldom seen in the lane, or at the mill or in the courtyard. She never attended meetings or even a film show. Her perpetual excuse was either a back ache or a pain in the chest. Chest pains were a common ailment among women, but the busybodies started saying the woman was tired of widowhood. A marriage broker who called on her reported that she had become extremely thin skinned. Her face seemed masked with layers of shame, and her eyes were always downcast. A few of the astute ones recalled the idiot's poster. Perhaps there was something worth investigating. They watched the widow and her nephew. Once again the villagers had something titillating to occupy the tedious hours that hung on their hands between sleeping and waking.

Four months later Judou quietly left the village to live with her sister at a place near Shijia Village called Four Horse Terrace. Yang Tianbai accompanied her a distance, and came back looking like a thunder cloud. He ignored all enquiries, and expressions of concern and solicitude. The eighteen year old youth swaggered through the village, his nose stuck in the air. He had become a ruffian and a bully just as Yang Jinshan had been. People were predicting that one day some unfortunate soul would meet his death at Tianbai's hand. And it would be the blood line of Yang Jinshan exerting itself.

Yang Tianqing the bachelor became more and more confused.

One day Tianbai was picking peppers and pricked

his hand. The wound was not deep but it would not stop bleeding. Tianqing who was gathering cabbage went over to him as if he were sleep walking and took hold of the injured hand. Tianbai tried to squirm free, but his cousin was too strong for him.

"What's the matter with you?"

"Let me fix it...."

He smiled kindly and held on to Tianbai's finger as gently as he would a baby rabbit, stuck it in his mouth and sucked. Tianbai tried to push him away but could not. In the struggle, Tianqing was knocked to his knees. But he still would not release the finger.

"I'm your father, Tianbai."

Tianqing's pale face twitched horribly. Tianbai stood stock still. "I'm your father, son."

"Damn it! You're mad! Mad!"

A wave of nausea gagged him. Tianbai could not shake him off. In a panic he lashed out with his foot. A vicious kick to the chest sent Tianqing rolling into the cabbage patch. Tianbai ran to the edges of the field and looked back at the man sprawled there. He seemed to be listening for something, or trying to remember something. The man who lay shuddering on the ground had become a terrifying thing, and he was frightened.

"You're mad...."

Tianbai stumbled toward the stream. Suddenly he was running as fast as he could along the stream and into a grove of willows, and he did not stop until he was deep in the forest. The man lying in the cabbage patch rubbed the painful spot in the middle of his chest. The cabbage leaves stroked his weathered cheeks, like the hand of a woman on one side and that of a child on the other. In his mind's eye he saw the plump cheeks of his infant son, and the firm round breasts of his woman. The clouds parted, revealing a brilliant sky beyond that dazzled the eye. He was at peace.

Another four months passed. One morning the loud speakers in the village crackled to life calling on each household to send one representative to the brigade headquarters for a meeting, in which the leader's instructions would be handed down. Tianbai left the house early and did not notice any unusual activity about the side room. A little later, the man next door came by to borrow some tobacco. He noticed the north room was empty, and pushed open the door to the side room. Tianqing's tobacco pouch was lying on the *kang* next to the pillow. The neighbour helped himself, and filled his pouch as well. As he pulled the door to, he glanced briefly at the north wall, as he headed for the gate. He sensed something out of the ordinary. As he went through the gate, he looked back. What he saw made him drop his tobacco pouch. For a moment he stood there shaking helplessly. When he pulled himself together, he ran, straight for the brigade leader's house, yelling like a mad man.

"The bachelor has drowned!"

The piercing screams roused the villagers from their *kangs*, rubbing their eyes and grumbling. The day was dawning beautifully and there had been heavy dew. The crops stood ready in the fields.

The cadres rushed to the house. The platoon leader stood blocking the door to the side room, arms folded across his chest and confronted Tianbai. When he spoke he waved his arms like an orator inciting rebellion.

"Report to the brigade! Report to the brigade!"

"Report to the commune. We want it reported to the commune."

"Don't touch anything. Cadres step forward...."

"Everyone clear out. Especially the women!"

The ones who had their wits about them pressed forward, and clustered round like a mass of black worms.

Yang Tianqing was oblivious to all that. His naked body was bent over, his head stuck in the water jar standing against the north wall. Water trickled from the jar and fanned out across the ground. Someone had seen him carrying water from the stream after dark the night before and wondered why one person needed so much water. Now he knew.

Yang Tianqing presented his bare round buttocks and a pair of heavily veined legs to the world. Something like a worn out wash cloth and a pickled carrot dangling between his leg lent him an air of romance and dignity.

Yang Tianbai was dazed. For the first time he was invited into the side room, which he could not bear to enter before. He stared at the strange lifeless figure. His eyes moved boldly between the dead man's legs. Finally he stared unblinking at the primitive yet beautiful thing there. He studied its contours and the beginnings of recognition sent a shiver through him. A dim memory stirred, that here was the mysterious and narrow passage he had traversed eighteen years earlier. This was the savage and mysterious place whence he sprang. He pushed his way through the throng. Outside he found a stump of apricot wood and sat on it. Later he took an axe and split the stump into dry sticks. He was still splitting wood when the villagers left. When the cadres of the commune waddled into the courtyard, Yang Tianbai was drenched in sweat and tears.

Yang Tianqing's suicide caused an unprecedented stir in the village. He was a bachelor, whose loneliness had become too much to bear and he sought escape in a strange, unthinkable way. Those who bore the same surname as he tried to put a better face on the incident. The elders claimed that he had suffered a heart attack while he was having a drink of water. They maintained that his end was swift and not unpleasant. Others were of the opinion that he saw something in the water, and wanted a closer look. Whatever it was enchanted him. When he ducked his head into the water, he found he could no longer pull himself free. Just what the enchantment was, nobody could tell, nor did they bother to give it much thought. In the months before he died, they recalled Yang Tianqing sitting on a knoll on the South Ridge, gloomily smoking his pipe and gazing off to the south. Whatever he was longing for, he must have found in the jar of water. It was not an unpleasant end.

Wang Judou did not attend her Nephew's funeral. At the time she was giving birth to a premature baby, a scrawny boy. The news which raised many knotty questions did not reach Floodwater Canyon till six months later. The villagers' reaction was first anger, then glee, then sadness, and finally indifference. After a while Wang Judou could no longer stay in her sister's house, so she brought the second child back to her own home. The villagers greeted her coldly at first, but gradually they warmed to her. The village elders went back to the old family tree, and gave the child the name of Tianhuang or Yellow Sky. No matter what, the name had to include the word "Tian" or Sky. Thus after all his trials and tribulations, Yang Tianqing ended with another cousin, just like the first. However, everyone recognized the second child as Tianqing's offspring. But they did not know that he had left another offspring as well. To them Yang Tianbai was Yang Jinshan's son. The second one was an entirely different matter.

Whirlpool

I

From the windows of the second floor conference room of the Qinglongguan Hotel one has a panoramic view of the farm land and a ribbon of road shimmering under the July sun. On the highway, a small car moved along like a shiny beetle.

Zhou Zhaolu had finished speaking. The air-conditioner hummed in the silence that followed. Someone at the back of the room coughed. In fact the coughing had punctuated the reading of his paper. By the time he was reaching the end, Zhou's throat was tickling too.

"Thank you!" Zhou croaked. His voice was giving out.

A desultory spatter of applause followed him. As he left the platform he tripped on the microphone cord. The audience came alive with a short burst of clapping that quickly died.

"Thank you," he said again. He was not embarrassed.

He nodded calmly as he made his way back to his seat. Only when the audience's attention was once more diverted did his face redden, and the corners of his mouth drooped.

There was not a familiar face in the crowd. They

were mostly elderly chemists and factory managers full of airs and graces. He expected higher standards. The treatise which he was so proud of went right over their heads. He had been casting pearls before swine. The conference was a waste of time.

The speaker that followed was an old chemist from the venerable Beijing firm of Tong Ren Tang, manufacturer of herbal medicines. The old man spoke in Beijing vernacular, regaling the audience with the misadventures of his apprentice days, evoking peals of laughter. Zhou Zhaolu felt abused. Still his hands came together to join in the applause. He was not arrogant.

Until a brief letter a fortnight ago informed him that he had been elected to its board of directors, Zhou Zhaolu did not know a municipal Society of Chinese Medicine existed. Soon afterwards a hasty phone call invited him to deliver a paper on Chinese Medicines. If he did not have a suitable treatise on hand he would have refused. At one time invitations to speak flattered his ego. But the novelty wore off. He came to realize that his position as a researcher of the Chinese Medical Research Institute was being used as window dressing for a handful of societies no one had ever heard of. He was already a member of the Qigong Society, The Sino-Western Medical Exchange Society, and a half dozen other societies. This was one more. If he did not watch himself, he would soon be lassoed into every nondescript society that popped up. He was accommodating. Nevertheless he resented being used. The only title he valued was member of the National Chinese Medical Society; the only title that opened doors when career opportunities arose. Though such opportunities were rare, he constantly reminded himself to be prepared to leap at the right moment. At forty-four years of age, the door of opportunity was not yet closed. The trick was to be alert to the possibilities hidden behind events.

He clapped and smiled, though he had not been listening. He lifted the lid from his cup, and emptied the dirty looking, yellow jasmine tea on to a bit of waste paper and replaced it with black tea which he carried in an envelope in his vest pocket. He only drank black tea. The tea had come from his mother who lived in Fujian Province. The hillsides near his village were covered with tea plantations. When he walked to school along the winding footpaths as a child, his belly was always warm with cups of black tea. It was the only part of those early years he had not shucked off. He could not be without his black tea. He was not like his wife who followed the fad of drinking coffee. She was from Shanghai, but led a simple life. However, in matters of food, she had an instinctive yearning to be fashionable. He did not consider it a fault. She was a kind and gentle woman, and he loved her. It was not difficult for a man of his placid nature to fasten his affections on one woman for life. He saw it as a duty. And he had been dutiful for the almost twenty years of their marriage. He was a good husband. Everyone said so.

A voice rumbling at the edges of his consciousness was expounding the latest advances in the manufacture of herbal medicines. Zhou Zhaolu's mind wandered. The sun was low on the horizon. A stream of traffic sped along the highway. He followed them out of sight. The road was empty for a while, until another lot appeared like metal beetles out of nowhere. He took a mouthful of tea.

"Delicious ... " his daughter's voice sounded in

his mind.

It was Xiao Ling's favorite word. She had picked it up from television commercials. He hated commercials, but he loved every word she uttered. He had a son too. Xiao Lei was in grade five at primary school. Although he did not do as well as his older sister, he was more mature.

"Sister don't be a copy cat!"

"What do you know?!"

"Look, mum and dad, she's mad because I hit a nerve!"

He told himself early maturity was nothing to worry about. He was proud of his children. He loved them. Yes, he loved his family. Nothing could ever change that. Nor did he want it changed.

Finally the meeting was over. Zhou Zhaolu got heavily to his feet. He found the convener and made his excuses. He would not be able to attend the banquet, he said, as he was expected at home. He felt a twinge of conscience even as he spoke. It was the second time he lied that day. The first time was to his wife in the morning. He had told her not to expect him for dinner as he was going to a meeting that was likely to drag on. He wondered whether his expression betrayed anything. Even if it had his wife would not have noticed. She was not the suspicious kind.

He was a good husband.

In the corridor someone stopped him, wanting a copy of his treatise. He hesitated, groping for an excuse. Finally he said, "It needs some more work. There are bits that are not quite clear...I can't possibly give it out as it is...."

"We need your support," the editor of the municipal medical journal said earnestly.

"We'll see...."

It's all very well to be mindful of other people's needs. But one has to protect the fruits of one's labour as well.

"I'm not sure I can do a good job on it. I'm not an expert of pharmacology and it would be a disaster if there are mistakes...." Actually Zhou Zhaolu was thinking the treatise should be published in a national journal.

Zhou Zhaolu extricated himself by asking for the man's address and promising to keep in touch. The other was disappointed. Zhou looked sincere, and did his best to make the editor believe this was the opportunity he was longing for. He did not want to be misunderstood, but he also needed to hide his true feelings in a place so deep and secret that even he would not discover them. He hoped that in the eyes of his older colleagues, he would appear compliant and diffident. He had learnt in university that people preferred that type to the the brilliant but hard-nosed.

The editor was placated. Zhou Zhaolu seldom upset anyone. He was an old hand at smoothing things over. The two men parted happily. But the minute the man was gone, Zhou's face fell.

He went into the washroom, and while he was relieving himself, took a neatly folded slip of paper from his wallet. His hand trembled so much that he could not get it unfolded. He had already read the message many times over. Still it disturbed him. Lights dimmed and flashed before his eyes. He had never before encountered anything to equal its effect on him. He discovered the note the day before in the drawer of his desk. The drawer had been locked, but there was a crack wide enough for a work permit to slip through. He resented the invasion of privacy as much as the mental disturbance it caused.

The row of neat characters at the end of the message were quite clearly etched on his mind: Saturday night, 7 o'clock. on the south-west corner of Dong Dan cross road, under the Monkey King's staff. I'll be waiting. He had noticed the billboard from the bus. Some Japanese electronics firm had used the Monkey King to break into the Chinese market. Now the Monkey King was invading his private life. He disliked advertisements.

He pondered the message a long time, and decided to test the invader with a gentle reaction. He was merely testing the water, not surrendering.

He left the Qinglongguan Hotel and took a suburban bus to the edge of the city. From there he went to Desheng Men and then to Zhongshan Park and finally to Dong Dan. He was caught in the after office rush. Getting off and on buses took an hour. It was six thirty by the time he reached the billboard.

The sun was low in the west, peering at the endless stream of traffic hurrying along Chang'an Street. The sidewalks were jammed with people. Now and then the svelte body of a young girl flashed through the crowd wrapped in some gauzy material. His eyes roamed wherever he pleased, followed whomever interested him. No one knew him. He was free and just a little wicked. The person he expected had not yet appeared, and there was nothing but iron railing beneath the Monkey King.

He bought a sweet roll from a street vendor, crossed

the street at the pedestrian crossing and stood beside the door of a tailor's shop munching it. He faced the showcase. He ate methodically. Customers passed him but no one took any notice. Suddenly he looked up and his own reflection startled him.

"Is that really me?"

He looked young. He was of medium height. His stomach was flat. His hair and eyebrows were jet black, and his skin was fair. His face was long and narrow; the features, regular. His wife particularly liked his nose. It was not the typical flat nose of the southerner, but delicately chiselled. However, the eyes were southern, large and lustrous. At the moment the eyes were fixed on the wrapper around the bun.

He seldom looked at himself. He had been a handsome young man when he was at university. But that was a long time ago. Looking at himself in the glass he wondered whether the mirror had some diabolical power that drew customers off the straight and narrow. He turned away from the mirror, but even as he stepped through the door he could not resist a backward glance. In the mirror he saw a worried, middle aged man. He was at a loss as to what he should do. He felt he was becoming degenerate.Just how low he would sink,he had no way of knowing.

The sun had set but the sky was still light. He stuffed the bun wrapper in a trash can, and when he looked up there she was. She wore a pale green frock fastened at the waist and white leather high-heel pumps. A white leather shoulder bag no bigger than a book was slung over one shoulder. A dark curl fell across her brow. She had a pair of long shapely legs. She was right on time.

He stepped off the curb and started across the street, absently dodging the traffic, muttering to himself and shivering. A cyclist yelled at him, but he was only conscious of a smile that sped toward him from under the billboard like a fatal dart. Escape was impossible.

"She's beautiful...." he groaned.

II

They shook hands stiffly. Her hand was small, hard and bony. His was soft and sweaty.

"Have you eaten?" he asked coldly.

"Yes. And you?"

"I have too."

They walked apart, heading south along the sidewalk. They drifted toward the east gate of Dongdan Park. They slowed and looked at each other. He wondered what sort of impression he was making. He had decided on this bland attitude in the split second before they shook hands. He felt he had no choice. Meeting surreptitiously was repugnant to him.

"Shall we go in?" she asked.

"Alright."

Most of the park benches were unoccupied. The ones that were contained young lovers tangled in each others arms, or sad and lonely old people. They had nothing to do with either. They circled the park. There did not seem a spot they could stop. Zhou Zhaolu picked a bench that was close to the street and near the gate where there were lots of passersby. Instinctively he guessed she would prefer a more secluded spot.

"It's cool today ..." she said.

"Yes, the breeze is pleasant."

"How was the conference?"

"Nothing special."

"What was the reaction to your treatise?"

"Just so-so. I don't think it quite hit the mark with that crowd."

A strange note had brought them to this spot, yet neither was willing to mention it. Zhou Zhaolu stared at the pair of long, smooth, slender legs beside his and his spine tingled. But he forced himself to be calm.

He had known her for some time. They worked in the same department. He was the Deputy Director , and she was one of the staff. She usually addressed him with the formal "nin" instead of "ni", or by his title. But now and then in a more playful mood she would call him "Lao Zhou" or "Master Zhou." She was vivacious, and witty, and her sombreness troubled him. He liked her, as many others did. The difference was that none of the others tried to understand her. Still she was a mystery; perhaps a trap. The question was would he be snared.

Actually it did not begin with the note. Two months ago she had come to see him about the thesis for her Master's Degree and he had given her some suggestions. Perhaps he had helped too much, but he enjoyed it. Anyway it was the last time, before her dissertation. There was no one else in the office. Old Mr. Qian Tongkui was on long sick leave and he alone occupied the room. She stood beside him, one arm draped across the back of the chair, and the other hand resting casually on his desk. Her closeness made him nervous. But there was no sound of movement in the corridor, and he did not object to her familiarity. Afterwards the thought his silence might have been taken as encouragement. Her body brushed his, and his spine tingled. He could not lift his head. He moved aside, unable to meet her eyes, suffering until she left the room. That day he stayed late in the office, brooding and feeling guilty. He waited till all the others had left, then slipped out like a thief. The next day he was more taciturn than usual. However, in the dining hall she was laughing and gay as usual. Her attitude was a reminder that he was overreacting. Nevertheless he could not force himself to be jolly. Then there was the incident on the bus from Beiyuan soon afterwards. By chance they sat next to one another. It was a bumpy ride. Under cover of her shoulder bag she reached for his hand. It was really too much. Though he did not object, he shot her a pleading glance. She answered with a smile that was half triumph and half teasing. He did not know what she wanted, or why she pursued him so brazenly.

The lights came on. There were shadows everywhere. The flower beds became dark masses. Somewhere in the depths of the park a fiddle whined and a tremulous old voice practised scales. A streetcar rumbled by. The cry of a popsicle vendor sounded forlorn.

Zhou Zhaolu sighed. They had been talking about children, but the conversation petered out. He knew her husband was an instructor at the Iron and Steel Institute, but she never spoke of him. If there was a problem between them, he preferred to let her bring it up. He did not want to pry. Somehow the conversation kept circling back to children.

She had an eight-year-old son whom she seemed

fond of.

"Xiao Hong is a clever kid, but unfortunately he's inherited his father's jutting lower jaw."

"At least he's clever."

"I saw your daughter at the spring picnic. She's a pretty little thing. Looks a lot like you."

"But she's a bit spoilt. I often scold her."

"Scold? My husband gives a hiding. A boy needs a good father."

"That … is only…."

"I'm very unhappy. I wish I could cry, but there aren't any tears left. My heart is dead."

"You're still young."

"I'm thirty-six. My youth is wasted…. Life is meaningless."

"You're quite optimistic!"

"I try! I pretend!"

"I don't believe that. You're an optimist. Since we're here, and we are colleagues who get along well, we might as well talk. I'm a bit older, maybe I…."

"No. Don't say another word…."

She cut him short. She sounded tense. In the dark he could not see her clearly. Her small, chiselled nose was grey, and her lips were black in the half-light. Her small mouth was as vulnerable as a young girl's. Suddenly she took his hand and laid it on her rounded knee. She bent over and pressed her face into his palm. Where the tip of her nose touched it tingled.

"I just want you to be with me for a little while. We needn't pretend. You're a man and I'm a woman. I like you…. That's all. I know you won't refuse…."

"I have no way of knowing your misery.... What I mean to say is...."

"Please don't move. Just be still for a while."

His palm was moist. He was not sure whether it was sweat. He did not move; nor did he want to. A current rippled through their bodies. He was amazed how simple it was. It was not as he imagined. He did not have a heart attack. Instead he was serene. He stroked her hair with his free hand. His fingers strayed to the nape of her neck; the smooth round neck that he had looked at so often before, and his mouth went dry.

"This ... is not ... right."

"Tell me what is?"

She was wilful but tender. Her lips traveled slowly upward from his wrist. Their lips sought each other instinctively, yet they dodged and parried putting off the inevitable. When they met he kissed her deeply, searchingly.

People crossed the lawn, and passed into the distance. Others came and went, their footfalls fading along the path. No one disturbed them. They were ageless, without identity. They were male and female. Zhou Zhaolu wondered how someone else in his place would react? The summer night was full of reasons for him to kiss a beautiful woman.

"I'm so happy! Are you?" she spoke in a small voice.

".... I don't know...."

"Then say nothing."

"I don't feel quite right."

"Where...."

"In my heart."

"Why?"

"I'm not sure."

"Guilt?"

".... What came over us? I didn't think we could behave like kids.... Forgive me...."

She smiled, and her row of small white teeth glowed in the dark. She snuggled against him. She was all movement now. Actions spoke louder than words. Words bred confusion, but actions brought gratification. They were busy. At least she seemed to be. He sensed she was beyond misery. She was too hungry, and desire shattered the fragile aura of romance. She was soft, rounded and sensual. And he responded to her every whim. Her lips parted like the petals of a night blooming flower beneath his. They kissed till his mouth ached. She had slid onto his lap and he was awkward under her weight. Her hands were everywhere. He was amazed at his own response to the strange innocence of her body. Perhaps she felt she had gone too far, for suddenly she snatched her hand away. She felt his forehead, and dabbed at his face with a handkerchief. She leaped from his lap and stood on the footpath studying him, her head tilted to one side. She was silhouetted against the street light, with her face in shadows.

"Lets get a cold drink."

"A cold drink?"

Zhou Zhaolu took her arm and they left the park. She shrugged free of him reluctantly. It was quite natural and he did not mind. He could find nothing to say. But the silence was not oppressive. What he wanted to say and what he felt contradicted each other anyway.

They crossed Chang'an Street, and at the north end of the over-pass almost under its metal skeleton they found a cafe. He ordered a crabapple drink for himself and a pineapple soda for her. The lights were very bright. There were a few people waiting for seats. They glanced at each other casually. There was a soft tender glow in her eyes. He could lose himself in those eyes as if he were plunging down a bottomless well. Even so it was possible to climb back up un-noticed. Life is full of awkward situations, he thought. But they pass. One must brazen it out, without shirking or forgetting one's priorities. He fervently hoped this little interlude would pass as quickly as it began. Right now there was just a bitter-sweet after-taste to savour.

At nine o'clock they parted at the trolley stop on the west side of the street.

"I'm responsible for what happened...." he said carefully.

"We're both responsible."

"It was too sudden. In future we mustn't...."

"I know what we must do."

"... I don't understand you enough ... I just want you to be happy."

"I think you're unhappy."

"I...."

"I have no regrets, so there's nothing to worry about."

"You're so naive."

"You're not blaming me, are you? You see, when I decide on something, I do it. I'm never sorry afterwards."

"We're both married...."

"It won't harm our families. If families could be destroyed so easily everything would be simple! Don't look so crestfallen. Nobody was at fault."

"The trolley's coming."

"Don't torment yourself. Nothing's changed." She got on the trolley, turned and waved. " See you Monday!"

Her home was at Dongsi Liutiao. In less than half an hour she would be home. She was coquettish. He could imagine her sensuousness in that setting going through the door with the scent of another man on her. It would be the same for him. Nothing had changed, yet he was a different person from the man who left home that morning. The new sensations he experienced had made him despicable. However dishonour is a state of mind, that can only exist if he allowed it to. And dishonour can be disguised.

Zhou Zhaolu lingered in the streets beset by bittersweet memories that were more poignant than the evening had been. How could a proper gentleman who had spent half a lifetime cultivating a persona slip from grace so quickly and completely? Perhaps the seeds of sinful pleasure were buried in his bones all along, waiting for her touch to bring them to the surface. He had become a caricature of himself.

He went home to the apartment at Sanlihe. He stood outside in the corridor hesitating to knock. The slip of paper was still in his pocket.

"I am miserable and need a friend to talk to. I think of you and only you. You already know the place you occupy in my heart. I have told you. I am going to try something that may shock you. I am prepared for the consequences, including the possibility of your rejection."

He did not reject her. He had become her accomplice. But until that moment the contents of the note still evoked all that had been inconceivable.

He read the note one more time before tearing it into tiny pieces, and throwing it down the iron maw of the garbage chute from which swarmed a cloud of mosquitoes and the stench of rotting tomatoes.

He knocked, and for some reason, or no reason at all he thought of the white smoothness of her neck.

His wife was waiting for him. She was already in her shapeless pyjamas. Her face was lined and the skin was dull. She seemed to have aged since morning.

"You're late," she said in a soft querulous voice.

"The conference dragged on."

He forced a smile, but she had already turned away to fix his coffee, her soft, padding footsteps were a slap across the face. He ducked into the bathroom.

III

Hua Naiqian finally earned her Master's Degree. The title of her thesis was "The Study of Arterial Innoculants and Their Effects on Circulation." The rather cumbersome title had been Zhou Zhaolu's suggestion. He felt her original title was inadequate. Hua Naiqian had some difficulties defending her paper. Some of the examiners felt the fact that all eight case histories cited were males made the outcome questionable. The objections almost shook the credibility of the thesis. Hua Naiqian did not have sufficient mental preparation beforehand. Had she appeared less confident the panel might have gone easier on her, or even given her a helping hand at crucial moments.

Zhou Zhaolu was ready to leap to her defence everytime she turned a pleading glance his way. But he held back, forcing himself to be detached, waiting for someone else to make the first move. He did not want to be involved. At the crucial moment, Liu the assistant dean of Research into the Diseases of the Alimentary System launched a surprise attack. He had probably picked up Zhou's scent in the title of the thesis. And he never let an opportunity to snipe at Zhou go by.

"The fact that the case histories used all involved men makes the outcome inconclusive. That cannot be denied. It may be overlooked in view of Hua Naiqian's inexperience. However, the thoroughness of research must also be considered...."

The audience was quite large. Many had come from the out patient ward of the affiliated hospitals, and were still in their white smocks. He guessed that a good number had come out of curiosity to see just how much water this decorative vase of the institute could hold.

Zhou Zhaolu could not remain silent any longer.

"The sex of the case histories does not have any bearing on the conclusions of the thesis. That will be apparent when the paper has been read through."

The statement was short and to the point, not open to discussion. The older researchers in the front row nodded sagely as he sat down.

"For the time being we can assume it does not influence the conclusion, but can we be sure? I feel the effect could be negative...."

"Research is always hampered by restrictions. And all conclusions are subjective. Hua Naiqian's selection of material was limited by the case histories themselves. The fault was not hers if the records are inadequate. The fault lies with the department, and we are all responsible. It has nothing to do with the thesis...."

"I agree."

Liu's spectacles flashed malignantly, but he backed down. Zhou Zhaolu was sickened by his performance. It was clear that Liu's intention was to embarrass the whole department. But why take it out on the woman? Still he smiled and nodded kindly. He could afford to be generous. His opponent had exposed himself shamelessly. At least eighty percent of those present supported the woman.

"You can't win over me!" Zhou Zhaolu thought grimly.

Old Liu graduated from Beijing Medical College at the top of the class of 62. He was ahead of Zhou by two years. They were the two stars of the institute, and rivals from the start. They followed each other into the Party, and soon afterwards both became assistant deans. But Zhou was made a Researcher before Liu. At that time there was only one vacancy. The criteria for the selection of candidates were vague. Liu was sensitive and indiscreet. He had as many enemies as friends. On the other hand Zhou Zhaolu had a smile for everyone. Also his ability to translate English and Japanese put him several notches above Liu. In the end the decision was based on personality, and Zhou was selected. However, the two men had been friends for a short while during the Cultural Revolution, when Zhou was cooking and Liu was scrubbing toilets. Circumstances threw them together. But things changed afterwards. With rehabilitation, Liu re-

entered medicine like a ravenous wolf. Zhou Zhaolu
felt menaced at first but he was resolved not to be left
behind. He always considered himself the better man.

The defence of the thesis was over. Liu was surrounded by his jabbering coterie. Zhou was a bit uneasy as he edged his way out of the crowd and headed
for the stairs. Liu sidled after him. Something was on
his mind. Liu's skinny frame was bent like a shrimp,
and the spectacles perched precariously on the bridge of
his nose seemed in imminent danger of sliding off.

"I'd like to consult you on a question."

"What is it?"

"I believe Beijing Medical College's graduate studies
program ended last year." "That's right. Three of
the graduates were posted to our Institute. Hua
Naiqian was one. She's been with us a year." Zhou
Zhaolu smiled. How he would enjoy smashing his fist
into that ugly face. Liu was obviously trying to create
problems for the laboratory.

"Aren't some of the case histories Hua Naiqian
used more than a year old?" Old Liu shrugged.

"Some...."

"How many?"

"Three ... maybe four...."

"But as a separate research project...."

"That's perfectly normal. The case histories are in
the public domain and anyone can use them."

"You misunderstand me. At least two of the case
histories have been used by you in the past. How did
they fall into Hua Naiqian's hands? Were you aware
of it?"

"I helped her select them."

"That's it. She made no mention of it in her bibliography. That detracts from the seriousness of the thesis. She should have acknowledged the original researcher...."

"Why didn't you bring it up earlier?"

"There was no need. I felt sorry for her. Her standards are deplorable but she is pretty. I suppose we can consider ourselves lucky that way. I mustn't keep you."

"Not at all...."

Liu was out to embarrass him. Perhaps he sensed something between him and Hua Naiqian. But Zhou dismissed that thought. There was no proof. There couldn't be. He was the head of the laboratory and she was one of the staff, and it was his job to supervise her work. No one could fault him on that. Though he tried to convince himself that everything was alright, he quaked. He might fool others, but he could not fool himself. From now on he had to be on his guard.

Hua Naiqian was waiting in his office. She was flushed and her mouth was drawn in a tight straight line, on the verge of tears. Her confidence was badly shaken. In the last phase of defending her thesis, her voice became that of a timid child. Watching her Zhou Zhaolu had the strange impulse of wanting to stroke her head and comfort her. Now she seemed about to throw herself in his arms. He deliberately left the door ajar. It was the right thing to do, for it prevented them from doing anything stupid. Still he desperately wanted to take her in his arms.

"Better get back to your office."

"I'm so ashamed." She was depressed.

"There was nothing out of the ordinary. The reaction was good as a whole. There's nothing to worry about."

"I didn't think they would be so picky."

"It had nothing to do with you. These little things aren't worth worrying about. In the future ... you have to be careful...."

"I understand. Thank you...."

"Better go now. And be happy. Naiqian I like it when you smile...."

She shot him a hurried glance, touched the back of his hand quickly and was gone. He caught a glimpse of her smooth, rounded calves as she went through the door. He was fascinated by her every move, whether on the bus to work or in the cafeteria. He found himself thinking constantly about the look in her eyes. He had no defences. He was like an adolescent again in the throes of puppy love. In his second year of university he had fallen in love with a girl who was a year ahead of him whom he never got up enough nerve to speak to. The pain of unrequited love stayed with him a long time after she graduated. Though it had been buried a long time ago, it haunted him now. The pain he was experiencing was the same although it was Hua Naiqian who started the affair. He was caught in a whirlpool of emotions. He was as afraid of the present as he was of the future. He was lonely. They had met a second time the Saturday following their first assignation. They had slipped away separately from a meeting of the Public Health Ministry and spent the afternoon in a secluded spot in the park around the Temple of Heaven. He thought he had a firm grip on himself, instead he had said a lot of things that made him blush afterwards. It was so unlike him. It was as though he was possessed.

"Qian," he had called her. Coming from a middle-aged man, it sounded incredibly callow. He had a clear, sharp notion that he would someday possess all she had to give. He desired her warm, soft body. She had tempted him, and she was a lovely woman. There was no romance in it.

"I'm finished," Zhou Zhaolu muttered to himself.

A vision of her rounded naked body danced before his eyes. He was a lost soul trapped in an empty tomb. He left the office in search of the elder researchers determined to finalise Hua Naiqian's thesis as soon as possible. He was using his concern for the department as a camouflage for other motives. It was all he could do for the time being.

He went home listlessly. Home had become distasteful. Once he crossed the threshold of the comfortable three-roomed apartment he assumed the guise of a good husband and father again. He helped his wife with the house work, cracking the odd joke that brought peals of laughter from everyone. He supervised his son's homework, giving him an encouraging pat on the head when he needed it. He chatted with his daughter. Even when she was obnoxious he smiled, never changing the timbre of his voice. He was the centre of a loving family. When they settled down to watch television, he would read, or work on an article for some medical journal. Or he would pore over the fine points of a research paper. His wife would quietly put a cup of coffee at the corner of the desk, and he would pat her hand absently.

"Don't stay up too late," she said.

"Go on to bed," he said gently.

On the surface nothing changed. His wife was not aware that he could make no sense of what he read, or put words effectively to paper. He sat there torturing himself with thoughts of him and her. None of it made sense. A vision of Hua Naiqian shimmered in the lamplight, while his wife's soft, even breathing sounded in his ears. A wistful smile congealed on his face. He was reluctant to get into the bed he had shared with his wife for twenty years. Another woman's body lay between them, urgent, and tender. He burned with desire and he longed for respite.

His wife did not have a strong sex drive. Still she noticed his disinterest and it troubled her.

"You've been very tired lately."

"I've been busy. There's always someone wanting something. It can't be helped."

"Why not cut down on social engagements. You're a researcher not a politician."

" It's expected."

"You've lost weight. You must take care of yourself...."

His wife's hand glided down his chest. Her familiar touch set his flesh tingling. He seized her hand and drew her into his arms. Afterwards the smell of guilt that clung to him made him want to weep. But there were no tears. Instead he quickly fell asleep.

IV

The general office announced the second list of personnel due for rest and recreation leave. Among the instructions was a rather comical item: bring enough toilet paper for ten days. Rumour was rife that toilet paper

could not be had for love or money in Beidaihe. But
there were all sorts of rumours these days. People
dying from food poisoning after eating crabs, and
drowning, and being robbed on secluded beaches. Rest
and recreation was becoming an adventure.

Hua Naiqian was not on the list. Although she had
applied, she cancelled at the last minute saying her
child was sick, and asked to go with the last group instead. Zhou Zhaolu was listed on the last group.

When Zhou Zhaolu saw the name list he could not
decide whether to cancel his trip. There were plenty of
excuses. For instance he had been invited to a number
of conferences, and the invitations were still lying on
his desk. Besides he suspected that Hua Naiqian's
child was not ill at all. She was merely creating an opportunity, without considering the effect it might have
on him. The other day, he woke from a nap on his office sofa to find the door locked from the inside, and
Hua Naiqian sitting in his chair. He broke into a cold
sweat.

"What if somebody comes?"

"Keep quiet and they'll think you're out."

"..... Be reasonable...."

"I just wanted to watch you sleep."

"That's ridiculous...."

She kissed him searchingly, and stole from the
room. His nerves were stretched taut. He strained for
sounds from the corridor, but there was nothing. There
was something lewd in the way she kissed, and he was
afraid.

We are all monsters behind the masks we wear for
faces, he thought. Ugly instincts hide behind labels
like "emotion" and "reason" that are nothing

more than a smoke-screen. A year ago a beautiful young woman was posted to the department as a graduate student. She was clever and vivacious. Who can tell what impressions she made. We really don't know each other he thought.

At that time he could not imagine that they could shuck off the bonds of society so easily. Looking back it seemed everything had been preordained. They were mere players in a drama that fate directed. They had revealed a side of themselves to each other that was hidden from the rest of the world. Perhaps their real selves would never be revealed. He did not understand her. She was a contradiction of sensuality and innocence. Only the beauty of her body was real. He too was unreal. He neither understood her nor himself, for they were freaks. He did not know whether sensuality brought joy. Life is full of problems.

After she got her degree, Hua Naiqian invited him home for dinner to celebrate. It was her way of thanking a clever and dashing boss for his help. But Zhou Zhaolu could not fathom why she arranged it as she did. They could have celebrated quietly in a restaurant, instead of making a spectacle in front of her husband.

She said she could not afford it, and he did not know whether to believe her.

"I'll pay then."

"But it's my party."

"It's ... awkward."

"I want you to get over it. Can I meet your wife?"

He could not tell whether it was callousness or just her way of dealing with guilt. She was certainly more open-minded than he. He preferred to think of it as a flaw in her character. She was amoral. Probably she had never regretted anything in life.

She lived in two rooms at the foot of a ramshackle courtyard. A leanto had been built out front as a kitchen, making the rooms dark. The furniture was old. A huge wardrobe took up most of one wall. The sofa was littered with books and papers and a heap of dirty clothes. A toy panda lay on its back on the window sill amid a jumble of bric-a-brac. The desk was piled with papers and books and a few children's magazines. But the child was nowhere to be seen. He had been sent off to his grandmother's. Her husband Lin Tongsheng, was a taciturn man who cooked and did the house work hurrying back and forth from the kitchen with tea and food.

The surroundings did not fit the image he had of her. While the husband was busy in the kitchen, she sipped tea and chatted with him. Zhou Zhaolu was on pins and needles.

"Your little nest is full of life," his attempt at lightness fell flat. "That's what you think."

Lin Tongsheng poked his bristly head out of the kitchen, his eyes dull from lack of sleep. He was physically and emotionally exhausted. He lacked vitality. He was an unhappy man. It was obvious that in this household she wore the pants.

"Go light on salt. Old Zhou is a southerner."

"I'm going to fetch some water."

"You go ahead. I'll mind the stove."

She leaned against the door jamb of the kitchen, and shrugged helplessly. The husband went out with a green plastic pail, his shoulders hunched. Zhou Zhaolu pitied him. At the same time he could not help feeling superior.

"It's a tomb," she said.

Zhou Zhaolu let the remark pass. He set the toy panda on his haunches, and discovered that one eye was missing and an ink stain covered most of its body. Hua Naiqian's misery filled the room, giving it an air of utter hopelessness. She was a floundering boat, and he had leapt aboard without weighing the consequences. It had gone beyond feelings or even amusement. He had embarked on a dangerous path. She was sinking and he was the straw she was clutching at. Her need was great but she stood to gain more than he could afford to lose. She was a threat to all he held dear.

What could he offer her?

She was unpredictable. Had she been bored and merely looking for excitement, he would have taken her for what she was. They would have had a quiet fling and parted. There would be pain but no danger. But this was destructive and therefore, unthinkable.

The meal went off without incident. At table Zhou Zhaolu talked about work, and even went so far as to comment on the impracticability of some research, and reminding Hua Naiqian that she needed to show more initiative. The husband took everything in, nodding from time to time. He had been drinking steadily, and it was beginning to show. He grumbled about being passed over for an associate professorship, and consequently not being assigned living quarters. Then there was a heavy teaching schedule and housework that left no time for self-improvement. He was maudlin.

"If only I had an understanding boss like you!"

"Everybody has ups and downs."

"In this family, success belongs to Naiqian. I'll never be more than a teacher."

"Don't drink so much! Old Zhou have some more fish...." Hua Naiqian pushed the husband's wine cup aside.

The man blinked at her, his chopsticks hovering in mid-air as he tried to decide where they should alight. The dishes were well prepared, but they had lost all savour for Zhou Zhaolu. He did not understand the pain of failure, and the icy gleam in Hua Naiqian's eyes shook him. If a man was despised by his woman, then he would never be able to hold his head up anywhere. Perhaps Lin Tongsheng realized that his wife did not love him; that he was not worthy of being loved.

Although Zhou Zhaolu could not understand the feelings of such a man he could accept the woman's misery, and excuse her wantonness and therefore, his own. He came away from Hua Naiqian's home in a state of turmoil. No one was to blame for what was happening. It was the mysterious doing of fate. Thus far his life had been smooth sailing, but the tiny boat that was his family was also in danger of being swamped. For he was not happier than the other two. He was tormented by love born of chance. Though blameless he was beset by guilt. They were as helpless as Lin Tongsheng.

She saw him to the bus stop. She tried to take his arm as they strolled along the sidewalk in the last rays of the setting sun, but he shrugged her off. They walked apart as it was too close to her home.

"Are you tipsy?"

"I'm alright. It's just that I seldom drink."

"What was your impression?"

"He's a good man. But a bit soft."

"A weakling!"

"I wouldn't go that far. After all he is your husband."

"I pity him sometimes. If you were a woman you wouldn't tolerate him."

"I understand...."

"It's been ten years.... Don't let that hang-dog look fool you. Actually he has no ambition. A monotonous life suits him. Nothing makes him perk up more than going fishing! You should see him then! If he buys something at a bargain, it'll brighten his life for days. It amazes me that he teaches drafting! I think he'd be content to go on like this forever...."

"Can't you talk to him?"

"I'm so tired of scolding I can't be bothered anymore."

"Naiqian, you're unlucky...."

"I'm content as long as you understand a little of it."

"I understand everything."

"Not entirely.... Zhaolu, I've made up my mind to seize happiness wherever I can. Otherwise I'll stifle."

"I know...."

"Zhaolu...."

They passed the bus stop without noticing it. In the shadows of a tall building, he put his arm around her shoulders, and he knew the affair would not end abruptly and sensibly as he thought it would.

"Naiqian, you must be more reserved in the office."

".... I can't keep a grip on myself...."

"We can always meet somewhere. There are too many prying eyes in the office. We mustn't give them any reasons to suspect anything."

"I'll be careful.... It's just that I can't bear the thought of losing you...I've made up my mind, I'll never let you go."

"In the future ... don't come to my office alone so often...."

"Alright. Kiss me...."

But she hadn't kept her word. She sensed his desire. Caresses no longer satisfied her. She needed the ultimate. He held back teetering on the brink between despair and exultation.

Temptation and terror loomed over the trip to Beidaihe. He dreamed of walking along the cool sandy beach with the salt tang of the sea in their faces. The year before, he had been there also. The nights would have been magical except for the mosquitoes that turned his legs into a mass of lumps. The sea was placid in the light of day, but mysterious in the night. The endless lapping of the waves lulled him into a sighing fantasy; a sweet melancholy whose utter stillness held him in thrall.

He decided he would go with her.

He packed early. His wife had prepared a few changes of clothes, mosquito repellent, and a packet of a special blend of black tea from Daling Mountain at twelve yuan an ounce. He had gone to a number of stores and finally bought a pair of trunks with brightly coloured squares. After dinner, he tried them on. They were a bit too snug. He folded them and stowed them at the bottom of his bag.

"I wish I was going with you," said his wife.

"Can you get time off?"

"Of course not. The semester is starting soon. Besides the Ministry of Education also has a recreational program, but who knows when it will be my turn."

"There'll be other times. It's really not much fun."

"Why don't you take Xiao Lei?"

"There mightn't be a bed for him. People have waited years for a chance to go. But if you like, I could ask the general office...."

"I didn't really mean it."

The wife never mentioned it again. Someone introduced them in '65 right after she graduated from Normal College. She was from Shanghai and had no one in Beijing. They hit it off right from the start. He was just starting out on his career then and marriage was the furthest thing from his mind. She taught high-school literature. However, she was nice looking, and genteel. They started seeing each other, and within half a year they were married. Everyone thought they were well matched. They seldom quarrelled. Nor did they share much passion. Theirs was a placid life. When they disagreed, they retreated into separate solitudes, ignoring one another. After a while they spoke again, and the storm in the teacup was forgotten. Aside from their honeymoon, they had never been anywhere together. Although business had taken him to many cities, she never ventured beyond Shanghai where her parents lived. She never made use of her school holiday, nor did she mind. Her entire life was taken up by her students and her family.

Now he was about to travel again, but there would

be another woman with him. Watching his wife pack his suitcase made him flinch. That night he was ardent. Though they were both exhausted afterwards, she was happy and surprised.

"I thought you didn't want me anymore," she said shyly caressing him.

"You were wonderful ... Really...."

"You must promise to take care of yourself...."

"Wasn't I strong just now?"

"Watch what you eat. Don't get the trots...."

"I'm a medical expert, remember?"

"You're teasing again...."

They lay in each others arms whispering and giggling until they finally fell asleep. He was as passionate with her as if they would never meet again. He tried hard to shove the trip to Beidaihe to the back of his mind. Just the same there was a premonition of disaster. The ghostly shadow of the woman loomed out of the darkened beach, her ghostly white arms reaching out to him. He wanted to hide; to vanish into that safe haven in the arms of his wife. But he could not evade her. As he reached his volcanic climax, it was Naiqian's face that floated in his mind's eye. He wanted to seize it and tear it to shreds.

V

Not long after the train pulled out of Beijing the sky clouded over. Past Changping the landscape to the north of the tracks was a tender green. Further north a blue smudge of mountains rose on the horizon, capped by billowing grey clouds that fanned out in all directions. The sky lowered. A few spatters of rain tumbled down the window panes. Then it poured. A swarm of coloured umbrellas surged across the platform of Beidaihe Station to meet the train. Many held back, impatient to be gone, but unwilling to brave the elements.

"Have you got an umbrella?" she asked casually as she passed his seat.

"I do,"

"Better roll up your pants."

She stepped off the train swinging her shoulder bag. All through the journey she stayed at the far end of the coach playing cards with the young girls of the Service Department giggling like a youngster. Her laughter was like a caged bird that had been set free.

Zhou Zhaolu followed the crowd out of the station, carrying two suitcases. The larger of the two belonged to an elderly researcher from the gynaecology department. He saw the old man struggling with it as he got off the train, and grabbed it.

"It's alright. I can manage."

"No. Let me. I'm a lot younger."

"Thanks for your trouble."

"Not at all." He glowed in the old man's grateful smile.

Carrying two suitcases through the teeming rain was no problem. It is these little attentions that make all the difference sometimes. He was pleased that he had not let this opportunity slip by. He gave himself a pat on the back. There was a tang of the sea in the air. He filled his lungs with it.

She waited beside the bus. Zhou Zhaolu lowered his umbrella. She wore a flimsy pink blouse, the shade of water lillies over a pair of snug grey shorts that set off her long, shapely legs. She had changed into a pair of sandals with wedged heels. He had seen young girls dressed this way. But the effect was different. It was the way she carried herself and the way she moved. She had a knack of looking smart in whatever she wore, even in the office. She had taste.

She got on the bus ahead of him. He noticed the skin of her rounded heels was dark and coarse. He had never noticed her feet before.

He deliberately chose a seat away from her. There were only the two of them from the same department and he had to watch his step. He chatted animatedly with the people around him, but he was constantly aware of her. He took a few Japanese journals from his bag. The others had come for a good time, but Researcher Zhou planned to translate some material. No one could criticize his professional integrity.

The sanitorium was beside the sea. Across the lawn and beyond a grove of pines was a narrow gate that led to the beach which sloped down to the water.

Researchers lived in an old fashioned building that was set apart. The rooms opened onto a wide verandah on which were scattered rattan chairs interspersed with spitoons. The windows were screened. The room was not big. There was a soft bed and a sofa. There were bald patches on the carpet and the pattern had disappeared long ago under the grime. A door in the corner led to a tiny bathroom. The tub was jammed against the toilet. There was no paper, so the rumour was probably true. But the towels were fresh. Last time he was here he stayed four to a room in the building where Hua Naiqian was billeted. But he wasn't a researcher then.

After the rooms had been assigned most people headed for the ocean. He went to his room and from the window watched her walking down to the beach with the others. She was gnawing a huge apple, and her mouth was small and red. She flashed him a glance as she passed.

He was pleased with the room. He filled the tub, bolted the door and got out of his clothes. By standing in the corner he could see himself in the mirror from the knees up. His body was firm and the belly still reasonably flat. But the skin was embarrassingly white. He added a bit more hot water, and slid in. He lay in the tub up to his chin. He was relaxed. Strange images which he could not shake off flitted across his mind's eye. He breathed in the steam through his mouth. His eyes were tight shut. His hands kneaded and caressed every inch of his body within reach.

He lay in the tub till it was time for supper. His body glowed and he felt alive. The cafeteria was crowded with strangers. Most of the guests were from hospitals affiliated to the Ministry. Hua Naiqian was seated at another table. She had changed into a white frock with a pattern of flowers splashed across it. Her hair was pulled back and tied with a wide red ribbon at the nape of her neck. She caught his eye, and deliberately asked in a loud voice, "Master Zhou have you been to the beach?"

"No. It was raining too hard."

"Not much fun otherwise, book-worm!"

The others laughed. He glowered.

"I'm too old to keep up with you young people."

"If you're old, where does that put us?" A few of the older ones chimed in. The atmosphere was like a family gathering. The rain petered out towards evening. Music wafted from the clubhouse. According to the staff there would be dancing every evening till nine o'clock. As he was not fond of dancing, he wandered into the reading room and then the chess room, but there was nothing that interested him. He went back to the dancing. A few couples wheeled about the floor. Hua Naiqian glided by in the arms of a fiftyish man he did not know. The man was a bit short but he danced well. She was having a good time. The man had a lascivious look that Zhou Zhaolu did not like. But he did not object to her dancing with a stranger. He was not jealous. He considered himself the only man that had the right to look at her in a certain way.

The waves crashed against the shore. The sea was brighter than the sky. In the distance there were pinpoints of light, probably a freighter or crabbers. The rain had started again, falling so softly he hardly felt it.

He went to his room and leafed through a few magazines. His thermos was empty but the room attendants were all gone. They had a better time of it than the guests.

He could not concentrate. There were a few phrases that escaped him and he had left his dictionary behind. He continued turning the pages but his mind was a blank.

Someone knocked. He stepped to the door. Hua Naiqian was silhouetted against the screen door clutching a small plastic bag.

"Come in."

"I brought you some fruit. I hope you like grapes."

"You ought to keep them for yourself."

"I've got more. Actually they're cheaper here. Where do you want them?"

She looked about the room, opened a dresser drawer and stuffed them in. She picked up his notes, glanced at them and put down again.

"Why do you work so hard?"

"I've been here before. There's nothing much to do except swim. So I might as well get some work done."

" The air is so marvelous here, why not have some fun?"

"I could do a bit of sightseeing with you. But I'll beg off of group activities.... They get tiresome."

"You're like an old man."

She glanced in the bathroom, before settling onto the sofa. Her skirt was hiked up revealing a length of bare thigh. He quickly shifted his gaze.

"The atmosphere at the dance was quite nice...."

"Don't bother! I literally fought my way out of there. Some crazy old coot from the Peking Union Medical College just wouldn't stop. He'll dance himself to death one of these days...."

"There's your chance," he said meaning to be funny. They laughed.

"Just to keep me on the straight and narrow, hide me in your bathroom till the coast's clear."

The grin congealed on his face.He swallowed hard, wondering whether she really meant it. Actually he had been thinking the same thing. Though he knew it was impractical the thought persisted.

"I've upset you."

"You have to be joking."

"Let's say I am.... Who's next door?"

"Old Li from gynaecology. He isn't well and is probably in bed."

"To the east of the verandah there's a path that goes around the wall." She pointed out the spot. He didn't quite grasp her meaning. Though she was in a light-hearted mood, he sensed a foreboding in what she had to say.

"There's a screen door that's locked from the inside. I know because I took a turn around this building in daylight. I was going to come in but didn't.... There seems to be a rest house for the army on the other side of the wall.... It's very quiet."

"What are your quarters like?"

"I live on the third floor. I'm the only one from our unit. The others didn't want to split up, so I have the room to myself."

She wasn't smiling now. Her eyes were fathomless. He had to tear his eyes from hers. The woman's sensitivity to her surroundings made him tremble. Her determination to satisfy her lust was cool and calculated. She knew what she had to do. He allowed himself to be manipulated. He did not have the will to resist. All he had was hunger, darkness, and a wild passionate longing.

"I'm liberated. Even if it's for a day. Here you belong to me...."

"I'm afraid...."

"Afraid it might ruin your reputation?"

"It's my conscience...."

"Relax. I'll protect you.... I love you...."

They unlatched the screen door, went down a short flight of steps and stole into the clump of trees. The rain had stopped again. The grass was wet. He kissed her long and hard, shaking with desire. Her fingers were twined in his hair.

"Naiqian, I'm going mad...."

"I'll give you peace."

"This isn't me anymore!"

"Then who is it?"

"I don't know."

"I know you. You're a greedy little cat ... but a scaredy cat ... Zhaolu!"

He let go of her slender body and watched her follow the wall into the trees and vanish beyond the gate where a gravel path led down to the beach.

He stood under the trees. The waves crashing dully on the shore seemed to ebb and flow at his feet. The night held him in a clammy embrace.

He could not sleep. He took a bunch of grapes into the bathroom and rinsed them under the tap. He stood in the middle of the floor, methodically stuffing them into his mouth. He did not turn on the light and the room filled with shifting, menacing shadows. For no reason at all he thought of her heel, tanned and coarse looking, but he longed to touch them. Something seemed to lurk in the room waiting to pounce. He forced himself to concentrate on the grapes, spitting the peels into the dark.

He spent the whole of the next day translating "In Defence of the Frail Constitution." The writer was a verbose Japanese who, somehow, managed to impart a certain liveliness to a dull subject. Zhou Zhaolu imagined the man must be short, bald and raspy voiced, an ideal companion for a rainy day. It rained intermittently all day. Hua Naiqian had gone sightseeing with the group. In the morning she had gone for a trip along the coast in a boat chartered by the sanitorium. She had asked him to go along at lunch, but he refused.

"What are you going to do?" She looked at him long and hard. "The translation's going well, and I don't want to break the momentum. I want to finish it in one go. I'll be at it till tonight."

"Are you going to stay up then?"

"I don't think it's necessary...."

"Get to bed early...."

"I will."

She danced all night. No one came near Zhou Zhaolu. Researchers are a law unto themselves. After he finished his work the lights were out in the Club House. The rain stopped, and a few stars were reflected in the murky puddles along the footpath. He walked a while under the trees like a lost soul. The vague but persistent desire that assailed him all day was gone. He was weary. He wondered how long the feeling of emptiness would last. He made up his mind to continue translating the next day.

But the next day he did not get much done. At noon Hua Naiqian came and insisted on dragging him to the beach. It was sunny, and half-clad bodies bobbed on the grey waves. Hua Naiqian wore a yellow bathing suit, a towel draped across her shoulders like bright coloured wings. He went into the change room and pulled on his trunks. He dawdled, putting off the moment when he would have to step out before the public practically naked. Part of his reluctance was because of the whiteness of his skin. It was for the same reason that he never used the work unit's bathhouse, or went swimming with friends. Once at university someone had remarked that his skin was as delicate as a girl's. He never got over that gibe.

He came into the sunlight hesitantly. Hua Naiqian stood at the water's edge with her back to him. She had shed the towel. The back straps of the bathing suit crossed at the small of her back. The skin-tight suit made her buttocks bulge. The man studied her with the unblinking stare of a dead fish.

"What took so long?" Her eyes swept down his flat belly.

They swam out as far as the shark nets where the sea glowed with blue light. There were few people around them. She swam with sure strong strokes. He struggled to keep up with her.

"Are you alright?" she tossed at him.

"My chest feels a bit tight. I'm out of shape...."

A wave picked him up and dashed him down. His breathing was harsh.

"Lets go back."

"I don't ever want to go back. Will you come with me?"

"I will ... but it's cold...."

"Lets not move, and see how far the tide will carry us...."

"If we don't move, we'll sink ... I'm tired."

The tide carried them in and a foot high wave tossed

them onto the shore. They found a patch of dry sand
and lay down. The sand was hot against his bare skin
until he got used to it. He lay on his back until the
bridge of his nose began to burn, then he flipped over
on his stomach. Her lips were purple from the cold.
She covered her face with a towel, and lay on the sand,
her hair fanned out about her head like strands of sea
weed.

"Unbolt the screen door tonight."

"Which one?"

"The one to your room and the one around the corner of the verandah...."

He was silent. Red and yellow spots danced against
his tight shut lids.

"Turn out the light on the verandah before you go
to bed...."

A big black ant crawled onto his hand. He brushed
it off and buried it in the sand.

"Just go to bed. There's nothing to worry about.
Did you hear?"

"Yes."

"Don't wait up. Just do as I say."

He turned on his back. His eyes were glued shut by
the red glow of the sun. He lay like that a long while.
All around them were men and women lying in rows
asleep or swooning with weariness.

It was only when they parted that Zhou Zhaolu
began to have doubts. He stood beside the gate, and
she leaned carelessly against a lamp post. His nose
was suntanned and looked red and sore.

"Naiqian ... are you sure...."

He turned away before she answered. But he thought

he saw her nod. She's laughing at me, he thought. He was sure if there hadn't been people around she would have laughed out loud. The mischief in her eyes told him so.

He shouldn't have asked. He berated himself while he bathed. Afterwards when he had changed into the underwear his wife had packed, that smelt fresh he felt differently.

"Where's the switch of the verandah light?"

The light of the setting sun flooded through the screen door. It was still early but he was already on edge. Desire and fear roiled through him.

He shut the window and after a while opened it again. He drew the blinds and went outside to see if he could peer in. The verandah of the second floor made him nervous, but a grove of trees formed a blind. He breathed easier.

He moved the rattan furniture away from his door, and shifted the spitoons where they would be out of the way.

He studied the screen door around the corner like a thief. His heart pounded wildly, but his eyes were steady, and without fear.

VI

Nothing happened that night. There was no disaster, nor was there a miracle. He went to bed early and lay staring at the ceiling until his eyes became too heavy to stay open. He slept fitfully. He had shut the windows and drawn the blinds. The room was pitch dark. The pounding of the waves sounded in the distance. The bare walls, and the white bedclothes glowed in the dark and he was alone. He slept more soundly during the latter part of the night, and woke refreshed.

That morning there was a group tour to Shanhaiguan. After breakfast the rest of the group gathered on the shady footpath waiting for the bus. As usual he stayed behind, but he joined the others to chat while they waited. Someone mentioned that Hua Naiqian had gone swimming alone after midnight. Her companions from another organization claimed she had gone as far as the shark nets. They thought she must have been suicidal for no one in her right mind would have done such a thing.

"Who went with her?"

"Some of the girls."

"Swimming in the dark might be fun...."

Zhou Zhaolu tried to sound flippant. At first he thought it might have been the strange man who was with her. He knew she was brazen, but he could not understand seeking excitement in that way.

Hua Naiqian hurried out of her building. He spotted her as he came up the path. He was deliberately cool.

"There's no hurry. The bus hasn't arrived."

"I got up late."

"Was the water cold."

"No. So you've heard. What are they saying?"

"They said you were probably trying to kill yourself."

"Idiots! You should've seen the ninnies, carrying on! It was a hoot!"

"What was the point?" -

"Zhaolu, I'm sorry.... I got cold feet ... I had to do something to punish myself...."

He knew what she meant. He was glad she had lost

her nerve. He gave her a comforting look, as if she had behaved exactly as he had expected.

"Did you do as I said?" she asked softly.

He put on a puzzled look. The woman was too sure of herself. She did not consider his pride or all that he stood to lose. He could not tell her he had followed her instructions to the letter.

"Zhaolu, you know what I want.... You can see I'm not afraid...."

She went to the bus, her skirts swinging with her light, quick step. She was greeted by peals of laughter. She was well liked. Although she was the type that could quite easily rouse jealousy, she had the knack of pleasing people. In that regard she was probably more adept than he. Everyone wears a mask. What sort of world would it be if all the masks came off?

What did she want? Was she driving him mad with desire and insomnia? Hua Naiqian's words bothered him. Perhaps she thought she had him wrapped around her little finger.

Zhou Zhaolu did not want to brood. Nevertheless he was thinking himself into a corner. Far better to accept the thing as it was. He was in love with a woman eight years younger. It was ridiculous, but true. And the world had not come to a crashing end as a result, so there must be some reason for it. Leave her to heaven, he thought. Neither of us can help ourselves anymore.

He finished translating the Japanese article, and selected a more difficult one on blood circulation as a follow-up. The Medical Journal once referred to his work as among the finest translators in the country. He earned as much with his translations as he did with his own works. It was a lucrative side-line.

He went to bed tired, but lay for hours staring at the ceiling,where he seemed to see strange shapes. His hearing became exceedingly acute. He found himself picking up the tiniest sounds; sounds that perhaps didn't exist at all. He woke listless after a second restless night. He told himself it was not disappointment. He was just over tired.

On the sixth night in Beidaihe he woke with a start. He had arranged the doors and windows each night. It had become a habit. Nevertheless he woke with a start.

Someone was standing at the foot of the bed.

He started to sit up, but a hand pushed him back on the pillow. A finger pressed lightly against his lips cautioned him to be quiet. He shifted to one side and a cool body slid onto the bed beside him. The bed squeaked. His limbs that were stiff and heavy became suddenly agile. He seized her, fumbling and clumsy, then he was as light and agile as a deer.

They both became aware of the bed squeaking. And they both knew what to do. There was no need for words. Or if there had been words, they were forgotten the instant they were uttered. He thought of turning on the light, but did not. His climax was shattering. He abandoned himself to it. He had never experienced anything like it. Perhaps it really was the devil in his arms. An hour later he was alone again. A delicious lassitude permeated his being. He thought of his first experience. She was his wife. She was legally his, but he failed miserably. He was still miserable about that initial failure years later. Now he compared the bodies of the two women, and felt no guilt.

He could not brush aside the memory of that sensuous body. He had no regrets. He no longer thought of himself as depraved.

He did not sleep well the latter part of the night. In the light of day his feelings changed. As the darkness receded a thousand insignificant details plagued him. Could he be sure no one saw her? Did the screen door make too much noise?

The patients strolling in the gardens seemed to stare at him. His secret hung like a pall in the air.

It took a while to get hold of himself. At breakfast he asked Hua Naiqian, "Did you go swimming again last night?"

"No. It was too rough.... I tried... but I chickened out."

Her smile calmed him.

He lost interest in the Japanese treatise. He wanted to have fun. He went to the free market with the others, and helped them bargain for sea-food. He played badminton and his antics on the court brought peals of laughter from the young girls. Translating had exhausted him. In conversation, he casually expounded his personal philosophy. He had the power to be whatever he chose to be. A young researcher has a lifetime to look forward to. He was steady and affable. That was the impression he wanted to make, and that was the way people saw him.

Hua Naiqian asked him to go for a walk in the hills. She wanted to see the famous villa of Lin Biao. He did not believe she could be interested in that bizzare building but he agreed.

They walked west along the narrow highway. Instead of going up the hill, they headed away from the tourist area. On the left there was the beach littered with dilapidated fishing boats black with age. On the right patches of low bushes were splashes of green and yellow on the hillside.

She was silent.

Suddenly Zhou Zhaolu thought of something she had said.

"You're terrific....." It was almost a groan.

She was pressed under his body. It was not yet over. At the time he did not grasp its meaning.

Was it an evaluation of his sexual prowess; or of morality? Or was it a sly dig.

He wondered what she really meant. He knew he had satisfied her, but what was in her heart was still a mystery. The things of the flesh are limited and incapable of reason. However, reason is unable to withstand the battering of pleasure.

They sat on the sand. Some local children paddled naked in the water. A speed boat sped along the coast, trailing a wide wake.

"Zhaolu, tell me something," she began, "you're always so cool, yet...."

She can't fathom me either, he thought. Zhou Zhaolu concentrated on the fine lines criss-crossing her lips as she talked.

"We ought to talk about us."

"What can I say?"

"Whatever you feel. There's nothing to hide...."

".... I don't understand...."

"Meaning what?"

"Me and you."

"Are you feeling guilty?"

"Yes. But I don't blame you."

She squinted at the slate grey sea, so cold and clean.

Zhou Zhaolu sensed the next question would be even harder to handle. The best dodge would be pretence.

"What do you want?"

"Somethings are only attainable when you come right up to them...."

"Does someone put them in front of you?"

She trained her pert eyes on him.

".... It's more like a feeling...."

"When you've had it, do you turn to something else?"

".... Sometimes you realize it wasn't worth it...."

"Be specific. What did you get?"

He blushed, suddenly confused.

"What did you think you got? A woman, a body or emotions?"

"Naiqian, this is very tiresome."

"I'm sorry it's tiresome. Did I seduce you?"

".... I think you tried ... No. I'm not saying it right."

"Alright I seduced you, because I'm in love with you. Never mind. You're too devious for me. You're not only a greedy cat, you're scared. What's there to be afraid of?"

"You're upset."

He felt he was coming apart at the seams. She did not look angry, but she sounded heavy. Her smile was derisive. You're terrific. He recalled the way she looked when she whispered those words in the dark.

The children had left the beach. It was damp and lonely. She stood up, sniffed the sea air, and stretched out a hand to him.

"Zhaolu I'm not going to blame you, even if it's only my body you want."

"You know I love you."

"Don't say anymore. You know I won't give up. But I'll never do anything to hurt your family."

"Naiqian...."

"I've taken all the chances.... But you were terrific...."

This time he knew what she meant.

"Naiqian ... you embarrass me...."

"There's noting to hide. If we can do it, surely we can talk about it. What was it like for you?" Her words cut him to the quick. There are things one does not talk about. Words desecrate it; turn it into trash.

He wanted to tell her she was beautiful, and wanton. He could kill her. Maybe that's what she wanted, and needed, to hear.

He glared at her in silence.

"Careful. I have expectations," she chuckled.

He gripped her hands. She balled them into hard little fists and twisted hard against him, her small, even teeth clenched tight.

What " expectations?" She said she would not be a threat to his family. No doubt she had something else in mind and "expectations" was only a hint that she was a liberated woman.

She came to him again the night before they left Beidaihe . Before daybreak the group went to watch the sunrise at Pigeon's Roost. They stumbled along the darkened highway in twos and threes. Zhou Zhaolu and Hua Naiqian lagged behind. There was no one in front of them or behind. The street lamps were few and far between. The harvest rustled in the fields. The sound of voices drifted back from a distance.

They left the road, cut through a corn field, crossed

a dry irrigation ditch to a hollow where the grass was tall. A few short trees loomed out of the dark like ghostly sentinels.

The dew was heavy. Everything was damp. She steadied herself against a tree, and the dew drops spattered down on her head.

There were mosquitoes everywhere.

She was dressed as she had been the day they arrived. The tight fitting shorts roused him to fever pitch. Aboriginal desire made everything simple. A thought flashed through his mind and congealed into action. There were no preliminaries. He took her like a wild beast. Afterwards he wondered whether this was the behavior of a man, or a savage ritual of self destruction.

When they parted on the platform of Beijing Station, he was still haunted by that dark encounter. He watched her vanish into the crowds, a female animal wearing a human mask. He had also donned his. In the subway train, he shut his eyes. The superior man he had always considered himself to be was no longer. She had destroyed that. He saw the two of them in the field again the moment after passion. She was calmly rubbing mosquito repellent on her bare legs.

VII

Zhou Zhaolu went back to the office tanned, rested and cheerful. He always brought back souvenirs for the staff, usually some local edibles that didn't cost much. The recipients did not feel unduly obligated, and everyone appreciated his thoughtfulness. He was a caring boss. This time he brought a basketful of cooked crabs, which were snapped up before he was half way across the office.

At lunchtime the corridors reeked with the smell of crabs.

"You ought to thank Hua Naiqian. If she hadn't badgered me, I wouldn't have bought them. You have no idea of the prices these days!"

A cheer went up for Hua Naiqian. She knew she had nothing to do with it, but she accepted the thanks with a smile. She told him with her eyes that she would always take note of his way with people.

He was plagued by irritating ailments. He had stomach pains, sensitive gums and insomnia. However, after a good night's sleep all the aches and pains vanished.

But the feeling of well-being did not last. His wife joshed him saying that a period of rest and recreation had done more harm than good. When he lay awake, his wife would prop herself up on her pillow and chat with him. He was having a hard time dealing with the warmth of family life. Sometimes a casual remark from his wife would stab him to the quick. She was completely ignorant of his adultery. That made it all the harder for him to accept her solicitude.

He wanted to be alone, without light or sound, to separate himself from the world around him with a black void, in which he could examine his true self. He had to understand what he had done.

He had betrayed his wife with another woman. He was not the only adulterer in the world, but he was not without honour, otherwise he would not be suffering remorse. He hated the circumstances, but he was bound to the other woman who had carried him to

new heights of ecstasy. He would happily continue the
affair if he were sure it would not affect his family. He
vacillated between joy and fear, afraid that the price of
ecstasy would be higher than he cared to pay. He
thought of breaking it off. It seemed the most logical
solution. However, she was flesh and blood and he
wanted her inspite of himself.

Zhou Zhaolu was mired in conflict. It was useless
worrying. He could be neither objective nor philosophi-
cal.One thing was clear: he loved himself above all. A
fact that was not hard to accept, but took courage to
admit. Aside from family, career, reputation and social
standing, he could do without the rest.That was his
basic philosophy in life. He would put up with moral
degeneracy as long as the status quo could be
maintained. What concerned him was the long-term effects of adultery.

The secret must be kept at all cost.That much he
had decided.He believed that Hua Naiqian was not
careful enough.He relived the nights of passion in
Beidaihe again and again.He was convinced that the
woman was less rational in the throes of lust.She was
willing to take chances that frightened him. He felt he
had to stand aloof from her, at least as long as it
took for her to regain her perspective. Then perhaps
they could renew the relationship on a clean slate.

A schoolmate of hers had a vacant apartment.She
showed him a big, shiny key. There was an education-
al film show every Saturday afternoon. They could slip
away.There were precious stolen hours to be shared.
The city was not as easy to cope with as Beidaihe.

Her eyelids drooped as she turned the key over and
over in her hand, like a precious jewel. He controlled

himself.

"The film is important. It's a documentary about the development of Chinese medicine in Japan and Southeast Asia. You ought to see it too."

You're not giving me a chance. Are you tired of me already?"

"You mustn't misunderstand.Who is this schoolmate of yours?"

"She's studying for her doctorate. An old-maid. She lives somewhere else. Her family has several apartments...."

"What reason did you give for borrowing her place?"

"She knows I don't get on with my husband...."

"Won't she think that you and another man ... what I mean to say is ... did you borrow the apartment for yourself alone?"

"I borrowed it for us!"

"You told her about us?"

He blanched. There was a humming in his ears. She grinned, tossed the key and caught it.

"How could you do it!" He sounded edgy. "You're thoughtless!"

"Have you forgotten I said I would protect you? I borrowed the apartment to study in."

He breathed a sigh of relief.She was in control right from the beginning. Tiny veins fluttered at the level of her collar, barely visible under the translucent skin of her neck. The rise and fall of her breasts under the fabric of her blouse was familiar yet mysterious. He faltered.In his mind he was already exploring the secrets of that apartment.

"Naiqian I really can't get away.All the supervisory

personnel are meeting for a panel discussion after the film.I have to be there.''

"Alright.''

"There'll … be other times…..''

She put away the key, disappointment in her eyes.Perhaps it was the effect of his last remark. He was sorry, but under the circumstances, he felt they needed time to cool off. They had to be careful. He refused to meet her again through the early part of October.

He was active. He held himself ramrod straight, and took the stairs two at a time. He was confident. When he spoke at business meetings, his words were lucid and concise. All that was needed were a few minor changes to the secretary's notes and they would be readable articles for the Institute's newsletter. He was often invited to speak at other Institutes. He was always hurrying hither and yon. Zhou Zhaolu was a man on the move. Nothing could block his rise to the top.

It was much harder to maintain the same unruffled calm at home. He was ashamed of play acting. His family's trust and admiration was unbearable, for he had betrayed their love.

He was no longer a good husband and father. He was not even a reliable lover. He was a weakling who had been seduced. He did not want to hurt anyone, but he had already hurt everyone who loved him, except, perhaps, Hua Naiqian. He loved her with a love that turned his life topsy turvy. He suspected it was only her body he loved.When he thought of her, he thought of her body, free, unrestrained, independent. It had no personality; was not worthy of respect. It existed because of Hua Naiqian.

The children felt that Zhou Zhaolu was distant. He seldom spoke at table, and no longer watched TV with them.In the past he used to set one evening aside to spend with them in front of the TV.But not any more.He was remote and preoccupied.

One evening his daughter crept up on him as he sat at his desk.He smiled at her absently.

"What is it, Xiao Ling?"

"Nothing. Just wondering how much wisdom you're putting away, when there isn't even a teacher hovering over you."

"Go play with your brother.Father's busy."

"Xiao Lei's been bad, and you don't even care."

"Has he been fighting?"

"I saw him smoking in the flower beds behind the building...."

"You should've told me right away."

"Mother said not to.She says you have too much on your mind right now, and you're tired...."

He pushed himself away from the desk.His eyes glittered with a peculiar light.He was going to do something that would set the household on its ears.

He dragged the boy away from the television set. He had never laid a hand on the children before. The thin little arm struggled in his grasp.

He saw red. Without realizing it, his fist thuded into Xiao Lei's back and sent the boy reeling into the corridor. The boy lay on the floor. His wife was too stunned to intervene. Finally Xiao Lei scrambled to his feet, silent tears spilled down his face.

"Traitor," the boy spat at his sister. "You promised not to tell! You promised!"

Xiao Lei's face was beet red.The wife took the boy

in her arms, and glared uncertainly at Zhou Zhaolu.

"Mother, you promised not to tell!"

The boy burrowed against his mother's breasts and cried.Anguish filled the house.Zhou Zhaolu regretted what he had done, and he could not meet their eyes.

"What's the matter with you today? Is something the matter?"

"Picking up bad habits at his age! He needs a lesson he won't forget!"

"You've never been like this…. It's not only the kids…. I can't stand it either…."

"Forgive me. I over-reacted."

"Has something gone wrong at the office?"

"No."

"Problems with the boss?"

"No."

"Aren't you getting along with the others? You used to say…."

"I tell you there aren't any problems. There's nothing to worry about. Everything's just fine…."

"I'm glad."

"Time for bed. I'll find an opportunity to apologize to the kids tomorrow. Do you think Xiao Lei hates me?"

"No. But he'll probably be afraid of you…."

Zhou Zhaolu was miserable, and his wife's understanding made it worse. He had not only frightened the kids, he probably frightened her too.A side of him had come to the surface that he did not know existed.He suspected that her tenderness was no more than doing what she felt was duty.He had been neglecting her,and that must have some effect on her.

He wanted to make it up to her but he couldn't. His

body was hampered by his emotions. It is a common condition among men. The senses are numbed by the monotony of repetition.But when there is something new and strange, the body responds with vigour.It is a fact often overlooked.

Zhou Zhaolu could still feel the roughness on his knees. The bed squeaked too much, but they could not stop, so they rolled off onto the dirty carpet, as though the thought had occurred to them both at the same instant.

"Like a pair of animals."

That idea flashed again through his mind.

He is an animal. At the right time and place anyone can revert to the primal state. An animal lives out his destiny just as a man. He eats, and drinks, lives and hopes, and the end is always a void. An icy cold corpse.

That is the great irony of life.

In his second year at university he had to dissect the cadaver of an old woman. The cadaver lay on its back, a dirty tuft of hair sprouting from its mound of venus, hiding the hideous folds of flesh between the legs. His curiosity was layered with sadness. The scalpel cut through layer upon layer of withered flesh as dry as parchment. He got an A. But he hated dissection. The cadaver was no longer a person, but a heap of rotting flesh. It was his first confrontation with the ugliness of death. Afterward the world seemed dimmer for it. Later he discovered the cadaver had been a professor of the medical school. She never married, and had donated her body to the profession a long time ago. She never realized the terrible nature of her gesture. It was a long time before Zhou Zhaolu shook off the melancholy the experience induced. It made him face his own immaturity, and it spurred him on to working harder. Since life was such a pitiful business, he must take care of his; he must love himself. That notion never left him. He loved himself.

"Like a pair of animals." That dark thought stirred up all the emotions he tried to keep bottled up, and took on the inevitability of relentless fate.

He was lost.

He apologized to his son. He admitted that it was wrong to strike a person under any circumstances.

"You shouldn't be smoking," he said gently. "It's bad for you."

The boy turned away from him. The whole family was silent. It seemed there was nothing he could do to win them back. He did not think that family ties could be so fragile. If a storm in the teapot could cause such grief, what would happen if they discovered his secret.

"Let's go to the Fragrant Hills on Sunday. The autumn colours should be at their best!" He sounded unnaturally cheerful even to himself.

He seldom cared to go anywhere. Nor was he in the least interested in autumn colours. It was just that he did not know what to do for his family.

The maples were turning red but the hills were still mostly green. They rode the chair-lift to the peak, and from that vantage gazed out over the city. The city lay under a pall of smog. The Institute was far to the north, an insignificant speck in that vastness. He lived out his life in that smog shrouded city that was without shape or borders. The city and the plains made him as a speck of dust, or a breath of wind that passed un-noticed. His life, his secrets, and his pain meant nothing. People are only interested in themselves. He had nothing to fear.

He was happy, and the kids were enjoying themselves.On the way down, they laughed and chatted, and tugged at him as though nothing had happened. His wife picked her way down the path cautiously, afraid of falling. She stopped every other step to catch her breath like an old woman. She was older than her age. Zhou Zhaolu was sorry for her as he took her arm. She flashed him a grateful smile. Even her smile was old, he thought with a start. Her clumsiness stood in sharp relief to the other woman. Involuntarily his thoughts turned to the other.

It was the differences that caused problems.

The grass was damp with dew.They leaned against a tree, and she applied mosquito repellent to her bare legs.The smell of it was everywhere.

He never intended to leave his wife.He owed her too much. She had given him two children, and much of his success was due to her inspiration. He had dedicated himself to her and the children. To abandon them was out of the question.

It was a happy family that came away from Fragrant Hills. Zhou Zhaolu thought he would wipe away the shadow that threatened their happiness before they became aware of it.

A few days later when he was confronted with the key again, he realized how fragile his resolve had been.It was not easy to free himself from a whirlpool. There were too many excuses.

His eyes raked that beautiful and lusty body.

"It will be the last time." He told himself that it had to end.

He hoped his actions would convince her the affair was over, yet he was tender and passionate. He lost himself in her as in a kind of death. Later he wondered whether other men who had betrayed their wives felt a soul-searing despair in the midst of ecstasy. He had no weapons against her seductiveness.

"This is the last time!"

It was with the same determination that he went to her a third time. It was the first Saturday in November, and the heating had already been turned on in the apartment. There was a comfortable bedroom. Hua Naiqian's schoolmate gazed out of a pretty picture frame. She had the querulous look of an old maid. Hua Naiqian assured him she only came home once a week on Sundays. But he was always afraid she might show up when she was least expected. He thought he could hide in the wardrobe, and slip out when she was unaware. He had given the matter of an escape route some careful thought.

He had a cup of tea after love-making. He had brought the tea himself. He flushed the dregs down the toilet, and rinsed out the cup. He had to be home for dinner.

"When will I see you again?"

She lay back on the bed, naked. He knew she wanted to be held a moment before he left. He was familiar with her body. He knew her needs, and though her hunger sometimes astonished him, he responded with ease. Even in their wildest moments he had never once said, "I love you...." He responded, as though to quiet her.

It must be ended he thought. He knew he did not love her. It was just a game they were playing that had gone on too long. The last time as he was leaving, she had come out of the bathroom naked.

"Zhaolu, there's something I must tell you."

He was pulling on his clothes, assailed by guilt.

"He's ... impotent...."

He wondered why she told him that.He was surprised then frightened. What was she trying to say. The whole thing had become a comedy of errors. She was toying with him. He was no more than a satisfying sex partner. That realization shed new light on their affair. His own wantonness rose to a new high. She became more desirable than ever. His sense of guilt almost vanished. Her clean white body was a vessel for them both.There was nothing to fear.

"When will I see you again?"

"That depends on you."

"We don't have to decide right now."

"Zhaolu, we mustn't part.... I love you...."

It was ironic. He kissed her eyes, her mouth, all the while sensing the imperceptible changes that had taken place. He still felt the power of her beauty, but the urgency was waning. She was a plaything. Neither really loved the other. Love had perished in the deluge of desire.

As he left the building he thought, "Maybe it is the last time; maybe not. It doesn't matter...."

It was only a question of time. The secret had to be kept now, and afterwards it must be buried without trace. He believed that it did not mean much to her, and she really did not have much respect for her body. I don't love her, he thought with relief.

VIII

The Ministry announced that Zhou Zhaolu's paper "The Study of Proof" was slated for the top award for scientific treatises. There were only five awards in Chinese Medicine and he was the only winner in the Institute. He had won over the paper submitted by Liu, the deputy dean of the Alimentary System Research Department.

"Congratulations, Old Zhou!"

"I didn't think I could win. It was a fluke!"

"You've broken the monopoly of the old fellows. It's a triumph for all us younger men...."

Old Liu was sincere in his good wishes. Zhou was embarrassed. Actually Liu worked very hard, but luck was always against him, "Next year it's bound to be yours...." he said.

"We'll see."

"You'll make it!"

"Of course. Congratulations again, and keep up the good work." Zhou detected a glimmer of envy in Liu's eyes not unmixed with disappointment and hurt. He was exhilarated. He did not need to be told to keep up the good work. He knew what was ahead, and what he must do.

Above all he must be self-effacing. Modesty becomes a man. It was a small enough price to pay.

Hua Naiqian suggested they celebrate together. He understood what she meant. She was tender and genuinely pleased for his sake, but his career had nothing to do with her. She was an unimportant decoration among his laurels; a pleasant interlude that fate provided which he had the right to enjoy.

On new year's eve there was the usual spring cleaning in all the departments. Zhou Zhaolu had gone into the lavatory to rinse out a mop just as the Party Secretary was coming out of one of the cubicles. The Party Secretary was an affable old fellow who had a high regard for intellectuals, an attitude not shared by the younger cadres in administration.

"Young Zhou, I suppose your year end report is finished?"

"It'll be on your desk as soon as it's printed."

"Fine, fine...."

The Secretary smiled as he zipped up his fly. When Zhou Zhaolu came out of his office again, the old fellow was still loitering in the corridor. He thought the Secretary must have something on his mind.

"Do you have an upset stomach?" Zhou asked jokingly.

"Not at all. When you're through I'd like a chat with you...."

"Alright."

Zhou Zhaolu knew the old man's habits. No matter how important it was, he always referred to it as a chat. The last time they had a "chat" was before he was named Researcher. The old man had warned him then that as a Researcher he would have to work twice as hard. Several hundred men with the same qualifications had their eyes on him.

Zhou Zhaolu sensed something in the wind, and he trembled within.

"Your career has been exceptional. So you must demand more of yourself. I've been a party member longer than you, and I am speaking from experience. Watch your step. See that you don't trip...."

"I understand. But...."

"You must not give anyone an excuse to find faults. Some trivia could cause a lot of un-necessary hassles...."

"What are you referring to?" He realized at once that he had said the wrong thing. He forced himself to be calm. His guard was up.

"When a man is exceptional, he draws a lot of attention," the old man was being vague.

"Please don't beat around the bush. If I've done something wrong please let me know what it is. I'll accept your criticism."

Zhou Zhaolu was smiling, still trying to make light of it, but he felt he was no longer in control. In fact he was floundering. There was a strange hollow feeling at the pit of his stomach.

"You intellectuals are all thin-skinned," the old man smiled too, as though they were close friends. "I believe you accepted a fee the last time you lectured at Tongxian County Hospital."

"I did."

"Someone accused you of being greedy, saying that you used office hours to teach elsewhere and demanded high fees."

"According to policy, I am allowed to accept a fee."

He seemed excited, but the knot within had loosened, and he deliberately put on an angry face.

"Let it go. In the future, limit outside activities to your free time."

"Then I'll demand a higher fee."

"We'll leave it. There's no need to go into it any further. Just be sensible. You're young and there's lots of work ahead...."

He broke into a cold sweat, and was a bit unsteady when he came out of the Secretary's office. At least he had not lost control, and blurted, "It's a lie!" But it was a close shave. The old Secretary had not mentioned the thing he feared most of all.

The old man's motherly good intentions perplexed him. Could the business about his teaching be a smoke-screen for something else? Would the Secretary believe rumours if there were rumours? Would the others?

He was convinced there were those who would welcome some dirt about him. He distrusted her and everyone around him. A host of faces crowded his mind. The treacherous one had to be among them, but he could not tell which.

It was Hua Naiqian who seduced him and put him into a tight spot, he ruminated bitterly. Now he was paying the price with his reputation and social standing. It was all her fault.

Henceforth he must tread softly among his enemies.

He was used to hostility. When he first came into the city to enter university he was a country bumpkin. His pants were made of rough cloth and his socks were darned. The other students despised him. When he rose to the top of his class, they laughed at his countryfied ways, and his awful accent. However he was determined to change all that. And he did. He became a proper gentleman. Hostility could not hold him back because he was exceptional.

In the meantime he went smiling and unruffled about his business.

His treatise won the first prize. The award ceremony

was televised. The children caught his smiling face as it flashed across the television screen but his wife did not. That night she sat up to watch the re-broadcast on the late night news. She was so proud.

He sent some of his prize money to his mother and brother in the country. They were not hard up, but he sent the money anyway. He made quite a tidy sum out of writing, but he never thought of sending money home before. Nor could he put a finger on the motive.

These days he caught himself thinking about his childhood, and how happy he had been.

One day he went to visit old Mr. Qian Tongkui who was ailing. The old man led a reclusive life and seldom saw anyone. Zhou Zhaolu went around to the famous stationer, Rong Bao Zhai and selected an ink stone for his mentor. The old man was a collector, and appreciated small attentions.

The old man was delighted with the gift but admonished Zhou Zhaolu for his extravagance. In return the old man made a gift of his own calligraphy to the younger man.

Zhou Zhaolu praise the scroll, saying that although he did not understand the finer points of the calligrapher's art, he was enthralled by the swirling vitality of the brush strokes.

The old man was flattered.

The visit was not prompted by any ulterior motive. A few years ago the old man had published the art of healing gleaned from a lifetime's experience. It was Zhou Zhaolu who helped compile and edit the tome. It was also Zhou's skill with words that made the book the success it was. The old man had intended to acknowledge his disciple's contribution in the book's foreword. But Zhou dissuaded him. He owed Mr. Qian a great deal for his success. He was made Deputy Director on Mr. Qian's recommendation. Zhao told himself he had to return the favour.

Mr. Qian had introduced him to the celebrities of Chinese Medicine. Once the old man had mentioned that he would bequeath his entire collection of medical books to the person he most trusted. Although no name was mentioned, Zhou Zhaolu was convinced the old man meant him.

He wanted to please the old man.

"Zhaolu, the various heads of the Institute visited me a few days ago...."

The old man hesitated. "There are things I shouldn't talk about, but I have no secrets from you."

Zhou Zhaolu smiled.

"The Institute is appointing a Deputy Administrator from within. They nominated several people and asked my recommendation...."

"Your opinion carries a lot of weight." "I'm old and useless. It's hard to know what they really think of me. But since they asked my opinion I gave it.... for what it's worth."

"Yes...."

Zhou Zhaolu's smile stiffened. He felt flushed, and the blood was hammering through his veins.

"I feel you are the best man for the job. Your record as an administrator is unimpeachable. You're the right age, and you're well liked. The leaders seemed to be in your favour too. They gave me the nod...."

"You've been most kind. But I don't think I am the right stuff. I'm better off doing research."

The palms of his hands were clammy. Thoughts raced helter skelter through his mind. He was poised on another rung of the ladder and knew he wanted to scale it to the top. He was exhilarated and scared.

"When opportunity strikes, grab it. But don't lose track of learning. I know all about youthful ambition...."

"I'll have to think about it."

"I've already sounded out some of the old guys, and there is a consensus. Of course, you must have time to think it out. But you needn't say so right away, unless you really don't want the job...."

"But am I suitable?"

"You're the right man. We're convinced you'll be good for the Institute. We wouldn't feel good about someone that's half baked...."

"I don't know what to say."

He was diffident and self—effacing, but ambition roiled within. He itched for action.

When he left Mr. Qian, instead of taking the bus, he walked. The noises of the city enveloped him. Passersby seemed friendlier. Even the cacophony of city life sounded pleasant. But all he was really aware of was the pounding of his heart.

The old Secretary's words sounded like a warning and a reminder that he must put his house in order while he could. He must garner all the support he could muster so that envy, false accusations and rumour and all the other pettiness that men are capable of would not touch him.

He recalled the Secretary's words. "You're young,

and there's a lot of work ahead of you...." the kindly old secretary had said. His intentions were quite clear now.

His standards and character were being appraised. The Secretary and Mr. Qian were good men. They understood him. He harboured no ill-will toward his unknown accuser. He pitied the man who tried to do him mischief. Zhou was convinced he was made of finer stuff than those who envied and feared him.

He also had a new understanding of Hua Naiqian. It was his success that she loved. It was he who captivated her and not the other way around. If he doubted his own prowess before, those doubts were gone. His ego had been given a jolt.

He had the power to captivate. But it was not the right thing to do. At least not yet. He could not afford to feed a woman's conceit with his future.

It was time to end the affair. He faced that prospect not without regret.

On Sunday he invited his colleagues for a meal at the Hongbinlo Restaurant. The excuse was the prize-winning treatise. Actually he wanted an opportunity to cement his relations with his staff. They knew the sort of man he was, so his elevation wouldn't upset them. Besides they would have to lean on him in the future. Still it was important that he make them feel trusted.

He did not pay special attention to Hua Naiqian who was seated at another table. She was teasing her tablemates for their manners. She laughed as easily as ever. She seemed to be trying to attract his attention. But he deliberately ignored her. She would have to get used to being one of the staff, no different from the rest.

The word "mistress" made him cringe. He disliked

the sexual connotations of the word. In any case the affair was over.

They arranged to meet after the meal. He would go to a used book store and she would go to a second-hand store, and they would meet in a furniture shop nearby. Hua Naiqian was disappointed because the old maid would be home in the apartment outside Yongdingmen, but he was not. Making love between the clean sheets of a stranger was beginning to bother him.

Objectively it was a revolting situation: without substance, melodramatic, and even farcical. His role had lost its freshness and excitement. Perhaps such roles were never intended to last.

He bought a magazine for his son at the used book store. As he came out he saw her in front of the furniture shop. They greeted each other with their eyes, and moved into an alley. Ahead was the Palace of the Nationalities. There were few people about. Because she had been in the company of colleagues, she wore less make-up than at their assignations, but she was still beautiful.

"I'm through with old Lin!" Her words surprised him.

"What happened...."

"I've had enough."

"You ought to be more level-headed about it...."

"I've been level-headed for two years. I can't go on any longer. I'm not going to throw away the rest of my life, because I'm sorry for the guy. I've lost too much already!"

She didn't look well. Her slightly up-turned nose was pale, tilted at a defiant angle but full of pain. He did not appreciate the woman's hatred for her mate.

The idea was alien to him, for he did not dislike his wife. What did the woman want?

"You have a child and a career. Old Lin is not a bad sort. You ought to think about it calmly...."

"You don't understand. Everything's going well with you. But what about me? I daren't think of the future."

"What will you do?"

"Divorce."

"Is there no other way?"

"No!"

"How does he feel?"

"Can't you imagine? He pleads, and he rages at me. But it's no use, I've made up my mind."

It was a woman of steel talking. She planned everything, and nothing would block the execution of that plan. This was the side of her that was at odds with the warm tender side of her personality. If she exhibited just a thread of regret for her choice Zhou Zhaolu might have pitied her.

He thought, this has nothing to do with me. The problems in the marriage had already existed. Their affair was not the wedge that was driving them apart, Nevertheless Zhou could not see himself as a completely innocent bystander.

He wanted to make his position clear, but he was at a loss for words.

"How will you live after divorce?"

"I'll be free. It will be better."

"You seem uncertain...."

"Any suggestions?" She was annoyed.

What did she expect of him? Surely she did not expect him to follow her example. She had promised she would never threaten his family. It was the one thought that he cherished, and bound him to her.

"You know I have expectations."

She had said that too before, and he never quite understood what she meant.

"What expectations?"

"To live with the man I love."

They were in the middle of a cross walk. The green and white mass of the Palace of the Nationalities loomed ahead. Cars brushed passed. Zhou Zhaolu kept his eyes averted, feeling sick to the stomach. The huge building wavered, and seemed about to tumble down around him.

"You're still young. You'll find someone."

".... I'm looking."

"You'll find him."

Inwardly he added, "But it isn't me." It can never be me. He breathed a sigh of relief, because she responded with a smile and changed the subject. Originally he meant to say that the affair was making him uneasy, and hinting at putting an end to it. But he had to put it off. Nor did he find another opportunity the same day.

They went to an exhibition of furniture at the Palace of the Nationalities. She had an eye for expensive furnishings. He was uninterested. When he thought of the messy apartment she lived in, he knew she would never be able to manage a well-ordered house. She was drifting, and she would only drag him down. He had to leave her.

"That sofa's very handsome, " she breathed.

"Yes, very handsome...."

"Do you like the colour?"

"…. It's alright…."

He didn't care. It was white, which she liked. She wore white frocks with matching shoes. Even her lingerie was white. However, white did not suit her. He was convinced she should always wear purple, like the rows of nameless flowers in the foyer. White is for purity. He wondered how she would take parting.

IX

It was snowing. His wife woke him early so that he would not miss the Institute's bus. By the time he was up she had already been out and bought food for breakfast. The hallway was covered with wet footprints. He went out on the balcony. The air was still. The snow drifted down gently. His head was still fuzzy.

He had a peculiar feeling of foreboding. It had happened to him a few times before. He recalled the time when he went home to his village after writing the university entrance examination in the county town. It was the same feeling of dread. What if he failed? But he never really considered the possibility. Life seldom disappointed him. Before one grasps what one desires there is always doubt that is akin to fear. It was the same with him every step of the way up. In the end he always got what he wanted.

This time he was not so sure.

The news was all over the Institute. People were whispering in the corridors, in the cafeterias and the offices, that he was about to be appointed Vice President of the Institute. On the other hand another candidate was also in the running. He brushed off all the talk as though it did not matter, but his nerves were on edge.

The more he thought about it the more he found himself at a disadvantage. He was not a good organiser. He lacked administrative ability. Although he was cool in crises, he lacked decisiveness. But what troubled him most was the affair with Hua Naiqian. That was a blemish on his record. Of course it could be hidden, but the spot would still be there. When he thought that she could be the cause of irreparable loss, his misery was complete.

"Are you really going to be the Vice President?"

"It's possible."

His wife was too excited to be any comfort. He had hoped that she would be calm, and urge him to go on with his research. That would at least relieve the pressure.

"Vanity, thy name is woman." They are all alike. Social position is the seducer that few can resist. It is only the hopeless who are disinterested.

"The ground's slippery. Be careful."

"Don't wait for dinner."

"You get on with your work. I'll wait."

His wife tucked the ends of his scarf under the collar of his coat. Her eyes shone like a bride's.

It was snowing hard. The snow was clean in spots and muddy in others. It had been churned into black slush on the road, but hung in white fluffy clusters from the trees. The air was clear.

This was the day he was going to break it off with Hua Naiqian. It was the first time he had suggested an assignation. When he asked her the day before, Hua Naiqian was thrilled. They would meet in the same place she did not know it would be the last time. Nor did he have the heart to tell her just then. All the same he was annoyed that she did not appreciate his position. If she really loved him, she would let him go. He was beginning to regret the whole thing.

Their parting should be once and for all. That he chose to do it in their old trysting place showed a kind of callousness. He was familiar with every soul-stirring inch of her body. To leave it abruptly out of boredom was not quite possible. There was regret for he was not ready to face his true feelings.

He thought of the mole below Hua Naiqian's belly.

He did not love her, but memory is unshakable, his assertion untrue and hollow.

The bus stopped at Dongdan and Hua Naiqian got on. She was wearing a wool coat a curious shade between beige and pink. He avoided her. He tried to read a magazine, which was his habit, but he could not concentrate.

He did not have a chance to speak to her all day. If he had he might have suggested meeting somewhere else.

But would she be hysterical in a cafe or some other public place?

There was a meeting of the Party branch to discuss the Institute's future expansion. The five candidates for Vice President were invited to attend. They would be interviewed by a hastily organised panel of examiners, and the job would go to the one who scored the highest. The meeting determined the perimeters of the interview, and such modish terms as the principles of administration were bandied about ad nauseam.

The air crackled with excitement. It was just another form of torture! Zhou Zhaolu felt that his fate was always in someone else's hands, and this interview was nothing more than another confrontation with the cruelty of choice.

Old Liu was one of the candidates. He spoke passionately, declaring himself ready for the challenge, and throwing himself on the wisdom and fair judgement of his superiors and the public. His plea was too urgent. He would not go far. He was defeated by flaws in his personality.

"I want a chance to give it my best shot. I feel it is a good thing to consider the overall picture when we speak of the administration of the Institute. I thank the leaders for this opportunity."

Zhou Zhaolu said what he had to say simply and clearly. He knew the sort of impression he wanted to make, and he had only one chance to do it.

Old man Qian phoned to encourage him. "You spoke well. That's a big help. Be prepared. If there're any problems, call me."

The old man had a lot of clout at the Institute. Of course he would go to him. What amused Zhou Zhaolu was the old man's parting remark, "You mustn't let me down...."

He knew complex personal relationships lurked behind each appointment. The old man could be useful in that regard. Therefore, he mustn't be let down.

In the evening he took the bus to Yongdingmen Wai. There was a light in the window. She was waiting. His footsteps crunched across the snow. He lost count of the times he had been there, but never had there been the hollow ache he felt now.

The corridor was cold and draughty, and he was always afraid of meeting someone, although no one knew him.

He went up five flights of stairs quickly. The door was ajar. He pushed it open without knocking. He had forgotten their usual signal: three knocks. They never came together. She always arrived first and prepared everything, for time is precious and he could not stay long.

The kettle was on the boil; the bed had been turned down. She was in a wooly sweater her face flushed with expectation. She hanged his coat on the rack and went into his arms. He glanced at the drawn curtains, the two pillows on the bed. She always lay against the wall, and he on the outside. It was the same at home. But there the resemblance ended.

He was never rough with his wife. But from the start this woman turned him into a savage. It did not embarrass him. The dividing line between beauty and the grotesque blurred. It was something that could not be experienced without taking chances.

He was covered with sweat. His breath came in harsh gasps of despair. They would part, and no matter how hard he strove, this moment was fleeting, a ritual of farewell. He was losing her forever. Her eyes were shut. There was a pinkness about her breasts. Her lips, faintly parted, roused in him a rush of tenderness and regret.

He got up and started pulling on his clothes with his back to her. She lay under the covers watching.

"What's the hurry?"

He did not answer. He tied his shoelaces and went

into the bathroom. Afterwards he went to the kitchen and made himself a cup of tea. He took it back to the bedroom, breathing in the aroma, and settled in a chair.

Her wide eyes were moist. She did not look thirty-six. Her languid sensuality was that of a younger woman. A stranger would not guess her age.

"Get up. I want to talk."

"About you?"

"….Yes…. It has to do with you too…."

"I understand…"

"Get up. We can't talk like this."

"I'm comfortable this way…."

She stuck a bare leg out of the covers, and quickly pulled it back again. Her smile was teasing, but she got out of bed. She watched him carefully as she dressed.

"You seem unhappy. Are you worried about the new job?" she asked casually.

"Naiqian, you know my position. It's time we talked about us seriously."

"What is there to talk about?"

"…. Although it's wrong…. I've been happy … and I'll never forget you…."

"What's all that about?"

She blanched. She was beginning to understand. Zhou Zhaolu quaffed a mouthful of tea. When he spoke again it was in a cold, businesslike tone.

"I've decided, we must part."

"…. You're joking…."

"I'm not."

"You make it sound so simple."

His hand shook as he put the teacup on the dresser.

The old maid gazed sadly out of her picture frame. Hua Naiqian leaned against a pillow, her cold, expressionless face framed by a cloud of rumpled hair. Her coolness surprised him. He went on doggedly, "It's best for the both of us. We have to resume our normal lives ... I'm too tired ... the pressure is unbearable ... I love you but ... I've never stopped being guilty...."

"You sure pick the right moment for guilt, why?"

"I feel a certain responsibility for the trouble between you and Lin. I didn't think it could become so complicated...."

"You know you had nothing to do with it. Our marriage was finished long ago. You knew from the start."

She leaped off the bed and stamped past him to the bathroom and slammed the door. She had pulled on a sweater over her panties. Her long slender legs seemed to grow out of the sweater. He had never seen her like that before and braced himself for hysterics.

He waited. Something drew him back to the photograph of the old-maid. She was innocent. She knew nothing about adultery under her roof, and a naked man between her sheets. These things were incomprehensible to her, or should be. She looked a proper lady. People are used to being sanctimonious.

When she came out of the bathroom her eyes were redrimmed. She climbed into bed again and pulled the covers over her legs.

"Have you anything more to say?" She sounded strained.

"That's all. I hope you understand...."

"You don't love me. You never did!"

"You're wrong...."

"I won't let you leave like this. I'm not something you can pick up and throw away. You can't treat me like that...."

"Be reasonable."

"... You disappoint me...."

Her voice shook. Finally there were tears. He had never seen her cry before. She made no sound, but there were a lot of tears. He wanted to take her in his arms and comfort her, but that would only make it worse. He tried to be calm. He picked up his cup again, and gazed at this fascinating woman.

The tears were probably proof of her love, or evidence that she had endured all she could. He did not want to hurt her, but he had to protect himself, and tears would not shake his resolve.

"Please don't cry. It won't change anything," it was the voice of a hypocrite speaking. "You'll still be my closest friend."

"That's all?"

"That's it."

"And if I disagree?"

"You won't."

"I don't agree. I won't!"

"That's childish. You'll only make it worse."

"... But I love you...."

"I know. I still love you. But it can't go on the way it has. It's too dangerous...."

They were quiet a moment. Outside the snow was whirling in the gusting wind.

She stuck a leg out of the covers in a final gesture of defiance as she slid to her feet. He stood too. His clumsy kiss was not put on, but born of awkwardness.

The whole ritual of farewell was awkward and steeped in misery. There was a bitter taste to her lips.

"Naiqian, forgive me…"

There was something more he wanted to say, but the mocking gleam in her eye cut him short. Her lips glided across his cheeks, damp and smooth as an orange. He knew she was not the only one playing a part.

He put on his coat and fastened his scarf. He flayed himself with his arms. It was like coming out of a conference. He was leaving and never coming back.

"I wish you success!"

Though her eyes filled with tears, the mocking gleam did not leave them. Of course she knew the real cause of their parting but the bitterness of her tone startled Zhou Zhaolu.

"I wish you the very best success!" she added sarcastically.

It was the meanest cut of all. Zhou Zhaolu had been fooling himself all along. She knew he would not leave her out of a sense of decency.

He hesitated. He was almost going to stay, to caress and comfort her, to make her take back her terrible epithet. But all it would achieve was a delay and more falsehoods. No explanation was possible.

"… what's the use?" He muttered and hurried from the room. The expression in Hua Naiqian's eyes was unbearable: mockery, hatred, lust for vengeance, but no compassion. She had become a stranger. It was only her body that he knew. He knew nothing about what was in her heart.

Would she vent her hatred on him, and destroy them both? In the wilderness of Beidaihe she rubbed insect repellent on her legs right after love-making. She was capable of anything.

Zhou Zhaolu slipped and fell under the railway bridge. He picked himself up and stamped on the hard packed snow angrily. There were few passers-by, and nobody took any notice. The bus to Chang'-an Street turned the corner, its brake lights flashing. He ran toward it gingerly, his coat flapping like giant black wings. He had reached a turning point in his life. He would not withdraw because a woman had gone over to the other side. He did not fear her. He was still the captain of his own ship.

He squeezed on board just as the gate shut. A great bird had landed on its nest.

X

Zhou Zhaolu saw his wife and children onto the train. Since the summer they had planned to take a family holiday and visit Shanghai as soon as winter vacation began. But he was too busy to get away. His wife was concerned that he would not be able to manage on his own. She reminded him again and again to have hot meals, and leave the laundry till she return-ed; to be sure the door was locked when he left for work. But he knew it was not these things that wor-ried her.

She pressed her face against the window as the train pulled out.

"Do your best. I wish you success."

He smiled confidently as though nothing could go awry. He waved a fist in the air in a gesture so youthful that it drew peals of laughter from the children.

He left the station and went to the home of Mr. Qian Tongkui. The administrative program was already taking shape in his mind, but there were still a few details that needed to be thrashed out. There was a difference of opinion between himself and the elders on the establishment of a consultation department. He felt that a Consultation Department made of elder practitioners should be a permanent establishment. Whereas Mr. Qian felt that if this department was to be financed at the expense of research, then it would be best left alone. Deep down Zhou Zhaolu did not object to Mr. Qian's way of thinking. However, his enthusiasm for the Consultation Department was not due to his need for the wisdom of his elders, but for their support.

One afternoon shortly before the final interview, after most people had left the office for the day, the phone rang. Zhou Zhaolu picked up the receiver and announced himself. There was no sound on the other end of the line. He hung up the phone, thinking it was a wrong number. But the phone rang again.

"This is Zhou Zhaolu. Who do you want? Speak up."

"Are you … assistant director Zhou? I asked the operator for the number, but I was afraid I might have reached someone else. I have a number of the institute here, somewhere. You are… Zhou Zhaolu?"

"That's me alright. Who is this?"

He was a little annoyed, but trying to sound amused.

"This is Lin Tongsheng. I really had to force myself to call. I'm sorry…."

"You're Hua Naiqian's husband. We've met. Is there anything I can do?"

The other's name set alarm bells jangling at the back of Zhou Zhaolu's mind. Something must have happened. He forced himself to be calm, and sound natural. The other's voice was low, and sounded depressed.

"I need to talk to you."

"Oh...."

"You are Naiqian's superior so it would be appropriate."

"What's happened, Lao Lin? Just take your time, and tell me clearly what it is your want to see me about."

"It's a family matter. I need to talk to you personally."

Zhou Zhaolu did not refuse to meet him. It is impossible to talk coherently on the telephone, besides Lin Tongsheng was so insistent it would do no good to refuse. Zhou Zhaolu did not feel threatened. If Lin intended to take him by surprise he would have used some other tactics. Nor would he be so plaintive if he had something on Zhou. He suspected that Hua Naiqian was up to no good. Perhaps she had drawn him into her marital difficulties, and forced her husband to approach him.

Zhou Zhaolu was once more agitated. In fact he was more anxious for the meeting now than Lin Tongsheng.

After they had parted, Hua Naiqian was her usual vivacious, friendly self around the office although she avoided being alone with him. In gatherings she still called him by his nickname. Nothing changed. He was ashamed of his mistrust.

He thought the worst was over, but once again he

had misjudged her. She was good at dissembling.
Perhaps she was preparing to attack him when it
would do the most damage.

He met Lin Tongsheng on the steps of a fast-food
outlet on Sidan. He had come directly from the office
without eating. Lin Tongsheng wore a short woolen
overcoat. His trousers were creased and lumpy, as if
they had been pulled over padded pants. His shoes
were scuffed. He wore a pair of wool earmuffs fastened
under his chin, that lent him a pathetic hang-dog look.
Zhou Zhaolu invited him for dinner. He nodded acceptance hesitantly.

They found a table at a restaurant in the under-
ground market. Zhou Zhaolu ordered the food, and
wondered what to say as they waited. Lin Tongsheng
smoked in silence.

"Will you have a drink?" Zhou asked.

"Please ... white wine ... you're very kind ...."

"Two ounces?"

"Yes ... you have some too...."

"I'll have beer."

Business was slack. The waiters working in the
sunless atmosphere were pale and wan. The food had
too much salt.

"Lao Lin, you seem unhappy."

"It's a long story ...."

"Fighting with Hua Naiqian?"

"She wants a divorce."

"Really? We haven't heard anything in the office.
What happened?"

Zhou Zhaolu was not a drinker. His face became
quite flushed very quickly. He drank quickly, tossing off
one glass of beer after the other. He was warm. Though

he was getting drunk, he was still in control. He was not sure whether he felt pity or contempt for the man sitting across from him.

Lin Tongsheng's brow was knitted into knots. He drank slowly, staring at Zhou Zhaolu with blood-shot eyes.

"I'm ashamed of bothering you with this.... But you've been a great help to Naiqian.... And when we met before, you struck me as a kind man.... I wonder if you would speak to her ... as a boss ... and ask her not to do this for the sake of the child and the family.... I'm sorry."

"I don't know how Naiqian feels about all this. Besides I am only her boss. I really can't interfere on that basis. It would not be appropriate."

"I've thought of that. If I took the matter to the Institute the whole thing would probably be solved, but Naiqian's reputation would suffer. And that means a lot to her...."

"I'm flattered that you have such faith in me, but I've never come across anything like this before, and frankly I don't know how to handle it."

"I'm sorry to trouble you...."

"Let's have another drink. Lao Lin, I really feel sorry for you....."

A half ounce of white wine, a plate of cold chicken and a plate of shreded tripe. There was no one waiting at home. He wanted to get drunk with this pathetic man and forget everything.

Lin Tongsheng began to open up.

"My marriage with Naiqian has always been difficult. At the time she was working at the Zhangjiakou Hospital.... Her home was Zhangbei. She had gone to the countryside and worked there first, and then went to Medical School. As soon as she graduated she was assigned to the city hospital. I'm sure you know all that....."

"I do...."

"At the beginning I was reluctant. But once I got to know her.... You know how it is...."

"I understand...."

"We were married in a hurry. I guess she was anxious to be assigned to Beijing.... Of course, it was a difficult relationship from the start; living apart and seeing each other once in a while ... We just weren't comfortable with one another. Also I am older, and not what you might call a 'good catch.'"

Lin Tongsheng smiled sadly. Zhou Zhaolu filled his cup and passed the food.

"I did everything within my power to get her transferred to Beijing. After the child was born, she was quite good to me for a time. Maybe she was grateful...."

"I believe she did well at the hospital in Yanqing County."

"Yes, she is very ambitious, but unlucky. I've never said this to her face.... Then she was accepted for post-graduate studies, and got herself assigned to your Institute. She's a very active person. I have no idea of her activities outside. Who knows, maybe I'm not the right man for her.... But I do love her.... This is very embarrassing...."

"Never mind. You're lonely, and emotional pain is the hardest to bear. I understand...."

Zhou Zhaolu was becoming a confidant. Hua Naiqian was becoming a stranger who had nothing to do with him. He was examining the secrets of her life with complete detachment.

Once again he felt it would be a mistake to be drawn into this woman's life. There was still time to back off.

"I was uneasy about her, but I never thought she would do anything to hurt the child. In the second year of her post graduate studies, I found some letters in her bag...They were from a young man at school ... I guess I lost my head ... I hit her.... She wanted a divorce then.... But it blew over ... and we went on as best we could...."

"Did she break it off with the man?"

Zhou Zhaolu realized immediately that the question was too urgent. He covered his confusion with a gulp of beer. His temples throbbed, and his chest was so tight he could hardly breathe. It was all beginning to unravel. What made him think that he was the first one..

"I love you!"

She had probably said the same words to many men. He was at once angry and glad. She really was trash, and he was well rid of her.

"She wasn't serious. From the tone of the letters, she was just stringing the guy along...."

Lin Tongsheng was drunk. He was slurring his words, as though he had a mouthful of cotton. He opened his eyes wide, trying to make everything clear, but he was losing control.

Zhou Zhaolu was not going to restrain him.

"She was a quiet person until she came to Beijing. Then she changed. She wanted to be fashionable. She went to all the dances for post-graduate students. She

even went to dances of other schools.... Maybe she
was making up for the lost years of her youth... Who
knows what goes on in a woman's mind...."

"But Hua Naiqian works very hard."

"That's true. She's better than me in so many
ways.... But I'm still her husband ... I will not give
her a divorce."

"Lao Lin, you have to pull yourself together."

Hua Naiqian had the man backed against a wall. In
some ways Zhou felt he too was responsible. It is tragic when a man loses his control over a woman.
What was it about her, that made her untamable he
wondered.

Love had turned Lin Tongsheng into a weakling.
Zhou Zhaolu felt a vague sadness and regret for this
simple, honest man.

"You have to make it up to her yourself. No one
else can do it for you...."

"In the last six months she's been constantly trying
to pick a fight. But I kept my cool. Lately she's been
coming home very late. Sometimes she stays out all
night. She seems very unhappy. The arguments are
fierce, and she's said some awful things...."

"What has she said?"

"She says she has many admirers, and every one of
them is better than me. She's trying to get me mad,
so's I'll hit her again. Then...."

"Aren't you getting the wind up? Women are
changeable. Let it go...."

"This time she's made up her mind ... I said I
would take it up with the Institute, but that didn't
faze her...." -

"Wouldn't that damage her self-esteem?"

"I don't know what she thinks anymore. I didn't want this to get out of hand, so I thought maybe you could talk to her, and obliquely suggest that the Institute might take a dim view...."

"I'll see what I can do."

"You mustn't let her know we spoke. If she feels she's lost face at the Institute, the whole thing could blow up sky high..."

"I'll know what to say. Leave it to me."

"I've never talked so much before. I'm sorry."

"Nonsense! I'm her boss, and I have a responsibility to help."

There weren't many people left in the restaurant. The waiters were tidying up. Lin Tongsheng seemed quite sober, but when he tried to pick up a sliver of meat, he could not make his chopsticks work.

Zhou Zhaolu was in an untenable situation. He was about to embark on the biggest swindle of his life. He was cheating a weaker member of his own species whose woman he had stolen, yet he was blithely mouthing platitudes.

The tunnel and the stairway to the street was interminable. Lin Tongsheng got half way up and his legs began to give way. Zhou Zhaolu took him by the arm, and the two staggered up like two long lost friends on a binge.

"I haven't many friends," Lin Tongsheng was saying, leaning against Zhou Zhaolu, and hanging onto the railing with his free hand.

"Me neither."

"All I do is teach. Never did anything worthwhile." "Me too. It's all so meaningless."

"... If it wasn't for the kid ... I'd kill her...."

"You're drunk."

"I'm not drunk.... I hate her ... hate her more than anything.... She's wrecked my life ... damned bitch...."

"You've had too much to drink."

Zhou Zhaolu was thinking the same thing. She really is a bitch. She ruined her husband, and now she was about to wreck his life as well. It gave him a certain satisfaction that he had thrown her over.

Lin Tongsheng revived a little by the time they reached the bus stop. He blinked owlishly in the cold night wind. The headlights of passing cars picked out the numb, resignation on his face. Zhou Zhaolu wondered what he himself looked like. They had been drinking for three hours. Everything that happened seemed unreal. It was all a dream.

"I might have said more than I should, Director Zhou. Please don't misunderstand ... I don't want you to have the wrong idea about Naiqian. Don't be too hard on her. She is ambitious...."

"I understand."

"It's just that she isn't very realistic when it comes to living problems.

She'll come to her senses...."

"I hope so...."

"I'll be in touch. Thank you."

"Not at all. Take care."

He saw Lin Tongsheng onto his bus, and took one headed in the opposite direction. The jouncing of the bus made him nauseous.

Lin Tongsheng was more likable when he was drunk. But he was a weakling. They were about the same age, yet Lin seemed a lot older and more depressed. Was a woman worth all that suffering? Lin always felt inferior to her; always pandering to her whims. No wonder she was dissatisfied. No matter how beautiful and sensual she was, she was his woman, and he had to tame her somehow.

Hua Naiqian had mentioned that her husband was impatient. It might even be true, but it should not be that important either. But for a woman such as Hua Naiqian perhaps it was important. Perhaps it was also the cause of her unslakable appetite.

If that were the case then Lin Tongsheng's tragedy was altogether too ridiculous.

Zhou Zhaolu staggered off the bus, and vomited on the patch of grass beside the road. A terrible sour smell filled his nostrils.

During his first year at the Institute, an old schoolmate from Tongren Hospital visited him. The friend had been drinking. He laughed and cried, and puked all over his dormitory. Later Zhou discovered that his friend was out of love. Zhou Zhaolu had no sympathy for the man. He looked upon other people's misfortune with indifference. Subsequently his friend married twice. Once to a university graduate in her twenties. Eventually the man went to the United States to study and never came back. Zhou Zhaolu knew instinctively that the man was no good, and all his wailing and carrying on was a comedy of manners.

But Zhou Zhaolu also had the premonition of the uncertainty of life, and he was overcome by sadness while he vomited.

He was thinking of what Lin Tongsheng had said. Hua Naiqian admitted having many admirers and sometimes stayed out all night. Had she been seeing someone else as well in their trysting place at Yongdingmen Wai. Did she flirt with anyone else aside from the post graduate student? Did she have a lover at Zhangjiakou? She had lived apart from her husband for a long time, perhaps her indiscretions had begun a long time ago.

He was just another harlequin trailing after her. The funny part of it is that he was completely mesmerized. He thought her wantonness was a natural outcome of long repression. He thought it was his magnetism that held her. He might have known better, even as long ago as on the carpet in Beidaihe. But up to the time they parted, he still believed that her tears were honest. In fact he had been duped.

He squatted on the ground, his head bent low, intent upon the stuff he had brought up. It was as though he had finally got the woman out of his system, and he felt better.

XI

Before the Selection Committee's decision was announced, the Institute was already buzzing with rumours. Members of the Committee had indicated that he was the best candidate, and the rest were only a formality. Zhou Zhaolu was definitely in.

Zhou Zhaolu also believed he would be selected hands down.

He had made a good showing at the interview. Old man Qian had raised some of the thorniest issues. He had deliberately left holes in his speech, making it easy for Old Qian to sink in his barbs. In fact the two had rehearsed the whole thing ahead of time, and the ruse went off like clockwork. No one could suspect anything. Old Qian had acted purely out of his love for talent. As for Zhou, he felt he had proved his own worth.

It happened that not long after the interview he was invited to lecture at the Medical College of Kyoto. The invitation came from the dean of Japanese Medicine, Okashige who had read some of Zhou's translations of his works. Okashige had written very flatteringly.

The previous year the Medical Society had organised a group to go to Hongkong. Due to tight money, his name had been struck off the list at the last minute. Zhou Zhaolu was unhappy for some time. Now there was a chance to make up for the disappointment. As all expenses would be paid by the host, Zhou Zhaolu expected approval would be quickly given.

He had never been abroad. Had he been practising Western medicine he would have had a chance long ago. Luckily there was an ally interested in China. Although the term Japanese Medicine was a misnomer, he could overlook it under the circumstances. He felt his Japanese was as good as Okashige's, whose writing was very pedestrian. It was another item for the Selection Committee to consider, and it was definitely in his favour.

Old Liu avoided him. He always quickened his steps as he passed the Cardio-Vascular Research Department hugging the walls. He was pitiful. When he got excited his speech became gibberish, though he was quite lucid when he was calm. He was used to asking questions, but when the shoe was on the other foot he became flustered. In fact no one was trying to trip him up. He tripped himself up. He was clearly not the right stuff for leadership.

Zhou Zhaolu was swept along on a wave of euphoria. But he was careful to mask his feelings. That was of prime importance. Lin Tongsheng phoned once to ask if he had spoken to Hua Naiqian. Zhou put him off by pleading pressure of work, and asking him to be patient. The other still harboured a shred of hope, but Zhou had no intention of keeping his promise. There was nothing to discuss with her. It was sheer foolishness even to contemplate it.

Lately she hasn't been going home. Nobody knew what she was up to. The thought of another man lying in the bed he once laid in did not disturb him. He was not jealous, for she was nothing to him. She and her family could go to the devil for all he cared. He was only sorry for the man who hoped against hope.

Though they would soon be together again Zhou Zhaolu wrote his wife immediately, giving her the news of the interview, and the invitation. Now she could show him off to her parents. Zhou's father-in-law was a retired engineer. At first he had been critical of Zhou's peasant up-bringing, and chided his daughter for marrying him. But in the twenty years that ensued, the old man was forced to change his mind. He was actually proud of Zhou, and treated him as a son. Zhou had not disappointed the family.

The apartment was not a home without his wife and children. He longed for their return. For a short while he had wandered off the straight and narrow and he was ashamed. How could he have allowed himself to be enmeshed in such a sordid affair. He was a researcher and a scholar, and soon to be the Vice President of the Institute. His position would not permit it. He had clearly not been himself.

Zhou Zhaolu had transcended the sordid. He was a man of ideals and integrity. He was pleased with himself. He was very pleased.

Sunday he stayed home to read. Around ten o'clock as he refilled his teacup, there was a knock on the door. He thought it was the old woman from the housing committee come to tell him about rat extermination. But Hua Naiqian stood on the doorstep. In his agitation he almost dropped the teacup.

She had come out of nowhere. How did she know his wife was away? She must have been watching his every move. What did she want?

"You bring food home every day, so I guessed you were alone. Where're the wife and children?"

"Visiting her people in Shanghai."

"I was right!"

She took off her coat and sat on the sofa, looking around the room. She was quite at home. There was not a shred of awkwardness. Her smile was natural.

"It's very comfortable."

".... Is there anything I can do for you?"

"I miss you so I came. Do you want me to leave?"

"Will you have tea or coffee?"

"It doesn't matter."

She looked at the wedding picture on the wall.

"You weren't so distinguished when you were young. But your wife was pretty."

"I'm getting old."

"If I could be the mistress of this household, I'd die a thousand deaths. You see, I'm jealous of her...."

Zhou Zhaolu was embarrassed. The teacup rattled in his hand. Again he wondered what she wanted.

"Zhaolu do you miss me?"

"Why talk about it. It's finished."

"I don't think so...."

"What do you intend to do?"

He had finally put it into words. He was suddenly angry. He wanted to dash the cup of tea into that pretty face.

"I am a woman with expectations. I want to divorce the man I don't love, and live with one that I do. But he lost his nerve. There are too many things he can't do without."

"What you want is impractical."

"I admit that, Zhaolu. But did you never think of divorcing your wife?"

"I love her."

"Do you love me?"

"No!"

"Then it was just a game?"

"What we had ... there was no need for love...."

"You're very cruel!"

"You are too."

They looked at each other: two people who did not understand one another. Neither could read the other's mind. She smiled. His face was blank. If she thought she had something on him that she could use to force him to continue their relationship, she was mistaken. He could not be threatened.

"I've made up my mind about the divorce. If he objects, I'll live apart from him...."

"What if he takes it up with the Institute?"

"He hasn't the guts. If he does take it to the Institute, my colleagues can prove I'm blameless.... So can you. You're my boss; you're supposed to understand me...."

"That I can."

"The painful part is over now. I still love you though. But I'll find someone suitable and marry again. It won't be you. You're too selfish...." Zhou Zhaolu was taken aback.

"Aside from that, you're a perfect man. Don't sell yourself short." He smiled sadly. He never underestimated himself. She touched the sleeve of his sweater, and he shuddered.

"Don't worry. You're still you. When I can't stand being alone, I'll still come looking for you...."

"You'll never be alone. Don't you have many admirers?"

".... What do you mean by that?" He avoided her eyes. That was hitting below the belt. Perhaps she wasn't the way he imagined.

"I'm not joking. Don't think just because you're the vice president of the Institute, you can treat me like a stranger. I gave you everything I have, and that's a fact!"

"I may have wronged you, but the responsibility was not all mine."

"In a word you don't want the responsibility. If I really wanted to hurt you I would have let the cat out of the bag long ago...."

"It wouldn't have done anyone any good."

"Who would it damage more?"

"Keep your voice down. There are neighbours."

"I have nothing to lose. I love you. But you threw me over for the sake of being the vice president. You never even thought of me...." Her face was flushed. Only the bridge of her nose was white. She had come to give him a piece of her mind; she had come to threaten. He never thought she could ever be as hateful to him as she was just then.

"What do you expect of me?"

"I want us to be the way we were. I won't destroy your family. I'll protect you, but you can't cut me off. That I can't stand...."

She got up from the sofa, and suddenly she was in his lap, his face pressed tight against the softness of her body. Everything went black. Perhaps she really loved only him; a sensual, irresistible love that held him in thrall, and he was lost.

"I could kill her!" Lin Tongsheng's words sounded in his ears. The man was not drunk when he uttered them. He knew what he was saying. Under the smooth skin of the slender neck on a level with his eyes, life throbbed.

"No. It's not possible here."

He thrust her from him.

"Why not here?"

"I won't permit it. This is my home."

"But you are mine."

"... Naiqian ... I beg you...."

Despair hovered between them unseen. He gave in. Darkness enfolded him. No matter how he struggled, the whirlpool sucked him under.

In the afternoon Hua Naiqian emerged from the

building looking radiant, a wisp of a smile on her lips. Later Zhou Zhaolu appeared, carefully groomed and dressed clutching a book, headed toward the river bank west of the housing complex. However, there was a curious stoop to his shoulders, and he walked with a stiff, almost sinister gait.

Before the Selection Committee's decision was made official, the Party Secretary had a private talk with Zhou Zhaolu in which he was briefed about his future duties. His appointment was to commence from the first of March, and he was to hand over his work in the Cardio-Vascular Research Department before that date. Zhou Zhaolu was always reserved, but his lack of excitement puzzled the old secretary.

"Is there a problem?"

"No. I'll do a good job."

"That's the spirit!"

The old man clapped him on the shoulder. Zhou Zhaolu remained impassive. He seemed already absorbed by the burden of his new post.

His family returned from Shanghai. His wife was concerned that he was over tired. He did not disagree. Indeed, he looked haggard, and could not shake off his weariness. Once in a moment of tenderness his wife plucked out a grey hair.

"My Zhaolu is getting old...." she murmured. His face was grim, and close to tears.

He cabled the University of Kyoto declining their invitation, "due to pressure of work," and expressing a hope that the opportunity would arise again some time in the future.

Professor Okashige replied at once, enclosing a Japanese magazine containing his translation of Zhou

Zhaolu's "The Study of Proof". The article was headed by a reproduction of his photograph from the original Chinese publication. In the introduction Zhou was lauded as a brilliant pioneer of Chinese medicine.

His inauguration speech on the first of March was a huge success. A vice Minister and other officials attended. He was a good speaker, who held the audience for forty minutes without a script. Not a word was out of place. There were even a few dashes of humour. It was a dazzling show of intelligence and ability. His future was ensured.

Zhou Zhaolu stood on the podium, filled with confidence. He knew the image he projected. He had fashioned it carefully for himself. The image was everything. What lay under the surface did not matter. No one knew his soul except Hua Naiqian.

The audience was applauding now. She applauded too. He could pick her lovely face out of any crowd, but he chose not to. He wanted her to vanish forever. Better still, that she never existed at all.

A shadow passed over the new Vice President's face. No one noticed. Not even she who was applauding the loudest.

He was drunk with applause. It was the only solace of his life. He had come to this moment one step at a time. He had a right to be proud. He felt as light as a swallow. There were no longer any restraints. He could soar to whatever heights he set his mind to.

He had arrived.

A small inner voice warned him: be careful! He smiled. He knew where that voice was coming from. But Zhou Zhaolu was no longer afraid.

Unreliable Witness

Prologue

OUR instructor in Logic was a young, eloquent and learned man who enjoyed calling the roll. This always created an atmosphere of tension that the older more laissez-faire teachers eschewed. They say a new broom sweeps clean, and the young instructor had a penchant for keeping the pot boiling.

The person whose name was called, popped to his feet, and barked, "present" like a child in grade school or a soldier on parade. Then he would be asked a question connected to the day's assignment. If he didn't have a ready answer woe betide him. I pitied the dullards who couldn't retain anything. I suspect the young instructor enjoyed taunting them, showing off his cleverness. When a name was called and there was no response, his pen would make a swift, triumphant hook on the roll.

"I'll say this one more time," the instructor, who probably saw himself as a stern teacher, said vehemently, "anyone who is absent three times in a row will fail the final exam." Wasn't that going too far?

The students of the special course were in their thirties and concerned about getting a degree. Few were actually interested in this new science of thought patterns. Many weren't even sure what Logic was ! As if humanity did not torment itself enough. The instructor was no more than a rubber hose that transferred the contents of a barrel into assorted bottles and jars. Milk, or dish water, it was all the same to him. Assignments, rollcalls, and tests were his refined methods of torture. He left you nowhere to hide. If he were my younger brother I'd thrash him, then boot him off to a monastery to mend his ways.

I bear no grudge against those who force feed us "the rhythm of thought" and so on. Nor do I harbour any malice toward the young instructor's habit of calling the roll. I could grit my teeth and bear it. One time I was almost thankful.

"Guo Puyun!"

It was the usual bland voice, but it seemed a bomb had gone off in the room. Outside, was the white, sunless sky of November. The room, being shaded, was gloomy. The radiator grumbled fitfully. It sounded like a power-drill working somewhere in the building. The silence foreboded someone was about to be caught playing truant. But this was different. The class had been thrown into momentary confusion by the name Guo Puyun. As an idea, intention and its execution the name would serve. But would it serve as well as a basis of judgement and reason? This interlude was so sudden and ridiculously bitter that I could not quite grasp it. The air had turned sinister, and nothing seemed quite real. I wonder what "rhythm of thought" was at work.

The instructor was making a mark against the name on his roll, and saying in his unhurried way, "Three absences will be treated as a failure at the end of term. Will the monitor kindly notify Guo Puyun that next week...."

The hissing was spontaneous. The instructor ignored it and went on speaking. The radiator suddenly sputtered to life. The rattling of the radiator and the hissing blended into a roar. A few titters set off peals of laughter. I was laughing too.

"What's so funny?" The instructor blushed.

"He isn't around anymore."

"Why?"

"... natural elimination!"

The remark came from the back of the room. The farce had been played to its bitter end where laughter was no longer possible. I too had been laughing a moment ago. Now I was a spectator. One person's discomfiture often evokes merriment in others. I have seen that time and again. However, this laughter was no longer directed at the hapless instructor. The wounding laughter had veered elsewhere. Guo Puyun was no longer a reality. He had become words, sounds, fragments of language, an idea deserving examination and judgement, beyond praise or blame. As spirit he did not matter much to anyone. As a physical manifestation he was a clod buried under three feet of earth. He would no longer cringe under the lash of cruel laughter. Perhaps he was better off where he had gone, than walking in the bright light of day.

The instructor finished the lecture listlessly. Afterwards the students scattered in twos and threes on foot, by bicycle, going home, cooking food, eating, reading, courting, making love. Doing all the things they did day in and day out. The incident in the classroom made not a ripple on their lives. Guo Puyun was nothing. But to refer to his death as "natural elimination" was heartless. The cruelty of that remark could not longer touch him. Only a name remained to suffer the barbs of unkind fate.

That roll call brought Guo Puyun sharply to mind. I suppose you could say we were friends. However, I did not often think of him, nor can I be sure whether thinking of him now evokes any sense of loss. In the beginning there was shock, and pity. It shouldn't have happened. As I continue muddling through life, complacency hardens the heart. I did laugh in the classroom that day, but that does not prove I am callous. The spontaneous outburst was frightening and shameful. I think I can face the memory of Guo Puyun without flinching. Yet I am groping for a fragment of humanity to clear away the debris that blocks well-springs of emotion.

Reason is objective. I am following a certain train of reason, and therefore, I too am objective. If Logic is not witch-craft, and the instructor not a charlatan then the results of my probing will be my talisman when I meet Guo Puyun in the nether world. I will either find the truth, or I will manufacture one. Somehow I feel it will be the latter. When that roll-call began who could have foreseen its outcome? Hearts are separated from each other by a veil. I am separated from Guo Puyun by the gates of hell.

Chapter   1

Guo Puyun killed himself on May Day. Why he chose the first of May is a mystery. I do not think he intended to blacken the holiday with a gift of death. However, his choice of date puzzles me, and makes his actions that much more intriguing. It is as though there was some hidden significance in his premeditation.

Early that morning Guo Puyun had gone to the market and bought a live chicken and a basket of fresh vegetables. He killed the chicken on the balcony with such finesse that his parents were not aware of it. A week later when they found his body, the bowlful of chicken blood was still standing in a corner of the balcony. It had congealed under a layer of dust, and resembled poor quality soya sauce gone mouldy. His father dropped the bowl down the garbage chute, and heard it shatter.

Guo Puyun plucked the chicken, but broke the gall bladder when he dressed it. His mother heard his groan and went into the kitchen.

"It's spoilt," he said standing over a mound of dripping red innards in the sink.

"What happened?"

"I spoilt it."

"Did you break the gall bladder?"

"I'm sorry. The gizzards are inedible."

He forced a smile, but his thoughts seemed far away.

"Is there fish in the frig?"

"Yes."

"I'll clean it now...."

"Why not wait till your sister gets home...."

"I'm cooking today."

"Alright then."

"Do you have anything to do?"

"Nothing special. You have a rest. Your father and I are going for a walk. We won't be long."

"The traffic's heavy. Be careful."

"... we won't cross the street."

He washed and went to his room, where he stayed all morning, reading. He was absorbed by the Japanese novel Snow Country. Whether it was coincidence or choice, is hard to say. The book was covered with margin notes, which made little sense at first glance. The writing was cramped and spidery. However, the line "He is a gentle liar" caught my eye. I doubt that it referred to the protagonist in the book. It was more likely his assessment of its author who had killed himself by putting a gas pipe in his mouth. He was fascinated with the man, and was probably probing for an explanation of his death. The line "His judgement is grotesque and romantic," which appears on page 53 had nothing to do with the contents either, which was largely a lifeless description of a body part except for one sentence - it was as vibrant as a freshly peeled leek.

His mind must have wandered far and wide. The book no longer held him.

At ten o' clock his sister came home. She opened his door and startled him. Later she recalled him lying on the bed, his back against the wall, with a book cradled on his chest.

"Didn't you hear my knock? Where's mother?"

"Gone for a walk with father."

"I have something on at lunchtime. Lets get together for dinner."

"Alright.... Can you get back a bit early?"

"You've got it! I must go. He's waiting downstairs. Bye!"

"Bye...."

At noon he ate some noodles and went back to his room and wrote five or six letters. He had never written that many letters at one time before. When his mother came to summon him to the kitchen, he was carefully pasting on the stamps. The envelopes were all neatly addressed and the stamps were pasted in the identical spot. All the letters reached their destinations. Each had been written with great care, announcing the most solemn decision of his life. He was serene.

It was a happy dinner. His brother-in-law was a witty fellow, whose chatter could not be impeded even by a mouthful of chicken bones. The old couple were completely captivated by his stories. Guo Puyun had little to contribute to the conversation, except the odd remark about the chicken, and the blandness of the fish. He quietly sipped his red wine. Nobody noticed that he had downed eight glasses. But they did notice that he fumbled as he picked the bones out of the fish, and that he was flushed. When the brother-in-law asked the recipe of the fish, he went into a long winded explanation. His father gave him the eye, and he faltered, adding lamely, "I believe the amount of wine and the timing are crucial." The brother-in-law nodded, and exchanged glances with the others. Guo Puyun could not hide his preoccupation, and the others were helpless at penetrating his privacy. They were used to his secretiveness.

Guo Puyun was the first to leave the table. He tidied his room and reappeared with his faded old knapsack and a few letters. His expression was bland but there was an under-current of excitement. He said he was using the few days he had off to visit his friends at his work unit whom he had not seen since he went back to school.

"How long will you be gone?" asked his mother.

"No more than a day or two."

He smiled. There were no lingering glances. Nor did he say anything unusual. It was no different from the hundreds of times he had left home before. His footsteps faded down the stairs.

He took a number 102 trolley from Baiwanzhuang to Yongdingmen Station. The local to the western suburbs stood at platform three. Platform 3 is on the far side of an overpass. He crossed the eight metre high steel bridge to the train, paying scant attention to either the overpass or the train below. There weren't many passengers. Most were miners going to work or village merchants returning home. He selected the last carriage and stretched out across three seats. Actually there were several of his co-workers in another carriage. Afterwards none of them recalled seeing him. In fact they denied he was on the train. When the train arrived at Xiaweidian, not more than ten people got off, and they swore he was not among them.

The letters were mailed from Xiaweidian. The station platform is very short, and his carriage stopped near the signal lights. He jumped off onto the tracks, and made his way northward along the storm drains. He crossed the street of Xiaweidian and stuffed the letters into the dilapidated green letter box attached to the wall outside the food store. The envelopes made small grating sounds as they disappeared in the gaping maw. The familiar letter box that had served him many years, had become part of his master plan. Most of the street lamps were out. The night was made desolate by the winds of May. He was filled with sardonic joy as he turned northwest-ward up a steep knoll.

The path ran across a suspension bridge and a branch of the mine's rail line. Finally it took him to the peak of Colt Mountain six hundred feet above sea level. There was a splash of lights at the foot of the mountain. To the right in a valley were the living quarters of the miners. To the left nearer the foot of the mountain was the Munitions Factory where he had worked for seventeen years. The narrow gorge leading to the firing range was hidden behind a ridge that glowed a dim blue. A convoy of coal trucks crept southeastward across the low land and into tunnel number 13, that led to the plains, and the mournful sirens sounded from the bowels of the earth. These familiar sights and sounds had no effect on Guo Puyun. He sat behind a rock, out of the wind, to watch, think and smoke, and prolonged his life till midnight. Beneath the north face of Colt Mountain there is a small reservoir. On his way there, Guo Puyun dropped a butane lighter that many people recognized, an empty packet of Changle cigarettes and more than ten half smoked cigarettes. He must have lit one, took a few drags, and lit another. He was anxious to get on with the job.

The eighth of May was a fine day. A middle aged farmer was out fishing on the reservoir. As he rowed his raft across the water, his oar struck something beneath the surface. He stuck the handle of his net in the water and stirred. A mop of black hair bobbed to the surface. Before he could gather his wits, it turned and a face broke the surface. Curiosity conquered fear. The farmer steered the body toward the shore with his pole, the end of which sank into the soft, white flesh again and again. Decomposition was already advanced.

Guo Puyun lay at the water's edge. Nobody bothered to lift him. The body was bloated twice its normal size. All the buttons of his clothing were undone and his singlet was pasted to his torso like a translucent dance costume. One shoe was missing. The other was embedded into the putrid flesh of the foot. Fish had been nibbling at the face. All the organs were torn. The body gave off a nauseating stench. Guo Puyun had shaken off his mortal coil. He was beyond thought, or pain, or even humanity. The dead fish in the farmer's basket, rounded, and glistening, were more inviting than he.

The farmer had been through the dead man's pockets and his knapsack before the security people from the Munitions Factory arrived. Finally he covered the hideously ravaged face with a sheet of plastic. Every new arrival on the scene lifted the covering for a quick glimpse, and leaped back in horror.

"What a stink!"

"Frightening!"

The same remarks were repeated over and over. They clustered together speculating on the motive, and expressing their own views on suicide. They did not bother to hide their contempt. The hideousness of death robbed them of compassion. Guo Puyun's fellow men were more interested in the drama than the voiceless actor at its core. How did he die, and why? Was it because of a woman? He could sink no further.

The security people found his knapsack filled with stones. The traces of rust on them suggested that they had come from the road bed of the railway tracks. Guo Puyun collected them on his way up Colt Mountain to weigh himself down. There were plenty of stones on the banks of the reservoir, yet he had gathered stones as he went. Was there some poetic significance to his action? Was he testing himself, deliberately adding to the difficulty of going up the mountain before he faced the final test? That action smacked of masochism, but it was completely in character.

Guo Puyun was back.

On the third of May the factory, the school and the family received his last letter. After the first shock, no one expected to find him alive. There was nothing to do but wait for developments. The discovery of his body in the reservoir was not a surprise. The tragedy had turned into a grotesque farce, and the ugly corpse became the object of jeers. He failed even in this dramatic gesture.

There were six letters. Perhaps there were others we know nothing about. In each he had used different ways of explaining himself, of trying to convince the recipient of the correctness, and inevitability of his choice, and asking their understanding. But his reasons failed to convince. Like most suicide letters, there was a surface calm; an almost perfect lie which no one but the writer would accept.

On going through his belongings, his sister came upon the Japanese novel which fascinated her at first. But as she ploughed through it, she came to realise that the poignant margin notes were really cleverly worded self justification of the dead man. She stopped reading then. Her brother, she concluded was really beyond the pale.

Guo Puyun's memorial service was held in an empty warehouse. Long ago the space had been used to store cannon barrels before shipping. Since the factory turned to civilian production, the warehouse stood empty.

There was only dust and air. There was no funeral

music.

Chapter 2

Guo Puyun was slim but not tall. Although he claimed to be one point seven-two metres high, I doubt if he actually was. He had a handsome face, with finely chiselled features. The eyes were wide, under gracefully curving brows. He was fair-skinned, and his teeth were even. At thirty-six, he was well past the first blush of youth. However, he seemed younger than men of the same age. He was reserved, and a bit feminine in his ways. His voice was pitched so low, that on first meeting him, one had the impression he was weak.

There is only one presentable building on the north suburban campus of the United University. Our special course took place on the second floor. Classes did not begin till the seventh of September, later than other universities. That day I had a class in Modern Chinese. I was a few minutes late. When I arrived the teacher was discussing *pinyin*. That got my back up right away. She was treating us like children.

There were six rows of desks with three aisles between. I tiptoed to the back of the room, and found an empty seat in the last row. There was dust everywhere. I was too embarrassed to wipe it off, so I sat on my satchel. I felt someone watching me. But when I turned he looked away. I noticed a pale face, and a high bridged nose. The ear lobes were thin and almost translucent. He was Guo Puyun. Ten ·minutes went by. Suddenly he tossed me a cloth across two rows of desks, and waved a slip of paper at me. I did not understand the gesture, but I smiled and he smiled back

I wiped the desk with the cloth before I realized it was a near new handkerchief with a pattern of blue squares on it. I went over to him during the recess and offered him a smoke. He refused at first, then changed his mind. He took out a copper plated lighter. The flame had not been properly adjusted, and flared two inches tall. I dodged. It was the same lighter that Guo Puyun later dropped on Colt Mountain. We introduced ourselves. He said he had seen me the day we reported and collected our text books, but I had no impression of him. He also said he was in charge of attendance and that he would not mask me for being late in the future.

"Where do you work?"

"The Writers' Union."

"Must be nice."

"I can't complain? What about you?"

"I'm from the country. Just another bumpkin."

The munitions factory where he worked had the innocuous name of the Hongdu Tool Making Co. Ltd. and he was chief of the publicity department. He told me he liked drawing and poetry. He seemed very open, yet his garrulousness was at odds with his reserve. His discomfiture a moment ago when his lighter nearly took off my eyebrows, indicated that he lacked self confidence.

The drop-out rate mounted within weeks of classes beginning. The classroom was never full. I took the seat next to Guo Puyun and when the lectures got monotonous, we chatted. Most of the students were in their thirties. Although some became quite familiar, I was not in the right frame of mind to strike up new friendships. Guo Puyun was the only person I could have a real conversation with. We were opposites. He got on with everybody. The women were especially fond of him. He was single. I could not tell whether he had never been married or if he had been married and divorced. He himself was vague about it, but he seemed content to be a bachelor. He avoided any mention of romance, yet he was friendly with the women, and gave the impression that he was not entirely averse to it. It was a contradiction I could not understand. Over a long period of time, I began to believe that he had remained single because he was choosey. There was no other explanation. His apparent disinterest was merely a means of deflecting unwanted attention.

I felt he was confident of his appearance and other attributes. He was not a sex fiend, who is usually ugly, and cunning. Nevertheless his flirting with the women struck some false notes.

He was sensitive. Once an old professor from Beijing University was invited to lecture on the poetic styling of Xin Qiji. At recess I sensed something was not quite right with Guo Puyun. His eyes were glued to the space in front of the blackboard. Only when a pretty girl a full time student, left the room did the tension go out of him. He turned away in confusion and muttered, "She's like Lin Daiyu, right out of the Dream of Red Mansions." When the pretty girl returned to her seat, he was flustered again. He could not keep his eyes off her. He sighed, lit a cigarette and smoked listlessly, unable to concentrate.

"The eyes are too far apart ... and a bit on the tall side. Wouldn't you say she's about one point six-eight metres?"

"Who?"

"That one just now."

"Which one?"

"The second from the window, with the red ribbon in her hair. She's talking to someone. She's turning around...."

"You think she's like Lin Daiyu?"

"A bit...."

"Too fat!"

"You're looking at the wrong one. The one on the left...."

"I know. Quite stylish."

"Stylish?"

He was captivated by the girl. The lecture flew over his head. He filled his note book with sketches of the girl's face: the nose, the tiny mouth, the eyes. She was pretty, and it would not be out of the ordinary for a young man to look at her. However, his absorbtion was unnatural. Surely it was not just that he wanted to sketch her? The way he drew her mouth again and again seemed as though he were sublimating the beauty of the opposite sex.

He had a knack for water colours. He was responsible for the wall posters of the class, and filled the empty spaces between the articles with drawings of flowers, animals and people. Our posters were the envy of the school. Other classes invited him to decorate theirs as well. He never refused. If one were late leaving school, one could almost count on catching a glimpse of him perched on a desk in an empty classroom, hard at work. He was usually surrounded by a coterie of young admirers. Once I saw the girl he called Lin Daiyu holding his paint box for him, her face all aglow. The two of them made a more striking tableau than Guo Puyun 's mediocre art could ever hope to achieve.

There is a narrow road that runs east and west past the campus. Students go in both directions. Guo Puyun lived in North Taipingzhong and would go westward. I went the opposite direction, except when I was on my way to my in-laws' then we travelled in the same direction. I had a monthly bus ticket. As the busstop was some distance away, he would give me a lift on his bicycle whenever I was going his way. He had an old Phoenix brand woman's bike with a low saddle and high handlebars. Riding it he looked as if he were lifting a weight. It became an established thing. His kindness and sense of responsibility was all embracing. Once we were half way to the bus-stop, when he suddenly cried out and fumbled in his pockets.

"Is something wrong?" I asked.

"No."

"Did you forget something?"

"… no."

"If you need to go back for something, I'll walk the rest of the way."

"It's alright."

He dropped me at the bus-stop. I saw him turn back and felt like a selfish fool.

"You didn't have to do that!" I cried out.

"It's alright. I just have to pay my monthly Party dues. I'm not like you. It's alright if I get home late. See you!"

He seemed more embarrassed than I. Watching that slender frame ride away, I felt a rush of gratitude, though it was not a big favour. It seemed a pity that such a kind-hearted person should be so alone. I was concerned. There are depths to a single man over thirty that no one can fathom.

But he was more concerned about me. He was a committee member of the temporary Party Branch of our course. After one of their meetings, he mentioned that the Party Branch intended to develop two lots of members, and asked if I were interested. I said I did not think I would be qualified. I lacked discipline and I was lazy. The competition might be too much for me. Besides I had no expectations. He shook his head and sighed, "You take yourself too seriously."

"It's not that. I'm not good enough to take it seriously, and if I don't it's a waste of time. Might as well just keep plodding along. I don't stand to gain anything by squeezing in.... Forget about me."

"Be serious. This is an opportunity."

"Give the chance to someone else. There are a few eager beavers in the class. Don't let them down."

"You really aren't interested?"

"Really."

"There are members that are no better than the average guy."

"You said it."

"But you do make snap judgements. If you change your mind, let me know. There's no problem between friends."

He never mentioned it again, and another candidate was selected. This fellow was in charge of teaching materials. He took his work seriously and was ambitious. If he continued the way he was, his expectations of joining the Party were bound to be deluged by envy. I wonder if Guo Puyun counselled him before he died. Somehow I think he did not. The fellow is plodding on in the same way to this day. The outcome is not optimistic.

I am more stubborn than Guo Puyun. There was an unmarried female doctor in my wife's work unit. She was pretty, fair skinned, modest and had been in the work force before she went to college. She came from an intellectual family;just the right sort for Guo Puyun. But everything had to be carefully thought through. With one slip up the whole thing would come down like a house of cards. Once we were discussing Lu Xun's works in our modern literature course. The lecturer had veered off essays and novels and concentrated on the great man's life, or more, precisely, on his love affairs which was much more interesting.

Guo Puyun muttered under his breath, "What's so wonderful about that...." He was bored. After a while, he tugged impatiently at my elbow and asked, "What do you think of "Death?"

"It's alright. What do you think?"

"It's a masterpiece."

"What about Ah Q?"

"Ah Q is another matter. Zijuan's tragedy is pure. Ah Q borders on farce."

"Zijuan is too soft."

"Really? But the sadness comes from the heart...."

"However Ah Q epitomises something...."

"Anyway after Lu Xun met Xu Guangping, he never wrote anything worthwhile."

"Knowing Xu Guangping changed his life. He was no longer pessimistic. Without her love Lu Xun would have been finished."

"I disagree!"

"That doesn't mean you're right."

"Love is un-necessary."

"Xiao Guo you are prejudiced."

"Be quiet...pay attention...."

His ears were burning. He smiled tightly. If we had been close friends we might have quarreled. But as we were not, there was nothing more to say. I felt he was childish and needed advice.

After callisthenic we strolled around the volley ball courts. The players were all in their twenties. The men were showing off and the women were vying for attention. I envied their youthful exuberance. He was unusually tense and preoccupied. When I spoke he jumped.

"Puyun, no one can do without love. It's like cooking without MSG...."

"I never use it. It causes cancer."

"That's why you're so thin."

"You're no more than a bundle of twigs yourself."

"Cut the nonsense. Tell me, do you have a girl friend?"

"What if I do, and what if I don't."

"If you do, then get on with it. If not I'll introduce you to someone that will suit you."

"Are you going into business?"

"That's right. How much are you worth?"

"Let's not talk about that. It's boring."

Guo Puyun ducked his head and smoked, only looking up to dodge the ball when it went wild. Just then one came flying our way. He took a stance, and hit the ball. It went wide, and the cigarette flew from his mouth. The young girls shrieked with laughter. Guo Puyun made a face, and his ears reddened. You couldn't help feeling sorry for him.

"You're stupid. You care about no one and nobody cares about you. Doesn't it bother you?"

"I'm just fine. And I'd be better off if people didn't bother me." "... I give up."

"We're friends and I don't want to hurt you. But don't mention it again. I really am not interested. You think my life is empty, and I need help. But I am really alright. All you can do for me is to read some of my poetry, and give me some pointers. I want to learn from you. Don't be mad. Forgive me if you can. Or bawl me out. I can stand it." He was very solemn. I was stopped cold. For the first time I was confronted by the peculiar mentality of a confirmed bachelor. My good intentions had been taken as an invasion of privacy. When I cooled off, I realized that perhaps I had been hasty. One has to know the other person's past. That was more intriguing than being a match-maker. We are all curious about other people's secrets. I am no exception, though not as dangerous as some others I know. I was not the only one trying to be a match-maker for him. He had refused all comers in the same way. It was the wrong move, for it only drew more attention to him. Inevitably it led to all sorts of conjectures and rumours. Guo Puyun was too naive and honest. Had he made up some romance, it would have saved him a lot of hurt. Instead he exposed himself to all the slings and arrows of gossip.

One Wednesday the instructor was ill and the class was dismissed. As I was leaving campus, a woman in my class caught up to me wanting to talk about the goings-on in literary circles. Who was divorced; who was suffering writer's block; who was unable to get permission to go abroad. She was a well of information. She rambled on, and it chilled me to realize that people got so much pleasure out of the misfortunes of writers. Big Sister was in her mid-thirties and she had a vicious tongue. As we approached the cross road, she suddenly turned conspiratorial.

"Do you know about Puyun?"

"What about him?"

"He's never been married."

"I know."

"But do you know why?"

"No."

"It seems ... he is defective...."

"Oh...."

"Physically defective."

"Is that so?"

"Didn't he ever mention it? I thought you two were close.... A good looking young fellow like that. What a pity. You must get him to see to it before he gets too old...."

Although she seemed sincere enough, I despised her conniving ways. I lost all respect for the woman. I thought what's it to you if he has a defect. Why don't you take the story home and amuse your old man with it. Then I wondered where she got the story from? Was she likely to go about prattling to anyone who would listen? It would amuse her, and possibly her listeners, but what of Guo Puyun?

"Big Sister, it's really none of our business. Whether it's true or not, lets keep it to ourselves. What do you say?"

"... That's just the way I feel...."

"Xiao Guo is choosey. Leave him alone. It's no

good worrying about him.''

"That's it...."

"My bus is coming ... you take care...."

I ran for the bus to be rid of her but Big Sister worried me. If she was a gossip monger then she deserved to be run over by a truck. That would silence her for good. What I couldn't understand is why someone had it in for Guo Puyun. I was more worried about him. He was too sensitive to stand up to gossip. To say that he had a physical defect meant, his thing didn't work. It was a terrible indictment, which amounted to saying he was not a man. Only an animal would spread such a story! And he was lurking in our classroom. The scurvy hound is probably well connected too. But he isn't human.

Guo Puyun you better find a wife soon!

I cooled down quickly. What if the story is true? The originator of the story might have been giving an objective account of an embarrassing situation. Neither derision nor pity could change that. If Guo Puyun could bear the reality of the situation, could he not fend off the idle talk? Still he was in an unenviable position.

Somehow he was untouched by it all. He did what was expected of him; was friendly, and did not suspect any unfriendliness toward him. He was like a child, totally unaware of the vicious whispers that followed him. I did not have the heart to tell him the truth, for I did not know how he would take it. So all I could do was to continue to play the match-maker, though I knew it was a waste of effort. He refused all my offers. Refused to meet them; wouldn't even talk about them. He was definitely not interested. I was at my wit's end. Perhaps he really had a defect.

In the mid-term exam both our theme papers were awarded top grades. He was overjoyed. All the other students crowded around us clamouring to read the papers. He smiled and handed it to me instead. I glanced through it quickly and handed it back with a few words of congratulation. Actually I thought my paper was better. The title of his essay was "Rainy Night." The style was lyric prose. His phrasing was stylish but too sentimental, and girlish. The essay was full of exclamatory passages: Oh, everlasting, gentle spring rain. He made mountains out of mole hills. At the age of thirty-six, it was not only a question of self expression, it seemed his emotions were still those of an adolescent. He had not matured. Perhaps love is still an ideal. If that was the case then Guo Puyun was in real trouble.

Later he showed me three of his poems all neatly copied on letter paper. Because I am not fond of poetry, I glanced through them and dismissed them with a few desultory remarks. They really did not grab my attention. Thousands of poets grind out the same stuff everyday. The poems quickly went out of my mind. Out of three I remember only the title of one: Oh, Colt Mountain. It never dawned on me that there might be a kernel of truth in that self-indulgent piece. All along I felt he lacked creativity.

Now I feel I owe him an apology.

Chapter 3

Not long after the fateful roll-call, I watched a new year's eve dance competition on television. A handsome young man was competing for the second place with a solo Tibetan dance. His boots flashed across the screen as though they had a life of their own. My heart skipped a beat. The dancer reminded my of Guo Puyun. My eyes were riveted to the TV screen. The dancer pirouetted to a halt as the music came to a rousing end. It took him a moment to catch his breath and execute a shy bow.

The program originated from Sichuan, and the choreographer's name, Hu Xiaofang caught my eye. I seemed to know that name....

The prize-giving followed. I breathed a sigh of relief when Hu Xiaofang appeared. She was a stocky middle aged woman, whose wide fleshy mouth was devoid of charm or beauty. The young dancer stood beside her like a dutiful son, hugging a television set that was his prize. The woman babbled incoherently into the microphone. She was not the person whom I had heard of, and whose photograph I had seen. But in the slender form of the young dancer I thought I caught a glimpse of a younger Guo Puyun. The traditional Tibetan tunic had been shortened. A pair of shiny boots were pulled over tights that revealed the contours of shapely buttocks with every movement. I wondered what inspired Hu Xiaofang to dress her dancer in this fashion. Perhaps Guo Puyun was costumed the same way once.

Guo Puyun's first love was neither painting nor poetry, but dance. His attachment to something so unmasculine was largely due to the influence of a primary school teacher because he was handsome, had expressive eyes, and long shapely legs. Most of all he was pliable. When he applied for entry to the Dance Class at the Palace of Youth, he was made to lie across the instructor's lap while she measured the distance from the nape of his neck to the tip of his tail bone. Then he was grasped by the heel and the knee and his feet forced up to touch his forehead. The pain was excruciating.

"He is a good-looking boy!"

He was aware of his beauty, and he knew that dancing enhanced it. He became fascinated with dance. By the time he was ten, he was accustomed to applause. He danced the roles of rabbits, foxes, chickens, Mongolian youth, and young farmers. Whatever he danced he stole the show. Once in a performance at the Palace of the Nationalities he danced the role of a Kazak girl. Wearing a wig, he appeared with the girls. His dancing was more stylish, his kicks higher, his hips and neck more supple than the girls.

He was the star of the troupe. He was popular with the girls but the boys envied and hated him. His aloofness on the one hand, and shyness on the other probably stemmed from that period. His natural weakness made him defenseless against his tormentors. He was easily reduced to tears, which immediately roused the sympathy of the girls with whom he had a bond of kinship. That only made the boys despise him more. Things went from bad to worse. At first his ties and handkerchiefs disappeared. Then his water mug vanished. Finally, one day on his way home from rehearsals, a group of boys beat him up, hooting derisively, "We're men! You're not. You're just a pretty face!"

He went home with a bloody nose. His parents hurried to the Palace of Youth. When they came back they told him he was not going back; that dancing would interfere with his school work. What they did not tell him was that his teacher had been very upset. She insisted that he was the most disciplined, and hard-working student she had. However, Guo Puyun thought she had abandoned him, and the girls had turned on him too. He wept bitterly over that. He withdrew into himself. He did not understand the problem, but he was determined to deal with it his way. From primary school and into secondary school he got on well with the boys. He never refused to help; never gossiped; was a great talker. The boys thought he was chivalrous, and friendliness dulled the edge of enmity. No one could call him a sissy. Although he was a top student, he had to be on his guard against becoming the teacher's pet, or attracting the attention of girls. It is hard to imagine what machination he used. In order to be one of the boys, he succumbed to the temptation of playing nasty pranks. Nevertheless he was gentle. When his so-called friends shot paper bullets at the girls, he rolled a few soft pellets, and laughed. However, he was probably ready to shield the victim with his own body. He was full of contradictions.

None of his schoolmates remember much about him except that he was honest and studied hard. Only one girl who became a fashion designer mentioned something more definite.

"He was handsome, and he had a nice body." The remark embarrassed her, but it summarized the way the girls saw him. The only other person I spoke to was a driver for a freight forwarding company. He was a coarse fellow who claimed to have been Guo Puyun's best friend in primary school, although he could not remember what Guo looked like.

"He could do splits forwards and sideways and leap to his feet from that position with the greatest of ease," he said. "I tried to learn. The first time I tried I thought I'd die!. It felt as though my thing was torn off...." The training Guo Puyun got at the Palace of Youth did him some good. He was small and lithe, and the only skill he had that would earn him the respect of his peers was doing the splits. The applause he got demonstrating his technique in the corridors, quieted the dreaded cry, "You're not a man!" His showing off was also proof of his love for the dance. Dance gave him his first taste of success, his first experience of joy and pain which he was not likely to forget. His parents could not cut off all connections with the art.

In his second summer at junior high, the National Ballet of Albania performed in Beijing. Guo Puyun left summer camp without permission, and got a returned ticket at the Tianqiao Theatre. He had put up his bus fare for the ticket as well, and had to walk home. On the way he practised the steps he had seen on stage, reeling about like a drunkard. The camp counsellor was waiting when he got home. His father slapped him hard as he came through the door. The father was usually a gentle man. The blow was a shock to them both. Years later Guo Puyun would speak of this incident whenever he spoke of his father or his family. He smiled ruefully and pointed to his cheek. "I caught it right here.... It stunned me...." It hinted that the difficulties between them went back a long way. The next year he persuaded his mother to let him apply for early admission to the Army Academy of Art. His reference was his teacher at the Palace of Youth. While other students were still preparing for entrance exams, he already had the red acceptance notice. However, shortly afterwards, another notice came announcing that admissions were temporarily suspended and all notices were cancelled. Soon afterwards turmoil broke out. Guo Puyun joined the Art Troupe for the Propagation of the Thought of Mao Zedong, and quickly became indispensable.

The troupe had various affiliations. Finally it came under the wing of a certain army unit. It was a large troupe made up of cadres, children of intellectuals, and red guards from a number of key middle schools. The second year of the Cultural Revolution, the troupe took over the rehearsal space of the Army Art Academy. Most people thought nothing of it, but to Guo Puyun it was miraculous. He felt that in this time of flux, he was captain of his own ship. He read with interest the big letter poster criticising the director of dance for sexually assaulting a young girl. He did not believe the staid officer who had been his examiner, would do such a thing. He was almost eighteen. No matter what was being spread around him, there were some things he did not believe could happen. He trusted his instincts and relied on his own judgment, not so much to persuade others to his way of thinking but as a guide for himself. Where his thoughts led no one knows. This behavior continued to the last day and the last hour of his life. The short period that he spent with the troupe was probably the beginning of his tragedy.

The radicals of the troupe supplied them with costumes and instruments, and sent them instructors of music and dance called "Military Representatives." The dance instructor was a vivacious young woman of twenty-four who was pretty and lithe, and the red guards swarmed around her like flies round a honey pot. She had graduated from the Army Art Academy and had taught for two years. Her technique was exceptional, and even her barbed criticism showed a wry wit.

"What's in your stomach? Did you swallow a bear?"

"Look at that drag queen! Let's see you swing those hips again.... I mean you ... and stop grinning...."

She probably noticed Guo Puyun from the start, but she did not show it, except that she was less critical of him. When she was dis-satisfied, she drew him aside and chided him softly. "You've got good from, but you're too tense. Try it again. Relax. Breathe...." and she would pat him on the back. As time went by it is possible that Guo Puyun sensed that the contact with her body was not entirely accidental or the demands of art. His ears were constantly red and hot. He put everything he had into the dance. I wonder what he saw in those black and lustrous orbs when their eyes met? It could not have been maternal tenderness. He discovered she was from Sichuan. Her home was in Wanxian County, only half a day's journey from where he came from. Being from the same province, they began calling each other brother and sister. They were rehearsing a Tibetan piece for male and female dancers. She showed him how to hold her by the waist. Their bodies were pressed together as they danced. Her mature body was a temptation and a threat. His ears blazed through the dance. His thoughts could not have been tranquil. Whether he felt any guilt is unimportant. The fact is she tempted him. It was the first time that he had experienced the signals of the opposite sex, quite different from the tenderness of young girls. A handsome youth calling a woman six years older, "sister" in private, and receiving pieces of chocolate wrapped in a handkerchief ought to be aware of some hidden meanings. Any brother-sister relationship that is not of the blood has emotional signals which only adults pick up on.

The troupe's rehearsal place was an old factory-like structure. There was a deep auditorium. The stage was comparatively low. The seats were movable. When not in use they were folded and stacked against the wall under the window to make room for rehearsing. The troupe slept on the floor. The men slept in the auditorium and the women occupied the stage. Before lights out, the curtain was drawn against inquisitive eyes. The toilets were in a corridor back stage, next to the dressing rooms and property room. The women's toilet was quite convenient but the men's was something else. It was not accessible from the stage during the night, so one had to go out the building, skirt around the boiler room and approach it from the back door. Those who were scared of the dark usually found a convenient tree in the yard, but not for a conscientious person like Guo Puyun. A communal flashlight hung from the door knob of the rehearsal hall for just that reason. It only threw a faint beam, that stirred lurid shadows in the long corridor. Late one night the female "Military Representative" was heard talking to someone in the corridor. The voice was pitched low but animated. She could have been talking to Guo Puyun.

There were many cold nights that winter. Everyone went to bed early. However, one snowy night the entire troupe had gone into town to celebrate the announcement of a new directive. A frail young girl, a dancer, went back early, and unwittingly stumbled on a scene in the dark corridor. The reflected light of the snow outside the tall windows beside the property room lit the corridor. She saw everything quite clearly. The dance instructor's great coat was opened. Her arms and the flaps of her coat were tightly wound around someone. The girl heard the sound of harsh breathing, and bolted. At the same time a figure detached himself from the woman's arms and raced down the corridor. She heard a clatter of footsteps cross the oak floor of the stage toward the auditorium.

The Woman Military Representative found the witness, and discovered that she left the others because she had started to menstruate. She took the young red guard to her bed, found a sanitary napkin, calmly and gently looked after the girl. The young girl did not mention what she saw that night till after the troupe had disbanded. She was never quite clear about what she saw. Finally she muttered something about kissing, which was probably the most delicate way she could describe it.

Years later a friend of the witness claims there was more to the story than kissing. Between a twenty-four years old woman and an eighteen year old youth things are not that simple. Particularly in times of turmoil. There was often a doomsday mentality of licentiousness under the puritanic veneer. It was a gesture of individual rebellion,and the wantonness was a despairing expression of personal freedom.

I do not agree that it was a shameful incident or that it contained any vestiges of freedom. It was a predicament, beautiful and intoxicating for those involved. It reflected the fullness and the limitations of human emotions,and demonstrated the seductive power of primeval feelings. Guo Puyun had wandered off the straight and narrow. More correctly he had stumbled upon bliss he had never known before. Guo Puyun would relive that incident when he was eighteen over and over. It was the joy he relived. The pain was in recalling the way he used to be.

Guo Puyun only mentioned a few isolated incidents from those days. The gift of chocolate; being nursed when he was ill; the intimacy of the dance; the long talks along the the quiet paths of the gardens.... He made it sound ordinary, trying to convince me that it was no more than sisterly concern. But there was a dreamy look in his eye, when he talked about the tenderness that time cut short.

"She was so good to me...." he sighed.

"Tell the truth, you rascal. Did she seduce you?"

He smiled without answering, as if he wanted to test my imagination. My curiosity amused him. Phrases such as she was so good to me sounded like the bragging of a thirty-six year old bachelor, trying to make a case of his relations with women. Yet it doesn't ring true. At the time I thought what he got was pitifully little.

One conversation took place a few months before he died. I bought six bottles of beer and a kilo of beef and went to the place he lived. I was hoping to get him drunk enough to loosen his tongue. As it turned out I was tipsy before him, and rambled on about an unhappy first love. Fact and pain were both magnified in the telling. Although I was embarrassingly drunk, the thought persisted that my story might cause him to open up. We talked and drank. Finally he was moved to show me a photograph. It was a group photo of the troupe. He pointed out a woman in military garb. Guo Puyun was also in uniform, looking like a doll. The woman was beautiful but one could not help noticing the difference in their ages. He claimed she was like a sister to him. She was discharged in '69 and repatriated to Sichuan. They had not been in touch for years. She was a beautiful woman of mystery. I was expecting some revelations, but his sighs told me more.

"She was so good to me!"

Yes, I still believe what he got was limited, no matter what he did aside from kissing. In the arms of a twenty-four year old woman all he could feel was fear. He had been robbed of his first kiss by a woman stronger than he. All that was left were the emotional scars that would haunt him the rest of his life.

The old rehearsal hall has been turned into a restaurant, an old and shabby one at that. The damp, sticky walls make the stomach churn. But traces of its former self remain. The deep auditorium, and dark corridor, the toilets are still where they were. The trysting place reeks with the sour smell of flour and left-overs. Not a shred of romance remains.

Hu Xiaofang on the television was someone else.

The woman in Sichuan was probably doing the same thing: teaching young men and women how to use their bodies gracefully. Does she know the life experiences of the boy she once kissed? If she had married, her son would be the same age as he was then. Would that son know how his mother once comforted or injured a younger "brother"? I hope she is not a wanton, or Guo Puyun's fate would have been pitiful indeed.

In the stillness of a snowy night, the corridor was lit by reflected light. Two people leaned against the wall, their heads close together. Moist lips pressed together struck sparks that lit up granite hearts, and rocked the foundations of their beings and sent the whole edifice tumbling down.

A suicide is often absorbed in fantasy. That is the judgement of renowned writers on law and psychology. Perhaps, in the winds on top of Colt Mountain, Guo Puyun had come face to face with that fascinating realisation.

Chapter 4

After a number of rejections, I gave up playing the matchmaker. Guo Puyun seemed content being alone. Perhaps there are advantages to the single life that an outsider cannot appreciate, and has no right to interfere with. Things were pretty much the same between us. I would drop in on him from time to time for a few drinks, and food he carefully prepared. Our conversation centred around the arts, poetry, economics, and society. We avoided discussing women. Our discussions were always an overview. Neither of us had the knowledge to give it any depths. Consequently we soon ran out of ideas, and the conversation would veer onto another topic. He was more voluble, and often talked himself into a corner. But he would doggedly press on, becoming completely incoherent. He liked movies, and managed to find redeeming qualities in the most pedestrian films. Maybe films stimulated his imagination. He could accept and transform what he saw on the screen to match the longings of his heart. It was the same thing that he sought in painting and poetry. In the end he might have discovered that art could not supply what he lacked in life. For all I know he might have known it all along. Then why did he cling to art?

In December he told me he was about to write an epic poem. We were in his messy little room. He sat on the bed, leaning against a roll of bedding rubbing a shoe nervously on the sheet. He was grave. I did not have the heart to tell him how I truly felt. Nobody needs an epic poem. Men who could write them have been long dead. These days people would sooner listen to nonsense.

"... You've got it all worked out?"

"Just about...."

"When will you start?"

"... I'm not sure. Every time I shut my eyes, I see the poem all laid out in neat lines.... The rhythms are just right.... But when I try to read the words, it vanishes.... If I don't get it down on paper soon, my head will burst...."

"Then what are you waiting for?"

"I don't know.... I guess I'm afraid of not being able to finish it. No use starting something you can't complete. What do you say?''

"Then don't do it."

He stared at me. He rubbed his head with his left hand, looking utterly lost. I couldn't bear that look of despair.

"If you want to write start right now. If you finish it fine. If not, don't take it too seriously. Writers of epic poems are extinct anyway. If you don't make it, it's not your fault. On the other hand if you do, it will be a real achievement. You have to think of it that way...."

"You don't understand."

"Cut it out. I understand. The poem is about yourself. Only you're not cut out for an epic poem. You're too shallow...."

"Leave it! Brother, you don't understand."

There was a new fountain pen clipped to his pocket, a prize he won in an essay competition to celebrate the December 9th Movement. He had won first prize. I did not compete. First of all I was not in the mood to write trivia. Then I did not want the embarrassment of losing. He flushed beet red when he accepted his prize. It was apparent that he had taken the competition very seriously, and winning was important. That small encouragement might have inspired him to try the epic poem. Also, we had been discussing the works of Lord Byron in our World Literature course. The long narrative poems of Byron might have fired his imagination. I thought I understood him, but all I had to go on were bits of disjointed trivia. I had no idea of the inspiration for his epic poem, yet I dismissed it out of hand. That was unforgivable. I dismissed his struggle to find relief from inner turmoil as self delusion. That

was far from the truth. It was only through his coura-
geous choice that I realized how wrong I was. I shall always respect those who are devoted to poetry, but des-
tined to fail, for they bear more than their fair share of
mankind's suffering. Like Guo Puyun they could have
lived happier lives.

But my responsibility or anyone else's for that matter, is limited. The obstacle to Guo Puyun's creativity
was his own confusion. Even if a poet's life is not sta-
ble, it must have some semblance of order. He must
know what he's doing, and have a fixed purpose.
Guo Puyun lacked those things. There were physical
signs of his mental confusion all around him. His
messy little room was a nest of suffering. A place
where a person without hope lived.

Whether it was poetry or love,the room showed he
could achieve nothing; complete nothing. He did not
lure women interested in him to his bed, to seize what
they both craved. He lacked the courage or the moral
values for it. All he could do was bury himself in his
confusion, and torment himself with shards of memory,
wrapped in the stale smelling bedding. The results of
putting together those bits and pieces only led to the
path of self destruction. He could not bring order to
that room. He could not make it more comfortable or
clean. Instead the room possessed him, and its squalor
combined with everything else finally drove him over
the brink.

I don't think anyone would want to live in that
room. The windows were thick with grime from
cooking on a kerosene stove. The furniture was never
dusted, and greasy to the touch. One door was missing from the old fashioned wardrobe. Inside was a

jumble of socks, gloves, old papers and a few changes of clothes. The door dangled on a broken hinge, like a bird trailing an injured wing. The dresser was heaped with rubbish. A cloth toy, some aluminum hooks, a small alarm clock, brushes, envelopes, magazines with missing covers, needles, medicine bottles. There was always something new to discover in that mess. The table was littered with empty beer bottles and cigarette packets, surrounded by peanut shells. The dreges at the bottom of beer bottles had gone mouldy. The litter of cigarette butts were like white maggots. The bedding was never folded. The blue squares on the counterpane were grey. The pillow case smelled of old socks. There were wine glasses and chopsticks in one drawer; waste paper covered with scraps of poetry and sketches in the other. There were books everywhere. New ones, old ones, torn ones, on the window sill, beside the pillow, on the floor, on top of the cooking pot, even under the bedclothes. There was no order. The room was a sinister ruin. Only a man beyond help could live there. And he was beyond help. Only he could pull himself out of that morass.

The room was the ground floor dormitory of a medical supplies factory in a tall narrow building. Although it faced the sun, a low nondescript structure in front cut off the light. His mother had been the factory doctor until she retired. Leaving him to live there alone was her idea. The place was a long way from Beiwanzhang, so he only went home on festivals and holidays. The mother seemed unaware of the squalor he lived in. Or if she knew, she didn't care. I hinted as much to him several times. He became very agitated, and defended her. But the more he protested the less believable it sounded. Besides it is not uncommon for mature bachelors to be at loggerheads with their families. They usually resent sympathy or help. She seemed a kindly old lady, but she was probably tired of Guo Puyun's stubborness and left him to his own devices. Her so-called kindness was probably self-delusion.

Guo Puyun's lair was unfit to live in. It was even less suited for writing or for entertaining. Some of the men in the class who had been there for drinks, mentioned that he was a fine cook, and that he led a carefree life. Some of them actually envied his bachelorhood.

Guo Puyun was not a heavy drinker. He only drank beer. Empty beer bottles littered the table and the bed, which was evidence that he drank everyday. However, even when there were guests he did not drink much. He nursed a glass of beer for ages. There was a subtle change in him at the least drop of liquor. He did not turn red or pale. Instead his eyes changed colour. The whites turned a soft porcelain blue. Gradually their corners became congested, but the eyes did not become bloodshot. A small dark spot under his left eye, close to the nose turned blue like a bruise. At first I thought it was due to lack of sleep. But then I noticed how he always shielded the eye with one hand, and that led me to think there was something wrong.

"There's always something wrong with me...."

He quaffed a mouthful of beer, and reached for a handful of peanuts. There was a slight tremor in his hand. His melancholy look was at variance with the philosophical mood he was trying to maintain. I was used to his moods, and the tension brought on by drinking. I knew he would not discuss what was on his mind. He was turning it over, carefully masticating it like some delicious dish which he was not about to share. It was useless asking. He would only give some superficial reply. There was no point wasting good beer.

"I'm unlucky...."

"Who isn't?"

"I'm different. Too many things have happened to me...."

"Everybody has ups and downs. But they go. Anyway you're the Chief of the Publicity Department. If that's not a break then I don't know what is...."

"You don't understand. Let's forget it...."

"Then what's wrong?"

"It's not worth talking about...."

"Keep it to yourself. Have a drink...."

I really couldn't be bothered asking. In any case nothing would come of it. The more you asked the more secretive he became. It did no good. On the other hand, if he felt you had lost interest, he might let fall a few tidbits.

"Brother you write. I need your help."

"Who's helping me?"

"Did you take the university entrance exam?"

The question took me by surprise. He was as pale as chalk. The expression was so tense that his face might crack.

"I did. I got forty for language, four marks for maths, and over ninety for politics. It was quite a show."

"They were subjects that don't suit us."

"Did you take it too?"

"My final marks were off by a few points."

"How much?"

His hand trembled as he picked up a few more peanuts. An invisible fist seemed poised in the air to strike him down. He muttered, "by six points."

"That's a shame."

"It was my fault. I wasn't properly prepared."

"I was prepared but I missed by twenty points. It's a trick of fate. When we should have gone to school, they wouldn't have us. Now they drag us into the classroom. It's sickening...."

"... six points."

"And that's what you call bad luck?"

"Think what you like. Forget it.... There's a bit of beer left ... and polish off the food...."

He leaned against the roll of bedding, his eyes fixed on something only he could see on the ceiling. There was nothing but dust and cobwebs. But to him it was a screen on which some pathetic story was unfolding, and he was a part of it.

The few missing marks were a middle school student's tragedy. After all these years, other worries should have softened the blow, and a man of thirty-six should have put it far behind him. Why think of it now. It was clearly a ploy to throw me off. I sensed the misfortune he was hinting at was something else. An unhappy first love; the loss of a childhood sweetheart; the end of a love affair he could not forget. Whatever it was it had no permanence. Lovers are the same throughout the ages, and making the loss of love a unique experience is foolish. No matter how much Guo Puyun pitied himself, I could not feel the same. He was tying himself in knots. To be honest I felt he deserved to suffer.

" ... too unlucky...."

It was making a mountain out of a mole hill. Maybe I had had too much to drink. In that mood everything is possible. I felt I could seize everything I deserved and everything I didn't. That is being lucky. Otherwise it is not. Luck is relative. Misfortune is absolute. It is unmanly to moan and groan over that simple truth. People who do are laughable. In that light Guo Puyun's melancholy is nothing more than greediness. He was handsome; he came from a good family; he had a good job, was getting an education; he could write poetry, and draw. What did he have to whine about? As for his lack of a wife, that was his own doing. He was sighing because he did not have enough of the things that came gift wrapped.

When I sobered, I thought I had been too harsh. Still I could not find a more honest way to understand him. Other classmates probably had the same experience. No matter how close two friends are,there are still instances when they do not see eye to eye. The relationship between people has its limitations. A frowning man might have a full bladder, or his hemorrhoids are itching. But all I see is the frown. Pain is exalted only to the sufferer. A peasant sleeping on the pavement will go un-noticed by his fellow man. The distance between human beings is like the head attached to the neck, and the feet attached to the legs. It's that simple. Guo Puyun was the living proof of that. Nobody could have stopped him from doing what he did; neither parents, nor friends. He did what he had to do, without any thought for others.

"Forget it ... it doesn't matter...."

He must have really despised me then. He had invited me for drinks, and cooked for me. but in his heart he kept me at a distance. He would not let me get close. In fact I could not help him. Not just me, but nobody could have made the least difference. There is no help for a shattered soul. He skipped classes the last two weeks before the first semester finals. Somebody else was taking attendance. He did not mention anything to me or anyone else beforehand. Only the Class Teacher and the monitor knew what had happened but they were reluctant to tell. It was plain that he did not want his classmates to know. A week before the exams, he reappeared wearing the same beige coloured down jacket, and carrying the same bulky satchel. He was as friendly as ever, borrowing the notes of the more studious girls, and flirting. On the surface nothing was changed. Before I could ask, he volunteered that he had been trying to get treatment for an eye problem. But why the mystery. I sensed there was more to it than he cared to reveal.

"Is there a problem with your vision?"

"It's been hemorrhaging."

"... It's not noticeable."

"I have to take sick leave every year. It aches. And when it does my head aches. I read a while then the pain gets unbearable. I'm afraid it's incurable...."

"Surely it's not that bad."

"I've been thinking that if I can't be cured, I'll drop out. I'm serious."

"What does the doctor say?"

"They don't know. They seem to think I'm lucky if I don't go blind. Maybe I could get an easy job somewhere.... What do you think of the reference room?"

"That's a woman's job. You'd be bored."

"I just want to hide somewhere, where I don't have to deal with people. Somewhere I can read a bit. I'm pushing forty. That sort of job would suit me."

"What happened to your eye."

"I told you I'm unlucky. Anyway, it's not worth talking about. By the way have you got your literature handouts? I'm missing page 3."

He rummaged through his satchel, carefully keeping his face turned away. The bluish spot was not particularly noticeable. In fact no one would notice it if their attention was not drawn to it. Now it seemed that everyone was looking at it, and it embarrassed him. It was something he tried to avoid but could not. Any other part of the human anatomy could be covered by clothing. But the face is exposed to public scrutiny. It was winter and nearly everyone wore a surgical mask. As soon as class was over Guo Puyun donned his. In his case it seemed to have more significance.

He was close mouthed, but the secret got out anyway.

He sat for the university entrance exam in '78. At that time he was a shift supervisor of the maintenance crew in the munitions factory. He had reached the turning point in his life, and his talents were not yet apparent. During the period preceding the exams he was not himself. He was impatient. It was obvious that he was weary of the life he led, and had great expectations for himself. He needed time to study, but he did not want to ask for sick leave so he asked for time off. For that he was criticised by the leaders. He took time off even after the exams. The time he took off before the exam was excusable, but afterwards was unreasonable. He went into the city every other day. It was not that he had any connections, nor was he the type to rush to the admissions. offices of universities to throw himself on some stranger's mercy. He was not capable of that. He was too weak. It was most probably a need to escape the pressures of the work place, and trying desperately to relax while waiting for the results. He rode around aimlessly on his bicycle as though he were trying to escape some dire punishment.

At dusk one day in August, he had gone to a few bookstores and was riding along Xizhimenwai Ave. As he approached the south end of Gaoliangqiao Road a truck was turning east. The truck was not going very fast, but Guo Puyun was riding even slower. His mind was elsewhere. Suddenly he looked up, and the huge green vehicle was bearing down on him. The driver slammed on the brakes. Guo Puyun swerved to one side but it was too late. A piece of wood protruding from the truck caught him in the face. Guo Puyun fell off his bicycle. The pain as his knees hit the pavement was worse than the numbness in his face. The driver of the truck asked if he were hurt and needed to go to the hospital. He refused, saying he was fine. A crowd gathered. He told the driver it was not his fault, and so the person that was at least partly to blame went off scot free. It is possible that Guo Puyun was deep in thought before the accident, and in the confusion, panicked, and thought he was solely to blame. He had a knack for blaming himself, a habit that was the result of his innate kindness. But in this case there was at least a grey area which anyone else would have seized upon to at least get some compensation for his loss. He let that opportunity slip by, and in the process suffered all the consequences that followed. Perhaps his constant harping of ill luck had something to do with the realisation of his mistake.

Three days later his mother noticed the swelling around his left eye, and the bruise. He looked in the mirror and was horrified. When his parents found out about the accident they were furious. But what the doctor had to say was even more alarming. The eye was hemorrhaging. If it was not properly treated he could go blind. Even if the driver had been made to take the responsibility, pay for treatment and living expenses, and make up the loss of wages and bonuses, or even go to gaol, it would not compensate him according to his mother. The psychological effect of this event was more serious. When he discovered that he failed the exam by only six marks, the news was more than he could bear. Guo Puyun was at a low ebb. Later when he searched for the roots of all his troubles, he would link these two events which had nothing to do with each other. His habit of blaming himself deepened. In the end it led to utter despair. Death was the only escape from the implacable web of fate.

Right now that fortunate driver is probably speeding along a highway somewhere. The small mishap might have made him more careful. Guo Puyun did not remember his license number, or for that matter, the type of truck it was. Nevertheless it did injure him. I wish the driver well. Although he is not without blame, Guo Puyun took too much upon himself, and he alone was responsible for the tragic aftermath.

Guo Puyun often mentioned the injury to his left eye

before he died. It was no secret to the people around him. He exaggerated its tragic nature. Privately many of the classmates laughed at him. His continuous harping about it seemed foolish, and trivial, even comical. I felt at the time that the exaggeration was symbolical. Actually there was something else on his mind that was too painful to express except in symbols.

It never occurred to me that it was death. If everything he said could be gathered together it would be a most specialised dictionary in which every word would be a declaration of war; a suicide's testament.

Chapter 5

After winter vacation our classroom hours were reduced to four periods in the morning. That meant we could go home for lunch. However, it also deprived me of a lift on Guo Puyun's bicycle. Lately he had taken to eating in the school cafeteria. Though the food was bad, he seemed to like it. I'm not a good observer of human behavior, and it took Big Sister's sharp tongue to put things in their right perspective. The woman was well preserved. Her fat cheeks were rosy. Her rather bulbous nose constantly rooting in other people's business. She swept all before her with the stink and hotness of garlic breath.

"Aren't you eating at school?"

"It's too expensive for what you get...."

"Guo Puyun eats at school."

"He can't be bothered cooking."

"I don't think so. Last semester he always had beef noodles at Taiji Restaurant. But he hasn't been there at all this semester. Since there aren't any classes in the afternoon, who doesn't want to get home early? Don't tell me institutional food is the only attraction!''

"What do you think it is?''

"If you leave a bit late after class, you'll catch a bit of drama at the back of the classroom. Mark my words. Nobody pulls the wool over Big Sister's eyes!''

She piqued my curiosity. One day I did not leave campus after class. Instead I went to the reading room and thumbed through some newspapers. When I thought enough time had elapsed I sauntered back to the classroom. Students carrying bowls of food passed me in the hall and on the stairs. I felt like a peeping Tom, creeping stealthily upon my victim. The closer I got the crueler my action became. I did not consider the distress my deliberate intrusion might cause. I did not make the slightest attempt to hide my purpose. My unflinching gaze swept to the back of the room at once. They sat close to each other. She was putting a slice of pork into his bowl, whispering. He saw me and moved aside. There was the look of a cornered animal in his eyes, and his small, well-formed ears coloured. She looked up calmly as though nothing had happened. She was pretty and intelligent, an experienced predator as slippery as an eel. All the talk of confirmed bachelorhood had gone up the flue. Guo Puyun had finally met his Waterloo. His embarrassment was that of a monk caught with his pants down, awful to behold. Human nature had asserted itself. He was no different from the rest of us.

I walked toward them nonchalantly, armed with a ready made excuse: I had been excused for half a day, and needed to borrow some notes on Chinese literature. Since his were incomplete, I took a few pages from her loose-leaf binder.

Before leaving, I asked him for a cigarette. He wanted a smoke too. As he pulled out his lighter, she stopped him.

"Wait till you've eaten."

He laid the unlit cigarette on the desk.

"Don't leave. Join us."

He clutched at me weakly, pleading in his eyes. I backed away. When I reached the other end of the room, I heard her loudly admonishing him, "You need more meat, to put on some weight." It seemed that she was speaking for my benefit. She was a woman to be reckoned with, and Guo Puyun had no defences. I wondered what was behind those solicitous words. Was she a trifle anxious? If she was confident of herself, would she try so hard to control him?

The classroom was empty except for a few young people from another class, clustered around the wall poster. They paid scant attention to the couple at the back of the room. Even if they did, they would make nothing of it. They looked like two cadres with things to discuss. The two bowls placed side by side meant nothing more than that they got on well. This was not the first love of adolescence that seeks out dark corners. No matter what Guo Puyun thought, it was clear she wanted everything to be in the open. Although the classroom emptied as soon as the lecture ended, there was always the possibility that some one would return, and anything out of the ordinary would cause tongues to wag. Big Sister had already done that. I had done the same thing. As far as curiosity goes I was no better. However, I can hold my tongue. I should have been happy for Guo Puyun, but I was troubled instead. This couple would face nothing but derision outside the classroom.

I felt she was not right for him. I can't honestly say what an average appearance is. But that is the only way I can describe her. You would not pick her out of a crowd. She had a nice figure, tall and slender, about the same height as Guo Puyun. Her features were regular. She was pretty; not coquettish, but serene, and faintly melancholy. The first bloom of youth had passed. She was about thirty; a bit younger than Guo Puyun. She was friendly in class, earnest and quiet. No one took much notice of her. She graduated from normal college, and taught high school maths, geography and literature in the western suburbs. She was not a good writer, and her profession did not make a difference. Out of eight essay assignments she did not produce anything worthwhile. She was grave, and the pallor of her brow and hair that was turning brown betrayed a caustic nature. She was the kind of teacher that students feared, and cursed behind her back. Such a woman is not fit to be the wife for a man such as Guo Puyun. She would be the one who wore the pants.

Zhao Kun is not a particularly feminine sounding name. I have no reason to suspect the sincerity of her love, but shortly after Guo Puyun's death she went travelling to some scenic spot in the south with a group of young men and women. Though the flames of love were smothered by death, surely sincerity would conquer forgetfulness. However, facts prove the inconstancy of emotions. They change as life changes. Change is just, intrepid, and unconquerable. My pain over Guo Puyun's death is due to my inability to discover the reasons that brought it about. More than his pathetic death, I am concerned with the whole process of reason and logic. I am dissecting his life to get at the truth. I could not do otherwise. I wonder what effect that ill-fated roll-call had on Zhao Kun. Perhaps it roused a faint surge of hatred. Tender-hearted Guo Puyun had made a mockery of her love and her desirability with his death. His corpse was a blow to her pride she would not quickly forget. That is understandable. Her going off to travel; to pose for photographs at well-known land marks; to find solace in a new love is understandable too. Death has pitifully little to offer no matter what significance one places on it. One derisive phrase summarises it all: "natural elimination." What must be lost is lost. What remains is waiting to be lost. The goodness is eternal. In the end none of us can shake ourselves loose from the murky whole. Guo Puyun drowned, and I sit at my desk, night after night pondering it, while others in other places do what they have to do. To live is proper, reasonable, and beautiful. To make it more perfect we have to do the task before us, to reveal secrets, to dredge up the withered life of the dead. As a survivor I have no right to refuse that heaven appointed mission. That is the greatest irony of all.

In March Guo Puyun had his last sexual encounter. There is nothing to indicate it was the only time, but one can be sure that it was not more meaningful than the others. It was a physical and emotional failure. It could not be otherwise. It could not have happened in the park or any other open space. The only safe place was his shabby room. Even that was not entirely safe. Classmates were in the habit of dropping in for a few drinks, talk poetry and settle the affairs of the world. It had to be at night. The room would be pitch dark. It was a night filled with odd smells and awkward movement. He did not have the courage to leave the light on. He was physically unable to initiate anything. His limbs probably knocked against empty beer bottles, an ash tray, books and clothes. All that would dampen his ardour. He was more engrossed with the reactions of his body, than the attraction of hers. The initial failure would swiftly lead to despair. He trembled with shame and self-loathing. There was a kiss of death in the terrible fatigue that followed. Despair became immutable. The scale of life tipped against him. The downward slide had begun. He was finished. His appointment with Colt Mountain was still sixty or seventy days away but the ending was clear. The fire of hell was already raging.

Zhao Kun's reaction to that encounter had remained a mystery. If her need was not great, Guo Puyun's failure would not have wounded, shamed or disappointed her. If she was experienced, she might have helped him overcome the shock of disappointment with tenderness and practised techniques. Surely she would not have scorned a man who had done his best and failed. I do not think she was so selfish as to consider only herself for she clearly loved him. Though their bodies failed the emotional bond would have remained. In the silence of the room, so dark that you could not see the fingers of your hand, the squalor and the filth enveloped them. Harsh breathing, and failure congealed in pungent bodily fluids that glued

Guo Puyun's naked body against the rough sheets. To preserve the last shreds of dignity, I believe Guo Puyun quickly pulled on his clothes. He downed the last dregs of beer, lit one cigarette butt with the other, and waited unblinking for the dawn. There was nothing else he could do, or, indeed, wanted to do. Damn it! He cursed poetry, art, women, thought, morality, mankind, history. He cursed everything and decided to kill himself.

His decision had nothing to do with what happened toward the end of March. But that incident illustrated the circumstances of his life, and proved that the fragility of his will to live was not entirely linked to his personality.

Zhao Kun lived in the suburbs and often stayed over at the homes of relatives and friends in the city. A week after Guo Puyun's failure, Big Sister invited her to stay over and she accepted. Big Sister's husband had gone to the north-east on business. The two women shared the double bed and chatted like a pair of school girls late into the night. Women discuss men as men discuss women. I was shocked by what I heard later on. Zhao Kun related Guo Puyun's sexual difficulties as though she were telling a dirty story. That she made no attempt to protect his reputation would seem to indicate the falseness of her love. Her audience was an over-blown middle aged woman, who never let a juicy morsel go. Gossip is often exaggerated. But I believe it must have come from her. It was too inhuman, too raw to have come from anywhere else. It left me speechless.

"Guo Puyun's thing doesn't work!"

His thing doesn't work.

The words are common enough. If one were to keep to scholarly expressions, then "thing" would be "bamboo shoot" or "lingam" and so on. But that lacked wit. My respected classmate who told me the story avoided the word "impotent" as if his ancestors had given them too many inadequate artistic terms. Nor could he bring himself to saying "he can't get an erection" because it smacks of Western medical jargon. We are the inheritors of Eastern wisdom and a proletarian wit, simplicity, and depths. He could not have found a more adequate expression.

"Guo Puyun's thing doesn't work!"

My classmates were not malicious. They were merely less careful of others than themselves. Besides when it came to "thing" there was always a fascination. That they took a joking attitude to the region three inches below the belly button lightly was not a crime.

Guo Puyun, I want to shatter your serenity in the nether regions with one thought. Your kind, healthy, clever, refined classmates disseminated your truth with this melancholy phrase: His thing doesn't work. I assure you they were sad for you; they meant no harm. You need not be ashamed.

I will never forget those words. Words that were more powerful than any poem Guo Puyun ever wrote. His poetry never took flight because he lacked a throbbing poisoned pen. He lacked imagination. I believe if ever the true value of satire is recognised, those words should be made as the epitaph of their creator, a monument to one that death did not snatch away.

Guo Puyun was not alone. The burden of guilt also fell on Zhao Kun's shoulders. She went on as usual not because she was stronger but because she had the strength to fight back.

"Did you know Zhao Kun is second-hand goods?"

"Guo Puyun was a real fool. After all his picking and choosing, he ends up with somebody's left-overs...."

"A leaking pot deserves a broken lid. They fit."

The classmates that said these things are not bad. They have merits. They were chivalrous in a pinch. They'd really put their shoulders to it building a kitchen for a friend. But some devil possessed them, and they spewed poison.

Zhao Kun was not driven to suicide though the secret of being abandoned, and her sexual encounter with Guo Puyun was making the rounds. She was not intimidated. Her counter-attack was swift and simple.

She was deliberately late for class by five minutes. She did not go to her seat but crossed the platform to where Big Sister sat. All eyes were on her. Big Sister looked up at her dully. The air crackled with tension. Zhao Kun was icy calm.

"Damned — fool!"

Big Sister never recovered her dignity until she graduated. Whenever Zhao Kun met her in the corridor or on the stairs, she would deliberately flatten her against the wall, a ballustrade, or against the garbage containers at the campus gate. Big Sister avoided Zhao Kun like the plague.

Zhao Kun lived a good life, a natural life. It was a pity that she could only master her own destiny, and could not help Guo Puyun. That proves women are not the weaker sex.

The two days when gossip was running rife, Guo Puyun was not at school. In fact he dropped out the day after the disastrous encounter. His excuse was seeking treatment for his eye. To avoid visits from classmates, or perhaps he was tired of the grim little room, he had moved in with his parents at Baiwanzhuang. A few cadres and his protege for Party membership visited him there, and reported that he was making arrangements at one of the better hospitals and was going under the knife. Zhao Kun was also there. It was said that Guo Puyun seemed in high spirits. He was lying on the sofa with his head on Zhao Kun's lap, talking and laughing like a contented lover. Everyone was relieved. He would have no trouble getting through the course with Zhao Kun to help him with lecture notes. Only his protege was disappointed. Guo Puyun had made arrangements to see his unit's Party Branch to arrange a transfer. Instead he had taken time off for himself. At graduation, the protege failed to be admitted to the Party, and he blamed Guo Puyun for his failure. But it was foolish to expect Guo Puyun to delay killing himself for the sake of another person. Selfishness is excusable when it comes to death.

I went to the dormitory of the medical apparatus factory twice, but did not see him. The door was locked, and the thin plywood door made a strange hollow sound when I knocked. I knew there was no one there, but I couldn't help feeling he was lying on the bed, or sitting at the table, his head propped in his hands lost in thought, or hanging in the wardrobe with a belt around his neck. He had mentioned death once before.

After his affair with Zhao Kun became public, I hesitated to mention it, even less to joke about it. Once the school borrowed the use of a military auditorium to publicise a document. At the end of the meeting, as we were going in the same direction, he offered me a lift. We passed Youth Lake Park, and he suggested stopping a while. I did not object.

We sat smoking. He pointed at the small island at the centre of the lake, and the arched bridge that joined it to the land, about to say something but changed his mind. The ice on the lake had melted but the trees along the shore were still bare.

He pointed at some old people moving about slowly on the island. I watched him take another few drags on his cigarette.

"There ... on that bridge was where Zhao Kun and I met for the first time...."

"Did she ask you to meet her?"

"She gave me a letter. I thought it was notes at first.... It was quite a long letter too...."

It was a commonplace beginning to an ordinary story. I could not be disinterested nor could I seem too eager to know everything.

"And you came?"

"I was not going to. But I wanted her to understand I was serious about being single."

"Of course."

"We talked till quite late. I didn't know it then, but she's been unhappy too...."

"What happened?"

He did not reply. Perhaps he felt he had already said too much. What he called misfortune was no doubt the rumours I later heard. I did not think that

Zhao Kun would reveal so much of herself so quickly. That she would bring up the delicate question of her lost innocence proves she understood and trusted him. It was not an obstacle to their friendship. On the contrary it gave Guo Puyun a feeling of kinship. The misfortunes of another took his mind off his own. In comforting the other, he eased some of his own inner turmoil. This was probably the motive for his continued friendship with Zhao Kun.

However, there were other complications.

The impression I got that day by the lake was that he did not fall in love. Rather he had been careless and slipped into quagmire. He stared at the bridge sadly. It was another symbol of the twists and turns his life had taken. I boldly voiced my doubts.

"Do you really ... love her?"

"Zhao Kun is a good person."

I did not say she was not. But that neutral expression could apply to any young woman. Zhao Kun ought to be more than "a good person" to him if she was to be his wife. That he was unable to say anything more satisfactory showed his hesitation. I wanted to say that at the age of thirty-six one should choose more carefully. However it sounded so pompous that I could not utter the words. He was trapped, and there was no use pointing out his folly. I could not do his thinking or suffer for him. He seemed lost.

He heaved a sigh and said, "What shall I do?"

"Do what?"

"I can't do anything!"

"If you've made up your mind, then get on with it. If you have doubts then step back. Don't do what isn't right for yourself just to please someone else...."

"I don't know what to do. I really don't!"

There is no admission charge to Youth Lake Park. To prevent cars driving through there are a few cement stakes blocking the entrance. As we passed them Guo Puyun scuffed his foot against one, and I did the same in a show of solidarity. There were probably similar obstacles in Guo Puyun's heart, just as cold, solid and implacable. We skirted the barriers and left the park. But Guo Puyun could not get past the hurdles in his mind.

"I wish I was dead...."

"You must be joking."

"Really! Everything would be resolved...."

"How are you going to manage it?"

"There're many ways. You tug hard enough at a string and it snaps...."

"Then go ahead and do it. Aren't you ashamed of yourself spouting that kind of nonsense...."

"You don't understand...."

It was the first time he talked about death seriously. I was shocked. Then I thought it was laughable. He was being dramatic. It was as if he felt his love affair was too ordinary and was deliberately being melodramatic. It was not the behavior of a mature man of thirty-six. Before he took his life, Guo Puyun repeated those same words a hundred times to whoever would listen. And nobody took him more seriously than I. We scoffed at him. He reminded me of something I read as a child: never cry wolf!

Everyone knew there was no wolf. Even if Guo Puyun had stuck his head in the wolf's jaw, we all knew it was just a prop, and he was doing it to get attention.

The ending was the same as the fable. He fooled us all.

He muttered about dying but he continued his hopeless love affair. What could he have been thinking of? Was it the hope that a woman's love would work miracles? Was it clutching at straws as life slipped away? Anyway, it was soon after that conversation by the lake that he and Zhao Kun stepped naked into his untidy bed. Perhaps the mysterious workings of his body responded for a moment. He had stripped, knowing it would not work but hoping it would, if only once. It did not. His classmates' verdict, "His thing doesn't work" was correct. He had the proof now. There was no other course than to end his useless life.

If his body had given him the satisfaction he craved, would he have the courage to live? Ecstasy is short-lived, and is not the only thing of value in life. Sooner or later he would encounter new obstacles, for which he would not find such easy excuses.

It was not possible to glean anything from Zhao Kun. The few people who knew the details were reluctant to tell, knowing the danger of gossip. When it comes to the living, there are certain considerations. Still I was able to gather bits of the story from one of her female friends.

"She doesn't care for 'that.'" I nodded understanding of what "that" referred to. "She dislikes it." I found that hard to believe. I imagined the encounter must have been one of unbridled desire, otherwise it would not have happened.

"She told Guo Puyun if they didn't have it, it would not matter, so long as they loved each other.

But he wouldn't believe her...."

"What did he say?"

"I don't know.... According to Zhao Kun he was apologetic ... kept begging forgiveness ... butting his head against the head-board...."

"Oh."

"... Now I didn't tell you anything."

She was embarrassed, by telling details like butting his head against the end of the bed. Even as I thanked her, I thought Zhao Kun was the sort that couldn't keep anything to herself. In a way it is just as well. If she was like Guo Puyun who kept everything in, life would be unbearable for her too.

"She doesn't care for 'that'."

I believe that Guo Puyun did not much care for it either. Nor do I believe he cared for pure love. He cared for something else too much.

There has to be something in this world that caused him greater shame than 'that.' It killed him, but remains hidden. I don't know what it is, but I must find it.

Chapter 6

Guo Puyun loved art exhibitions. I went with him twice. Once it was the work of a French impressionist named Peterson or something at the National Art Gallery. The frames were beautiful, but the paintings were another matter. A pair of breasts of different sizes were grafted onto buttocks. From a distance it resembled a heap of rotten fruit. However, it elicited groans of pleasure from Guo Puyun. The foreigner struck me as a charlatan.

The time at the Cultural Palace of the People was different. The artist was a young man named Wu Yan whom he knew and he was more objective. Wu Yan was an assistant professor at the Academy of Art. There was a photograph and short biography of the artist by the entrance. In the photograph he was solemn and unsmiling but pleasant looking. The biography explained that he had been a worker in a certain military establishment for more than ten years. He had been a carpenter, brick-layer and pipe-fitter as well. This unusual biography gave added interest to the exhibition.

"Will you look at that! Just look at that!"

Guo Puyun was excited as soon as we crossed the threshold. The first painting was an oil, about the size of two tabletops, a landscape with black mountains and white water.

"Great!"

As we moved from canvas to canvas Guo Puyun quieted down. There was pain in his eyes. "That guy's made something of himself...." he muttered.

He fell silent. He wanted a smoke, but a guard stopped him before he could light up. There was no one in the gallery as excited as Guo Puyun. I do not think it was the power of art that moved him. It was more likely envy of a talented artist who had emerged from the same work unit. They had been work-mates. Guo Puyun had a head start learning art. But Fate had played another prank on him. His friend was a full moon sailing across the sky, whose light dimmed the faint sparks of star light that he was. Standing in the gallery he could not avoid the merciless comparison. Envy alone did not explain his feelings at that moment. It was the awfulness of fate that assailed him. He drew me to the far end of the gallery. The light was poor, and no one else took notice of the picture hanging there. He took a step backward, and a few steps forward, looking at it from this angle and that. Finally he asked, "What do you think of it?"

The title of the canvas was "Netherworld". The whole canvas was black, like a black sail or a section of newly tarred road. Up close, you could see that there were many colours applied layer upon layer in some kind of order. But it was hard to tell what it was.

He shook his head.

"He is a representational painter. This won't do. I shall tell him."

"I think … it's not bad."

"No. This is not his style."

His mood lightened. Finding fault with his friend's work pleased him. After that he picked fault with everything he saw. His remarks were cutting.

"These little gimmicks he pulls will destroy him."

"I'm surprised he'd show this. It's at least ten years old!"

"I've always said he doesn't use red well. But he will fall into that trap…."

He seized the artist's short-comings with malevolent glee.

He was trying to prove something. His comments were not necessarily wrong, but his attitude was. I do not understand art, but I knew he was making a fool of himself. Bad as Wu Yan's art was made out to be, it was still a notch better than the crazy foreigner called Peterson or something. Guo Puyun was lavish with his praise then, but he had only barbs for a friend. He might say these things to his friend face to face. But not in the presence of strangers. At the time I did not think of it, but his reaction was probably a form of rebellion against the friend's success and a sop to the pain of his own failure.

The artist did not give him a chance to catch his breath. If he had not seen the next painting, he might have left the gallery a happy man.

There was a two metres wide canvas, hanging by the exit. It was placed there as a grand finale, and it shook me more than "Netherworld." A man's face peered out between bunches of huge yellow flowers. A lighted cigarette dangling from the man's lips, had set the flowers and the man's hair aflame. Everything was burning. The flowers were turning red, but they and the face retained their shape. The face was serene, expressionless, untouched by the flames. It was an uneasy blending of realism and fantasy. I waited for Guo Puyun's judgement which did not come. He stared at the painting for a long while. The pained look that I had come to know so well was on his face. His shoulders hunched and there was desolation in his eyes.

We left the gallery. He heaved a long sigh.

"Just look at him. When we were doing sketches he was far behind me."

"Why compare yourself with others."

"Those flowers were beautiful...."

"I've never seen such luscious flowers."

"That's woodshavings from yellow pine. We worked with it for many years.... Lets get a drink somewhere in Nanchizi. Art exhibitions exhaust me."

While we drank he praised his friend, and at the same time lamented his own lack of accomplishment. It was clear his friend's success did not give him much pleasure. He regaled me with stories about Wu Yan, making a great deal out of his friendship.

"Wu Yan loves chilli sauce. Every time he eats it he sweats.... We used to tease him...."

I tried to stop him from drinking too much. He said he would stop, but the next minute he was at the counter again, asking for another two ounces. His conversation became fragmented, and tinged with hurt.

"Wu Yan's wife doesn't cook. I used to cook for them all the time."

"Did you see them often?"

"I used to but not any more. He has many engagements, and I didn't want to seem to be riding his coattails. Several times I was on my way, but turned back before I got there. There was no point. Once I was there I didn't know what to say. I haven't seen him for a long time. He often asks about me through the work unit though. He's alright...."

"Don't you want to talk art with him?"

"Who am I? What right have I got? We're not in the same league."

"Actually, with a bit of effort, your water colours are just as fine."

"Don't fool me. I'm not much good. It's too late."

In fact he did not drink much that day. However, we had not gone very far northward along the road, when he suddenly dropped his bicycle, leaned up against a tree and vomited. Afterwards he ducked into a lane, probably embarrassed, and squatted with his face to a grimy wall for quite a while. His face had a greenish tinge when he got up. There were bits of food stuck to the corners of his mouth. He smiled sheepishly. I thought he was going to say, "I'm unlucky," again. Instead he bade me goodbye, and rode off shakily.

In the days that followed when he spoke of death, people would jokingly ask how he would do it. He was deliberately evasive. For a while I thought he might do something foolish with that old bicycle.

Guo Puyun once claimed that his failure was because he chose water colours instead of oils. That analysis avoided the real issue. But at least it explained the effect of coincidence on human life. There were six students that were assigned to the construction brigade of the munitions factory in the autumn of '68. They were full of enthusiasm, and not yet weary of physical labour. They hoped to work in the testing centre, where they would handle guns and cannons. That was heroic. Soon the booming sounds of the firing range palled, and they were doomed to the dull life of saws and planes. They often went to Colt Mountain west of the factory precincts, where they caught rabbits and snakes and roasted them over a fire. It was only after they met the factory supervisor on one of these outings that their lives changed. The man had been a famous artist once. In the late 50s he was reassigned to the main Trade Union. Then he was forced back to the countryside, and down a mine shaft. When he came up at the end of his shift, he would gather his palette and hurry up Colt Mountain before the light failed. No doubt his tenacity and stubbornness impressed the youngsters. Guo Puyun was nineteen, and Wu Yan was just over eighteen, just the age when art would fire their imagination. They threw themselves into it.

Guo Puyun once wrote about this teacher, covered in coal dust. I thought the essay was fictional. Lyricism robbed the piece of veracity. Wu Yan also wrote about his teacher in an article published in the third issue of Chinese Art in 1984. It was a retrospective in which he spoke of his teacher with great respect. However the main thrust of the article was how he had burst the bonds that limited his teacher's art, and the difficulties of forging ahead on his own, and achieving success. When that article appeared both Guo Puyun and the teacher were dead. The teacher died four years earlier of sclerosis of the liver. It was at a time when his artistic creations were at a low ebb and a new crop of artists were gaining recognition. His death was almost unnoticed. If not for my friendship with Guo Puyun I would not have known that he existed. His teaching had produced one success and one failure. Whether he deserved praise or blame, who can say.

The wood-working shop remains. It stands at the northwest corner of the munitions factory, near the wall. Behind the building, the hillside drops in a steep cliff. In front is the yard. It was quite a difference from the clean factory premises. There were tufts of grass growing out of the roof, and the walls were streaked with rusty stains left by leaky drainpipes. Everything was tumbled down, and neglected and smelled sad and musty. When the Deputy Supervisor of the Factory's Party Committee Office showed me around the men had gone off work. As the door was heavily pad-locked, I peered in through the window. Inside was a jumble of abandoned tools. Bright yellow coils of wood shavings were everywhere. Smooth blocks of wood were stacked against a wall. This was where

Guo Puyun and Wu Yan came to escape the noise of the dormitory to paint. Who knows how many lonely nights were spent there, painting, painting. I found every brick every blade of grass moving. How could one face failure after such a struggle. I doubt if I would have the strength.

The Deputy Supervisor had come to the factory at the same time as Guo Puyun. It was said that when Guo Puyun and Wu Yan became interested in art, he was interested in playing the fiddle. Since he was a clerk, he would often steal letter paper from the office for them to draw on. So he had a part in the thousands of sketches that the two made. Often he would pose for them, clad only in his briefs, sitting, standing or lying in the litter of shavings that prickled. After Guo Puyun's death a stack of sketches were found under an old mattress. One was of a naked young man playing a fiddle. The quality of the sketch was no better and no worse than those published in folios.

"There were several of us who came to the factory together. All of us posed for them. In the summer the mosquitoes were murderous. In the winter there was not enough heat. So we brought our quilts, huddled under them for a while, and then bared ourselves. It was punishing...."

The Deputy spoke enthusiastically. He was candid and open, a man of honour.

"Did you do it for nothing?"

"I was quite happy to do it. Xiao Guo provided lunch and Xiao Wu took care of supper. The money I saved posing went for drinks. Everyone had a good time. My fiddling bothered the others in the dormitory, so I played in here. They did their thing and I did mine...."

"You must play quite well."

"If I kept it up, I might have turned professional. But I haven't the patience of Wu Yan. One spring festival we all went home. He bought a basket of bread, and put a kettle on the stove, and painted. He didn't leave the work-shop for days. When we got back, his face was the colour of chalk, and his clothes were covered with paint." He did not mention Guo Puyun.

"He worked harder than Guo Puyun?"

"They were about equal."

"How come Guo Puyun didn't succeed?"

"I don't know. He did quite well at the beginning. His commercial art was exhibited by the Ministry. Later on it was also included in an exhibition organised by the Mine. He was getting a bit of a reputation in the suburbs. At that time Wu Yan was nobody."

"What was their relationship?"

"We all got on well. We were like brothers."

"Why did Guo Puyun give up painting?"

"I forget exactly when it was. Probably '75 or '76. He was always praising Wu Yan's work. At first nobody took any notice. Later it began to sound like sour grapes. He was always whining that he was not as good. Actually his commercial stuff was quite striking....The trouble was he was always comparing himself to somebody else. If he'd gone ahead and done his own work, he would have been fine...."

"Then he started writing poetry?"

"He wrote poetry before that. But he put all his efforts into it from then on. In '77 Wu Yan sat for the entrance exam to the Academy of Art. Xiao Guo had applied also. But at the eleventh hour he backed out. All of us persuaded him to try, but he wouldn't listen. Wu Yan got accepted. Xiao Guo got really drunk at the farewell dinner. It was pathetic but annoying too. The following year he tried for entrance into the faculty of literature, and was turned down. That finished him.... He was a good person, but...."

The Deputy had nothing more to add. He showed me Guo Puyun's old quarters and his office. A tidy bed and an equally tidy desk had been taken over by a living person. The surroundings had not changed. Although a life had gone to its end, there was not a hint of oppressiveness. The able Deputy who had been a young cadre at the same time as Guo Puyun, was well suited to being the Chief of Advertising. He would lead a healthy, placid and happy life while Guo Puyun rotted in the ground.

Is it worthwhile competing for the sake of competition? Or for its rewards? One sometimes gets drawn into competition in spite of oneself, and the result would either be triumph or defeat. But could one not be magnanimous about it. To give one's life for its sake is stupid. When Guo Puyun's decaying body lay on the shore, like a dead fish for all to see was the moment he had reached the pinnacle of stupidity. He was worthy of being despised by all those who competed and won.

I found Wu Yan's home in the Guanghua District of the city. He had gone abroad to study at the Bavarian Art Academy in Germany. I had a glimpse of him in number four warehouse at the factory the day of Guo Puyun's memorial service. He was taking an intensive course in German at the time. He had a pocketful of vocabulary cards, which he glanced at from time to time, while he chatted. The service was very simple. Some of Guo Puyun's friends wept silently, but Wu Yan was expressionless all the way through, his eyes fixed on something far away. He grimly refused to show the least emotion. At the time, I wondered how a person could be so cold. I felt there was something frightening and unfathomable about him. He and Guo Puyun seemed to have inhabited separate worlds. One was weak, and easily hurt. The other was strong enough to remove all obstacles that stood in his way. After Guo Puyun was laid to rest, I had wanted to talk to Wu Yan, but he had gone off with someone else.

His wife gave me an address and I immediately sent off a letter to Europe. It was more like a questionnaire. His reply was simple and direct. It was one more proof of the intrinsic quality between the quick and the dead, success and failure.

He wrote:

"I do not wish to remember my friend in this fashion. He did what he had to do. I respect his choice. Since we had no power to help him through his suffering, we have no right to chide him. I am still puzzled by his actions. But to understand I would have to follow in his footsteps. That to me, to you, or anyone else would be unimaginable. To probe for reasons is meaningless. This is not the only case. This is their choice, simple and irrevocable. There is nothing to be shocked at. If you can, I beg you not to disturb the peace of my friend's grave. This is the collective answer to your 24 questions. I have nothing to add.

At Colt Mountain, north of track 386, is the grave of Guo Puyun. You might like to go there. There is a headstone. I shall still be in Europe next Qingming Festival. I beg you to visit the grave on my behalf. The scenery is pleasant and it would make a nice day's outing.''

I wrote a long chatty letter back immediately, promising to visit the grave according to his request. I also asked a few questions to which I needed answers. Had Guo Puyun been in love, or out of love? Did he have a physical defect? The last was a firm but shameless question did he masturbate? Perhaps I had gone too far, for there was no reply.

The Deputy told me that in the more than ten years at the factory, Guo Puyun had never been in love. Whether he had someone in the city, nobody knew. He never talked about women. When the younger men talked dirty, he would quietly slip away. He was known for his purity. Many people tried to matchmake for him but he refused them all. In the end people realized it was useless and stopped trying. Even good friends didn't raise that question. I was too embarrassed to ask the Deputy about masturbation. Even if he knew, it was a matter of honour, and the Deputy would not have told.

Guo Puyun's grave site was indeed quite beautiful. There were many low bushes and wild flowers. Butterflies and insects hovered on the grassy slopes. Dew drops glistened, and the air was filled with the fragrance of flowers, and the dank smell of earth.

The granite headstone was about a metre high. The epitaph read: The eternal resting place of he who came and went too quickly. The characters were well formed and cut deep into the stone. The words seemed ironic at first reading. The "eternal" stood contrasted against "came and went too quickly." Yet it was exactly the pity of coming and going too quickly that added poignancy to the permanence of eternity.

The words could not have been better chosen to summarise a life. Although headstones are made for the dead, they are meant for the living. If later generations are to learn anything from it, it must be bitter, forceful, and shattering. This headstone should have read:

His Thing Doesn't Work

There is no need for shame. There will be more than one body lying under such a headstone. What does "thing" represent? Is it spiritual or physical? It is spirit and flesh. It is a reproductive organ: thought, and boundless human aspirations.

Whose thing works needs further examination.

Chapter 7

Guo Puyun's operation was fixed for April 7th. I suspect his real motive had less to do with correcting an eye injury than with removing the bluish spot. The rapid freezing procedure was similar to that used to remove unsightly freckles and black moles on a young girl's face. The apparatus was newly acquired from abroad, and mainly used against cancer. At present the techniques had not yet been perfected, and its use was tantamount to piercing ears with a laser.

Guo Puyun first had treatment for his eye at Tongrun Hospital, where his complete medical history was kept. But he avoided it. Instead he went to a military hospital in the west of Mashenmiao, that also treated civilians, and registered under dermatology. The doctor carefully explained that the results of fast freezing were erratic. People reacted to it according to their physical condition. Besides the tiny permanent bruise was hardly noticeable. The doctor insisted that Guo Puyun should think about it more seriously. But Guo Puyun was determined. "Please help me. I'm courting," he pleaded. He went back three days in a row. Finally the operation was set for April 7th, at nine a.m. He lay on the table and shut his eyes. The apparatus was wheeled into position. A narrow shaft was poised over the handsome young man's face. The doctor pressed the lever.

The Operating room became Guo Puyun's execution ground.

Two days later the bandage came off. His parents, his sister and Zhao Kun gasped at what they saw. He broke into tears and swooned. The bluish patch was gone, but in its place was a patch of colourless skin. From then on he called himself a clown. He gambled and made a fool of himself.

"He swooned right away!"

"As soon as the bandage came off, he went crazy!"

"It was white on white."

The students of the special course mulled this bit of news over. They agreed that it was unmanly to put such importance on one's looks.

"He shouldn't have done it. I wonder what made

him do it...."

Those with sharper tongues thought it was quite reasonable to compensate for his other defect by improving his looks.

They analysed the situation thoroughly. The conclusion was not important. It was a game. Nobody thought much of the white patch. It was not a great unbearable tragedy. Yet Guo Puyun swooned, and afterwards tried to impress others by threatening death when the real cause for failure in love was that "his thing doesn't work". Compassion is reserved for oneself besides it is not possible to maintain an air of solemnity about trivial things.

Many classmates visited him, prompted by sympathy, not unmixed with curiosity. Guo Puyun smiled at their solicitude but he did not let them look at the colourless skin which was still covered with white gauze. He explained the procedure and described the apparatus. It seemed that he was not the victim of a failed experiment but its enthusiastic salesman. He did not blame the doctor, or threaten to take legal action. It was not an accident, he was quite adamant about that. Nor was it the fault of the apparatus that cost in excess of two hundred thousand US dollars. The responsibility was his. The release form he signed had listed three possible side effects, and the chance of the happening was one in a hundred. It was his rotten luck. He had been unlucky all his life.

It was not clear what kind of trouble the patch caused him. He kept it covered with gauze and strips of tape, as though he were afraid that something else might go wrong. His classmate were piqued. They really wanted to see the white patch. Finally one fellow openly broached the subject. Guo Puyun immediately put him in his place.

"You can't see it! I look like a clown in Beijing opera. If you don't know what I mean go home and turn on the TV."

The questions became more and more stupid.

"Is it like vitiligo?"

As if that were not enough people were offering all sorts of advice: magic potions, ancient Chinese remedies, acupuncture. Someone even offered to take him to the hot springs at Xiaotangshan. Guo Puyun rejected them all. He realized rapid freezing procedure had dissolved the bruise, but also destroyed the skin pigment which could not be restored. The white patch became a mark of death. His eye injury was not cured. The skin pigment could not be replaced. He would never write the great epic poem. He would never have an erection or take charge of his destiny.... Problems were heaped upon him. Did he see some vague connection between them? He spoke dully of the meaninglessness of his existence. It was not that he was unable to go on living, but because he was fascinated with death. Although he was melancholy, no one took him seriously.

"There you go again!"

Zhao Kun reached over the back of the sofa and gave him a shove. The talk of death seemed to tickle the funny bone of the others. They took it as a joke. The conversation became animated.

"Xiao Guo when you're ready let us know, and we'll keep you company. I am tired of living too."

"You're always harping about death. How are you going to manage it? Maybe we can learn something."

"You take in a hundred odd yuan a month. What a waste. Why don't we swap places...."

"You're really hard hearted. If you kick the bucket, what's Zhao Kun going to do?"

Zhao Kun slapped the fellow soundly. She was neither sad nor angry, but calmly poured tea and passed around a plate of melon seeds.

Guo Puyun's mother looked in and quietly shut the door again.

The classmates rose to leave. He and Zhao Kun saw them out, and stood on the lawn outside waving. Zhao Kun leaned comfortably against him. It was clear that neither the white patch nor anything else would dampen her resolve to become his wife. As all the obstacles had been cleared there was no reason for Guo Puyun's despair. Everyone went away feeling confident about his future, and that he would surely be back in class within a few days. Then there would be pranks to play.

"Give my regards to the Class Teacher." Then he added as an after thought, "I won't pollute the city."

One of the older girls ran back toward Guo Puyun waving her fist as if she was really angry.

"Shut your filthy mouth! Any more nonsense and we're through with you."

The others hooted with laughter.

She turned and loudly asked if anyone would accompany her to the farmers market. She had seen some cucumbers that were tasty and cheap. No one would go, so she went alone.

"Have a good rest. We'll see you in a few days...."

The rest went their way, chatting about vitiligo, the dangers of plastic surgery, and why men were becoming more feminine. Finally they scattered each to his own little corner of the city that throbbed with life. Death was a fallacy. Everyone was madly searching for a better life. Guo Puyun was a bubble on the great torrent of human desire that would neither sink nor disappear, but flowed on with the current. He was far from death.

No one noticed that the alarm bell had already sounded. That visit was only a fortnight before May first. For the victim that fortnight was too long and too full of incident. Guo Puyun did not encounter any obstacles until he met his destiny. From start to finish he had not been joking.

"I'm a clown."

The patch of white gauze became a part of his face. He even took it to his watery grave. When he sank beneath the waters of the reservoir, and his hands clutched fearfully at the muddy bottom, the last message that flashed though his brain was, "A clown deserves to die!"

"I really am a clown"

He repeated it until it became tiresome. It was as though he was incapable of any other thought. Why did he consider himself only fit to play the fool in life? The answer was plain while he lived. Nobody can get through life without laughing at themselves some time. No one thought Guo Puyun was a clown. His insistence on that point was unreasonable. Which of us has not been tripped up by his own cleverness one time or another? He might pity himself over his medical history, and the failure of his organ, but lowering himself worth was going too far.

One cannot but suspect Guo Puyun's obsession. His self condemnation must have been based on something that no one else knew or recognized. The arts of a clown are predestined by his calling. What had a kind and good man done that could not be brought out in the light of day? What made him curse himself?

I almost feel the uneasiness of Guo Puyun lying under Colt Mountain. Don't be angry, my friend. The ruminations of the living can no longer touch you. The greatest injury done you is locked in your head. You are beyond pain. Death will compensate you for everything you have suffered. Sleep in peace. These disquieting thoughts have nothing to do with you.

Nothing at all!

What I want to say is that Guo Puyun's mother only became his mother in 1972. She brought with her someone with a different surname, different parentage, to be part of the family. That stranger became his sister. She was a capricious eighteen year old and he was twenty-three. From then on she had a handsome, melancholy older brother. Her natural father and his natural mother were dead. A newly-wed middle aged couple brought these two young people together in the three-room apartment in Baiwanzhuang. Fourteen years later when Guo Puyun walked out of the door for the last time, that almost perfect family had already disintegrated. Was his sister's laughter a death knell that followed him down the stairs?

In our first semester, I remember him mentioning her quite casually. He gave me the impression that she was head-strong, and unreasonable. She gave up the chance of a doctorate, and came home from the University of Jilin to plunge into the Physics Department with her master's degree. Her reason was that the winter in the north-east was too severe. She did not endure it for even a year.

"I wrote her persuading her to think about it. But she was home within a few days. She's childish...."

"She's probably a liberated woman?"

"I think she's spoilt."

"Was she always like that?"

"Yes."

"She's just your opposite. But brother and sister with completely different personalities is not uncommon. Is she beautiful?"

"She's alright."

He never spoke of his sister again. He did not even mention that she was married on New Year's day. Furthermore he never mentioned that his mother was actually a step-mother, and the sister was a step-sister. I only learnt these facts after he died. I cannot fathom why he hid these details. My informant also said that contrary to his story, the family did not get along. There was a deep rift between the step-mother and himself.

I had gone with some of the others to visit Guo Puyun, mainly out of curiosity to see the white patch on his face. It was the first time I met his mother. She had a kindly face. There were very few wrinkles for she had kept her age well. There was no smile in her welcome. She was coldly polite. She pushed open his door, stuck her head in as though she had gone into the wrong room, and quickly went out again. That was a clue. She fitted my imagination of the mother who would allow her son to live in squalor without any concern. The others were sensitive to it too. None of us stayed long. She was indeed that kind of mother.

She did not attend Guo Puyun's memorial service. Nor for that matter did her husband, Guo Puyun's natural father. The factory was far and the road difficult. Besides the father had had a stroke and had difficulty in walking and talking. It was understandable. Rightly or wrongly, the factory authorities had persuaded the old couple not to come. The disintegrating body was swarthed in bandages from head to toe. Only the half open eyes were visible. There was really little reason to come all that way for that sad sight. Seeing Guo Puyun lying on the ground like that might have moved them to realize something had gone horribly wrong. There should have been someone beside the dead man. If I were to be carried off before my time, I hope that I would have at least my mother beside me. I could not be without the person who had borne, raised and loved me.

Afterwards when I discovered she was a step-mother, I felt there were things I ought to understand. The more I thought the more confused I became. By what I knew of Guo Puyun, it was unlikely that he would raise objections when his father remarried. Nor was he likely to object to his father's new wife because of his memories of his natural mother. Even a shrew would be less demanding faced with Guo Puyun's gentleness. The old lady did not seem to be the sort that would be fault finding. In fact she seemed quite genteel.

But there was definitely a rift.

I accompanied the Class Teacher to the home in

Baiwanzhuang after Guo Puyun's death. His object was to get hold of some notebooks to study and try to understand what students thought about. I went along out of self-interest, hoping to glean some morsel from any material that he let drop.

Guo Puyun's father answered the door, leaning on a cane, his mouth twisted to one side. His sad eyes stared dully at us.

He mumbled something unintelligible, but his attitude told us we would not be allowed in.

"I am Guo Puyun's Class Teacher. I came to see...."

"There is no one home."

We understood that quite clearly. The door shut in our faces. The Class Teacher was not about to give up. We sat on the stairs and smoked waiting for Guo Puyun's mother to return. He was convinced that the old lady was out shopping. I was equally convinced that she was inside, and did not want visitors. The old man was sent to block us. He would not accept that, and said that I ought not to judge the actions of someone who had suffered a tragedy so harshly.

"We ought to be understanding," he protested.

The Class Teacher is a nice man. He was right. As we were about to leave, Guo Puyun's mother came toward us carrying a basket of vegetables. She recognized me and stopped to chat. As she made no move to invite us in, we talked on the lawn.

"The leaders of the school visited a few days ago...."

"Yes. I am the Class Teacher and I come representing the class...."

He looked around for a place to sit, but the old

lady had no intention of sitting. She stood ramrod straight clutching her basket, her eyes serene and attentive.

"It's like this. We are trying to improve our work with the students' thinking, and to be able to grasp their thoughts, we wanted to thoroughly examine this incident. There is a lot we don't understand. The difficulty is...."

"Is there some way I can help?"

"We would like to borrow Guo Puyun's note books."

"Did he keep note books?"

The old lady's question took the Class Teacher by surprise. Guo Puyun kept a secret diary that no one was allowed to read. Not even Zhao Kun. He also kept a notebook into which he scribbled poems, quotations and odd phrases, of his own. If we could not have the diary, the notebook would do. I tried to reason with the old lady.

"He always kept a notebook. He let me read it several times. We guarantee the contents will be kept secret and we'll return it as soon as we've finished with it...."

"That's not necessary. Last Saturday his father spent the whole day burning things. He wouldn't even let me see what they were. He made sure there is nothing left. Guo Puyun's diary was probably there.... Forgive us...."

"That's a pity."

"Even if it hadn't been burnt his father would not lend it. Neither would I. Puyun's business had nothing to do with anyone else. Therefore, you can do your work without him....'

"I'm sorry."

The Class Teacher was embarrassed. During the conversation he had taken the basket from the old lady, and stood listing to one side from its weight. I asked a lot of questions about May first before Guo Puyun left home. The old lady answered me at great length and with some detail. She did not seem to mind, until I asked one question too many. I wished I could take it back but it was too late.

"Was there some conflict between the family and Guo Puyun?"

"... What kind of conflict?"

"He lived alone in a filthy place.... I thought maybe he and you ... or...."

"That was his fault. He never told us what was in his heart. Nobody knew what he thought about. He didn't tell us and we didn't ask. He's over thirty and ought to be able to look after himself. If he did not make any effort to make things better for himself, who are we to interfere...."

"He was very even tempered."

"What's that supposed to mean?"

"Appearances meant a lot to him. The way you spoke just then would have hurt him deeply.... Did he quarrel with you?"

"I'm his mother. I have the right to criticize him when he's done something wrong...."

"What did he do?"

The old lady blanched. The Class Teacher was tugging at my sleeve, but this was the opening I had hoped for, and I pressed on no matter how insensitive I seemed.

"Did it have anything to do with his death? What

did he do?''

"Puyun had a lot of friends. The family was very good to him. You can ask any of the neighbours...."

Of course that was entirely out of the question.

"Puyun was a good son...."

The old lady glanced at me and the Class Teacher, retrieved her basket and disappeared into the building. There was no doubt about the truth of her parting remark. Guo Puyun was a good son. That was a fair assessment of him. The trouble was he did not believe it himself, and viciously branded himself a clown.

The Class Teacher regretted the loss of the notebook. He did not think it inappropriate to pursue the dead to further the students' education in political thought. I was not less callous; perhaps more. For I had touched a nerve in the old lady and wrested from her that Guo Puyun had done something totally unacceptable. I have always suspected that he fended off, however awkwardly, the advances of a member of the opposite sex, except for the dance instructor. Those fleeting experiences were probably only visual contacts but they left a lasting sense of guilt.

He died just over six months after his sister returned from the northeast, and exactly four months after her wedding. Those were coincidences. However, in '75 when he was competing against Wu Yan he suddenly lost all interest in art. That was exactly three years before his father remarried. Did something happen during that period? His disdain for romance was already established.

One of the friends of Guo Puyun, the Deputy Chief of the Party Committee Office at the factory had told me of an incident that was almost comical. But he told it so seriously that it was no longer a joking matter.

On the eve of Spring Festival in '76 Guo Puyun had gone to buy festive foods. The counter where frozen chickens were sold was crowded. He managed to lay hands on a chicken, and was either shoved or forced his way out of the crowd. He stood there clutching his chicken half-dazed, when he was grabbed by the civil militia and forced into the office behind the counter. He was accused of stealing. They had caught him red-handed. There was no escape. Unless he could give a reasonable account of himself, he would be sent to the public security. The triumphant shouting drowned out Guo Puyun's protestations that he was fully intending to pay for the chicken. No one believed him. Finally the market authorities phoned the factory's security people to come and fetch him.

Would Guo Puyun steal a chicken?

Nobody at the factory thought that accusation could stand up in court. Guo Puyun had public issued food coupons, which he distributed quite freely, and did not mind whether they were ever returned. He was constantly helping out the older brigade members who were having difficulties. A good hearted person such as he would not steal a chicken. It was a joke.

The factory eventually convinced the market authorities, and the charges were dropped. However the militia stuck to their guns. They claimed he was too close to the door and too far from the counter at the time. If they saw anyone like that in the future they would take him in too. They were professionals, and recognized the stealthy look of thieves.

Although the factory protected him, it took a long time for him to recover from the blow to his honour and pride.

"He was dazed. There was nothing anyone could say that did any good. So we just never mentioned it."

"You're sure he did not intend to steal?"

"That goes without saying."

"Then why was he unable to hold his head up for such a long time?"

"Honest men are like that. If someone was accused of stealing in a roomful of people, Guo Puyun's face would be the first to redden. Honest men can't bear to be even suspected of something like that. I've seen that a few times."

"But what if he wasn't as squeaky clean as you think?"

"I might have doubts if it were anyone else, but not Guo Puyun. He was one of a rare breed."

The Deputy's confidence in his friend was touching. I too have always felt people like Guo Puyun are rare. Still we must face the fact that before he died, Guo Puyun had repeatedly called himself a clown. It was not an ordinary self-deprecation. It carried with it a much deeper brand, indicative of despair and pain.

Guo Puyun seemed unable to recognize what was in his heart was the same as in everyone else's. His impotence was possibly not physiological, but a product of long periods of stress. There was no reason to believe that he did not have the normal desires of men, yet his moral concepts remained pure till the age of thirty-six. His only release was masturbation. The effects have been chronicled in scientific pamphlets and books of hygiene for young men. One side effect is a sense of guilt. Guo Puyun paid an awful price for relieving himself.

In the prolonged period in which he refused all contact with females, he seemed plagued by unbridled desire. The exhilaration at the moment of climax is the same for a man of refinement as it is for a ruffian. We are all subject to desires of the flesh. The broadminded take it as it comes, the depraved think nothing of it, and those like Guo Puyun feel guilty. But the fantasies that arise from these hungers are even harder to bear. Did he succumb to the visual seduction of a female body? And was he discovered?

On the partition wall between the stalls in the second floor lavatory of United College there is a line of graffitti written in blue felt pen, which is a distillation of a certain philosophy of life.

"After a day's refinement, a little lewdness is excusable."

Some clever youngster had demonstrated the connection between two opposed ideas. Although he might not have been refined all day, when it came to being lewd he did not try to hide it, but laughed at himself instead. He recognised that what he did had nothing to do with refinement. The form and content of what he did was indeed lewd. The unknown student's life might not be the model of propriety but it was carefree. So long as refinement and lewdness were kept in the right perspective that young man would have a good future. Even if they were disproportionate, he would not dub himself a clown as Guo Puyun did. Guo Puyun's problem was that he could not bear the least stain on his soul. The stuff in the latrine came from the human body. We carry that burden around with us and we are not ashamed. The blood in our veins is untainted.

Yet he did away with himself muttering clown, clown. Those who do not commit suicide must be thick skinned. Some lead pleasant lives without any shame. Morality and depravity live side by side. Guo Puyun vacated his spot on the stage of life, but he does not know what he left behind. His departure would not make the world better or worse. It remains unchanged.

There is only one good person less in the crowd.

CHAPTER 8

Guo Puyun visited me five days before he died. He was in good spirits. The patch of gauze stuck tightly to his face was grimy. I tried hard not to look at it. He leafed through some magazines on the sofa without comment. My wife bought ice cream and we ate as we talked. The conversation rambled. He sighed that his epic poem would never be written. I said if he really wanted to he could do it. If it was not a great success, it would at least be a small one.

"What can a dying man write?" He smiled serenely at my wife. He was getting tiresome.

"You've said that a thousand times or more!"

"This time I mean it."

"Because of that?" I pointed at the gauze on his face angrily. Suddenly I wanted to hurt him. Friendly persuasion was getting nowhere. His hand flew to his face is if he'd been struck.

"Someone suggested cosmetics. Someone else suggested a native doctor. None of it's any use. If there was a way I wouldn't.... Forget it. By the way when are you having a child?''

He did not stay long. Before he left we made plans to meet the day after at the class reunion at Taoranting Park. He joshed my wife saying, ''Sister, you're awfully thin. Not much appetite these days?'' She reddened. After he had gone, she remarked that the handsome young fellow was not thinking of dying at all. She liked his sense of humour.

I have often wondered if I had slapped him soundly and called him names, would it have shocked him to his senses? On the other hand, if the outcome was the same, would I be no better than a murderer? Therefore I was right in not striking him.

Only twenty odd people went to the reunion in Taoranting Park. Guo Puyun was waiting at the gate before anybody else arrived. He was the liveliest of the lot. It was his farewell to life.

We rented six boats. It was agreed we would race across the lake from north to south, and the occupants of the last boat to finish would give a performance on the grassy slope on the opposite shore. Sides were quickly chosen. Guo Puyun was slow on the uptake, and was left with three girls.

The Class Teacher suggested exchanging one of them for one of the men, but he objected. The girls too were noisy in their protests. In the end it was decided that Guo Puyun would have a five stroke head start.

His first strokes were steady. The boat cut through the water in a straight line. The other five waited for the Class Teacher's signal and shot forward. If he were alone, Guo Puyun would have maintained an even speed. With the other boats rapidly gaining on him, he faltered. The prow of his boat wobbled from side to side. The spray grew higher, and his ears turned redder.

One boat nosed ahead, then another. Someone in the second boat that passed, roared gleefully, "You're losing, Guo Puyun!"

My boat was the last to pass his. He sat facing the stern, eyes fixed on the ends of his oars, sweat gleaming on his face.

The girls who didn't mind losing, splashed us as we passed. However, winning seemed to mean a lot to him, and there was something tragic in the way he concentrated on the movement of his oars.

I waved, but he did not notice. "Turn back...." I shouted, laughing. He dismissed my shout with a wry smile. Suddenly the victors on the south bank let out a great whoop. I looked back. He had really turned his boat around and was rowing in the other direction. He raised an oar and waved it triumphantly at the others. "You lose! Come back to the north shore!"

Several boats set out at once. The race was on again. The competition was fierce. Finally Guo Puyun's boat nudged against the dock. There was a water fight. Guo Puyun staggered ashore. His pants were soaked. Even as he admitted defeat he covered his face to protect the gauze from getting wet.

Everyone clamoured for a performance, expecting him to refuse.

To their surprise he complied immediately. Afterwards when we recalled this incident, we thought it was a definite sign that he had made up his mind to die. He did a pantomime called The Drunkard.

He paced the lawn on the slope a couple of times,

and picked up some stones. Then he stood stock still and went into his character. The others fell silent, spellbound.

He mimed drinking. His eyes glazed. He swayed from side to side, back and forth as the liquor took hold. Finally, in a movement reminiscent of Beijing opera he did a few somersaults, and rolled over. His limbs quivered, and he lay still. The group broke into loud applause. He leaped lightly to his feet. Everyone was surprised by his performance which was probably inspired by martial arts. It was obvious that he was a trained dancer. The girls were especially impressed and begged for more.

He dusted himself off. "That was not a bad bit of clowning was it?" he said and quietly melted into the crowd.

At the time I thought he had rehearsed it. Anything would have sufficed, so why go to so much trouble?

He stood on the slope with the lake at his feet, his legs trembling with anticipation.

"I'm going to perform the Drunkard," he announced.

I recall the scene vividly.

It would be his last performance. He was doing it for himself. He had submerged himself in the character of the drunkard, and condensed the ups and downs of his life into five minutes. When the performance ended, his life ended too. He wanted to show through his art that he was in complete control. I have no idea what else to make of it.

When we left the park, he stopped his bicycle on the sidewalk and bade each person farewell. I noticed that Zhao Kun who stood beside him seemed unhappy, so

I did not stop to talk, but waved and left.

"Have a good life!" he called out.

I was some distance away and could not be sure whether he was speaking to me or the others clustered around him. It was the last time we saw him alive. I can't remember his expression as he stood on the sidewalk. We must have seemed a cold, unfeeling lot.

I believe it was at the gate of Taoranting Park that he broke up with Zhao Kun. He apologized, saying he wasn't good enough for her, and a whole bunch of other nonsense. She was upset. I don't know the details, but that was also the last time that she saw him. They parted quietly. Guo Puyun deliberately made it that way because he did not want what he was about to do to hurt her. He knew he did not love her. He had never loved her, and his confusion made it impossible for him to accept the burden of such emotions. It was proof that a woman could not deter him. For his action was dictated by a deep sense of guilt.

He did not speak of death that day. For death had already become a reality and was not worth mentioning. One of the girls in his boat during the ill-fated boat race recalls hearing him mutter under his breath, when he was at the end of his strength and it was certain they would lose, "This is fucking stupid! Stupid!" She was shocked because he never used coarse language.

His last words explain something of the nature of life and death. The others thought the activities of people younger than he bored him. Was he content to reveal his plans to a bunch of empty-headed youngsters? Or did he despise them for going on as best they could? He knew that his actions would raise questions, and a few hurts. He was secretly toying with their insensitivity.

Since he had already decided to abandon this world, he had no further use for any of them. He had that right. The classmates who enjoyed his entertainment, must have been clowns in his eyes. The streets were full of clowns, all driven by the same desires. He despised them all. His self pity and despair had been refined to a kind of arrogance, that drove him along the last stretch of life's path.

May first was the day he conquered himself and the world. It became his memorial. His victory was death.

From May third onward six letters were received one after the other. In each he spoke of the need, the rightness, the inevitability of death. He chose it because he needed it more, and understood it better than anyone else.

But his declaration did not rouse any compassion, but only a deep sense of the ridiculous. That perhaps is the greatest difference between the quick and the dead.

Letter to his parents (extract from letter No. 1)

Do not mourn me for I was not a good son. I have thought about this for some time. I have talked about it but you never took it to heart. There was nothing more I could do. When I thought of it before my mind was in a whirl. I did not speak of it to threaten you. It was not your fault that you could not understand. This concerns only me. No one else is to blame. Accept that. I know this will inconvenience you. But it will be the last time. Forgive me.

There are a few bags of clothes and books behind the door of the dormitory. Dispose of them as you see fit. You may sell or burn them. The few sticks of good furniture can still be used. The overcoat Father gave me is in a suitcase under the bed. It was too long so I hardly wore it. Please return it to Father. I had intended to clean up the place, but never got around to it. Please forgive the dirty windows, mother.

There are a few bottles of kerosene on the window sill. The people who live next to the latrine borrowed the stove and never returned it. You can ask them for it, Mother, if you wish.

To his sister (extract from letter No. 2).

You look good in jeans. Even though Mother may not approve, don't mind her. I hope you will always wear them, as long as it's the right season. Stay beautiful.

That incident might have frightened you. But it's passed, and forgotten. You are happy now. My decision has not harmed a single hair of your head. Just think of me as short lived. I am weak and useless. I think differently from other people. Don't curse me.

I have worried for a long time, but I am serene now, and empty. There are many things I want to say, but I don't know where to begin. I feel physics is not your vocation. Don't be stubborn or too disappointed if nothing comes of it. There's nothing wrong with being a good wife. When you have a child, don't mention me. Bring him up to be open, like you. Don't let him inherit any of your short-comings, or those of your husband. Let him be broad minded.

I am Father's only child. His is old and ill. Please look after him. There are things better left unsaid. Though his mind is not what it used to be, Father used to be a good engineer. Don't be angry with him. When he's irascible, take no notice.

I have done enough thinking. Now I feel good about myself. All my troubles and secrets I take with me. I am happy. This is the best for everyone. I can hardly wait.

To Zhao Kun (extract from letter No. 3).

This has nothing to do with you. You tried to talk me out of this many times, but I'm going through with it just the same because there is no other way. If anyone blames you, show them this. Don't torment yourself.

Perhaps you have already forgotten how I spoke of my pessimism when we first met. I had no clear goals in life, but you did. Although I tried to make things clear to you, you moved me so deeply that I lost control. That might have given you the wrong idea. I am not worth loving. You must believe that. I did foolish things, sometimes without realizing it. Don't think about them anymore. You are a good person. I believe sooner or later you will find what you want. When I think of all the things I cannot give you, it hurts me. Forget me. Live your life. That is the only thing left.

Our classmates are bound to discuss us. When I'm gone, the gossiping will get worse. You must be strong. You're old enough to have been through all this before. Don't treat it too seriously. On the other hand brushing it aside will not make things better. Be careful. I am serene now. I only worry about you. I wish you well. If you love me, forgive me, and bear this last barb with me. I have nothing to give, but the blessing from the bottom of my heart. That belongs to you alone.

Speak of me in the harshest tones to the others, if they ask. It's all I deserve. Time flies, and there are more letters to write. Give my regards to your parents and your brother. They have been kind to me, and I have disappointed them.

When I'm gone, you will be free to find happiness. I firmly believe that. Let me go. Just don't hate me. I couldn't bear it. This has nothing to do with you. You must believe that.

To the Party Committee Office (extract from letter No. 4).

Don't search for me. You will not find me. For I go to the only clean place left in the world. It is fitting. The factory is busy, and I have added to your burden. Forgive me. When you receive this, do nothing, and tell no one. Let me quietly depart. I have no regrets. In the decade or so that I have been there, the factory has been good to me. You've sent me to university, and I regret not being able to repay your goodness. You have entrusted the job of Chief of Advertising to me, but I have done little of value. Forgive me. Please select a successor, and erase my name from the Party roster. I have been a member for eight years, yet I am about to do this thing. I apologize to the leadership and to my colleagues, and ask that you do not search for a motive, but beg for your understanding. After careful deliberation I can find no other way. The only path open to me is not so terrible. I have waited, now it's time to act. This is what I want. I deserve your censurer. One day you will understand, this is the logical conclusion for me. I used to be hesitant about everything I did. Now I am filled with confidence. I will succeed and no one can stop me.

This has nothing to do with politics. It concerns only me. There is no point discussing the reason. For a long time these thoughts have plagued me. I don't know how it began. When I was six years old, I used to wake up each day longing for death. But it passed, probably because I was afraid.

I am no longer afraid. Please don't think that I am being coerced.

I did not collect my wages for April. Please send 50 yuan to my home, and use the rest to pay my Party dues. Please get rid of my personal things in the dormitory and on my desk. Return the things that belong to the state.

To the office of the faculty of Chinese Literature (extract from letter No.5)

I am not a good student. If I could, I would minimise the disturbance caused the school. I hope my teachers and classmates will understand my difficulty. I have always dreamed of going to university, and I was glad when I was accepted. However, there are many reasons that make it impossible for me to continue. I thank my teachers for their instruction. Knowledge is useless to someone like me. There are many others who will benefit from it, and live fuller lives. I am weary, and so, I slip away.

Zhao Kun is a fine young woman; clever, studious and warm-hearted.

My decision has already injured her.

I do not wish her to be subjected to more gossip.

Therefore, I beg the school administration and the faculty to protect her. That is my only request.

My teachers are thoughtful people. You will discover the reasons for my actions, so there is no need to explain. This is the only way for me. Yet I have hesitated so long. I must make haste for if I tarry I might not be able to take the final step. That would be a real tragedy.

There is no need to return my dossier to my original unit. It can be cancelled. I am unfit to live; and unfit to be a Party member. I can never hope to repay the debts I owe, so I have cancelled them.

To Wu Yan (extract from letter No: 6).

Don't laugh at me. We have known each other a long time, and talked of many things. But you cannot understand things that I have never said to you before. Finally I feel confident enough about my thoughts to stand up to any jeers.

You know how I blush in front of a crowd. Now I am ready to bare my thoughts to the world, when there is no longer a need. The only person I have to convince is myself. Besides there are only a very few who would understand. You are one. Do you understand me?

There is no need for us to discuss the meaning of life and death. That meaning is clear enough for everyone, but doesn't necessarily suit them. To me the meaning of life is its exact opposite. I did not realize it until now. At least I have got that much clear. That is my great good fortune. I must go. Sadness is almost all dissipated. There is a great emptiness. I am cleansed. I used to suspect that my understanding of things was wrong. Now I know it's not true. I am finally coming out of my corner. Very soon a strange new world will open to me. I can imagine death, and I am not afraid. These last nights I have been pondering the aftermath of death. It is comforting. You are going to scold again. The fact is I am not a whit afraid. Living is a hundred, thousand times more frightening. But death is comforting. No wonder so many great men seek it.

Your painting improves all the time. You are developing a style. Now I must say what troubles me. I sense an inner strength that you have not yet tapped. You no longer have the will to do it. You are exhausted. I failed before you. Although I never stopped loving art, I also knew I did not have the talent. You have read some of my poems. My pain comes from a heart that is easily hurt. Sooner or later you will face failure also. But in the meantime you will create many fine works, and your fame will last. I hope, for your sake, that failure will not be too harsh.

Today I read "Snow Country" again. It occurred to me that in committing harakiri the writer was admitting failure. It was a grand gesture, but it was playing to the audience. I did not like that. Let me go quietly.

I no longer envy you. When life becomes weary, please accept my prayer for you in the other world. I wish you a good life.

Those were Guo Puyun's thoughts before he died. Simple and confused, serene and passionate, they were the crystallisation of all his conflicts that nothing could cut through. The message had lost its superficial meaning. It was heard as a faint far-away sound, like a signal from Hell.

I have photocopies of the six letters. They were given to me by the Deputy who had gathered them with the hope of finding some clue to Guo Puyun's disappearance. One phrase caught the investigators' eye: "a very clean place." Someone had circled those words and those circles have been faithfully preserved in the copies, a mute testament of deep thought, and an unfathomable mystery.

Where is this clean place? Just how clean is this place?

In this great country, the frantic searchers could not find one spot that they had any confidence in. Actually there are many clean places, but they were so anxious to find him, none of the places would do. In a moment of frustration they might have cried out: damn it! There isn't a clean place!

Men swarmed over the mountains near the Munitions Factory like troops on maneuvers. They covered every inch of ground. All they netted was a pair of lovers, who turned out to be husband and wife out on an excursion who got carried away. Laughter swept the mountain. The luckless man's bare white bottom took precedence over Guo Puyun for the moment. Following the parents' suggestion the school contacted relatives in Sichuan and the northeast. The Chinese Literature faculty placed a missing persons ad in the newspapers. Zhao Kun went to Beidaihe with a few cadres from the factory, because he had once mentioned the sea. They were intent on saving a life. If Guo Puyun had mentioned the Himalayas, they would have gone there. On May 5th his lighter was discovered. That proved the clean place had to be nearby. The area of the search contracted. The game of hide and seek was almost over. The cleverness of the living lagged behind that of the dead. The searchers overlooked the reservoir where fishermen went, but concentrated on abandoned mine shafts in the vicinity. They crawled into these burrows no longer mindful whether they were clean or not. They were seized by the same mad urge that spurs treasure hunters in wrong directions. By then they were sure he was dead. The school and the parents also lost hope of finding him alive.

Their certainty was not surprising. They did not really care. Were they not ashamed? Did they not feel something was wrong? Classes were held as usual. The lecturer talked about an ancient poet. The bulletin board announced the time and place of guitar lessons, and the punishment of a student from the class of '84, who had been caught shop-lifting in the Wanfujing Bookstore and fined a hundred and ninety-three yuan. The old man in the gate house, bawled out a young man for leaving his bicycle in the wrong place. He was being difficult with the penniless student. Someone was practising high jumps on the basket ball court. Another was waving a grey bun and yelling obscenities outside the canteen. The faculty secretary was seen loitering in the corridors, her ear hoops bobbing merrily, her mouth painted like a monkey's ass. On the newly white-washed walls of the latrine, some artist had scratched the undulating outlines of his desire and disquietude. Nothing changed. The earth did not lose its gravity, and went careening through space with billions of living creatures clinging to it.

Meanwhile Guo Puyun had gone to the bottom of

the lake to feed the fish with his flesh.

Something was definitely wrong. The world is wholesome, so is life and people. It is people like Guo Puyun who seek death that have gone wrong. His grotesque body confirmed that fact. The clinic of the munitions factory examined the body with the latest scientific techniques. Their verdict was melancholia had led to a nervous breakdown. He could not voluntarily quit the Party or life. But as a madman his actions were at least acceptable. Their conclusion satisfied the leaders, and the friends of the dead. Now his friends could love him, respect, and pity him. They could quite honourably mourn him, and raise a tablet to his memory. Science is humane.

There were wreaths but no funeral music at the memorial service. It was not that he did not deserve any, it was just that number four warehouse was too far from the broadcasting room and the cables would not extend that far. The service was not held in the auditorium because arrangements were being made for a conference and the chairman's table was already in place. A ceremony of some sort in a tumbled down warehouse was not an insult to the unknowing corpse of Guo Puyun. Mankind had been generous with him. It would suffice.

The school phoned the city newspaper and cancelled the missing persons ad. The response was quite straight forward. They would have to pay half the price anyway for the inconvenience of having to remake the page. The person who went to pay the bill discovered there were dozens of ads waiting for space. If Guo Puyun had not floated to the surface, it might be months before the ad appeared. The messenger pounded his desk when he got back. "The trouble that rascal put us to is sickening!"

The Party Secretary of the United Universities came to the class. He was a large, placid man. It was the first time he had been there, and we did not see him or hear his solemn, reasonable voice again before graduation. It was just as well, for wherever you go you will find him before a microphone going on and on.

"As a member of the Party, what Guo Puyun did was inexcusable. However, there were mitigating circumstances. Still ... we must...."

We listened carefully. We had to. For it was a discourse on philosophy, analysis, and the most important items of our education. We could flunk Chinese Literature, and Logic but not this course.

"This matter has been concluded. The past is the past. We must not be disturbed. Work hard. The midterm exams are almost upon us. I hope you will all have good results. The Party members and key personnel must take the lead, and not let someone's actions disturb their daily tasks. Believe in the organization . This will be handled properly. In fact it has already been settled. I wish to express, on behalf of the Party, a request. I hope...."

He was sincere, kind and thorough. The fat man seemed affable, and a hard worker. But his talk stirred up tension. It was as though the shock he had expressed to the Ministry of Education and other higher ups had been transmitted to us. It was unnecessary. The past was indeed the past. I did not think the class was much affected by the incident. The monitor had just distributed tickets to the movies. I respect the

Party Secretary and agree with everything he said. But I wonder how he would react if his son had committed suicide. Of course everything passes.

Nevertheless there were those in the class that were indignant.

"Damn it where was his compassion!"

"Humanity was on the auction block. Who needs it?"

"It was unfeeling...." A classmate offered me a cigarette, his brows furrowed.

"Why do you suppose Guo Puyun died?"

"Someone killed him." The words just spilled out. He shook his head.

"I suspect he was hooked on drugs."

"Any proof?"

"Just a gut feeling. His eye was giving him a lot of pain. He could have been taking something for it. I hear it's addictive. Once you're hooked...." I was surprised. The classmate who had commented on the Party Secretary's lack of compassion was adding to the muttering that was like a clap of thunder in my ears.

"I think he was homosexual. There was a womanish air about him." Suddenly the air turned putrid.

He left behind things the living could not explain; a fascinating mystery that could be explained anyway one chose. People are always more interested in the dead than the living. To explain the dead they seized upon the most facile explanations, and the honour of the dead was the pawn. The uninformed guessing of the survivors was an insult the dead deserved. They stank. Whether it was the Party Secretary, the student with fancy notions, the rag picker in the street, all smelled alike. For they all came from the same pickling jar. We are all part of a cauldron of porridge. Guo Puyun was a bubble that leaped out of the pot. Even then he had not escaped. For his fellow humans put him back as flavouring.

And it's good porridge, is it not? I suspect my own motives in writing this. Guo Puyun, have you guessed my reasons for writing this? I will tell you, You friend is struggling with the double temptation of reality and imagination. He wanted the ecstasy of artistic creation. But what he got is the bitterness of human suffering. Forgive and pity him.

And give him courage.

Epilogue

I left the plastic flowers my wife bought on the train. I had intended to visit the grave on Qingming Festival but changed my mind. It happened that my wife had gone home to her people. And left alone, I was bored. Suddenly I thought of taking the night train up to Xiaweidian. It was the same night train that Guo Puyun took. Once the idea took hold, I was excited. Every muscle tensed. When I left the house with a parcel of food and the flowers for the grave, I was determined to retrace Guo Puyun's footsteps, to try and discover what he might have felt from my own observations and feelings.

It did not work. For starters, I was almost knocked down by a country bumpkin getting on the bus. I was about to bawl him out. I told myself to calm down; instead I smiled at him. Guo Puyun would have. The man glared at me. Fuck him. What would a man about to die do? Would he beat the fellow to a pulp? Instead I gave him a good shove as I got off. But the mood was shattered. I am just a little man without any of the sad resignation of one about to die. I would go on living as best as I can.

The lights of Yongdingman Station flickered like fox fire. The square was full of people waiting for the train, squatting, sitting, lying on the ground like so many grave mounds in the dark. I bought a ticket and squatted in a corner of the waiting room. I had just lit a cigarette when a claw-like hand appeared before me. A ragged woman pulled a piteous face and begged for money. I had some change in my pocket, but I hesitated. Guo Puyun would have given it all to her. A dying man has no use for money. I gritted my teeth, and gave her five coppers. I was immediately embarrassed. The other people around me had shunned her, and my generosity was a reproach to them. I felt badly about those five coins. I had no pity for the woman. I suspect she was a professional beggar. Guo Puyun would not have thought that way. I was a lesser man than he. But perhaps not. His kindness was destroyed by the world. If he had been stronger, the world might have one more person who rode roughshod through life.

"Get out! Get out!" The attendant drove the woman from the room like a dog. She fled clutching the coins like a dog with a bone. Guo Puyun would have pitied her. I did not.

The crowd surged forward as the train pulled into the station, shouldering luggage and carrying parcels. Everybody was rushing for seats, afraid to be separated from the others but not wanting to be too close.

One fellow who had shoved his way past the ticket collector, fell flat on his face. The crowd split and swirled around the prostrate figure. Guo Puyun would probably have stopped to help him. All I wanted to do was laugh, for the man was groping about blindly for something as though he had lost his dentures. I really did laugh in the end. It was funny.

I will never know why people choose to jam into the carriages at the centre of the train when there is lots of space at the ends. I found a seat in the last carriage, and opened the window. Suburban trains are old and smell of unwashed feet.It seems a dying man's senses should be dulled, unable to pick up on strange odours; blind and deaf to everything around him except the beating of his own heart. The train started. The steam whistle sounded a few sharp blasts. Steam hissed. The outer darkness began to move backwards faster and faster until it blurred. The movement was conducive to melancholy. As there was no one else around, I stretched out across three seats. I shut my eyes and concentrated on people and events that disturbed me. It was a good time to feel sorry for myself. There was a strange satisfaction in it. In my mind I shoved them all between the wheels and the rails, and was gratified by their screeches. It was not the way of a dying man. Guo Puyun would have behaved differently. He would have helped them. I did not have it in me to do that. However, I was happy before I dozed off, when I woke we were one stop from Xiaweidian. The attendant was mopping the floor. When she straightened to wipe her face I could see she was quite pretty. Guo Puyun would not have noticed. Beauty to a dying man is as useless as dog droppings.

But this was a gorgeous heap of dog droppings. My eyes were fixed on her. She was good enough to eat. Guo Puyun would not have cared. If he did he might be still alive. Life is beautiful. As long as there is life even dog droppings can be beautiful. Guo Puyun did not understand that. I do.

Because of these wild thoughts, I left the bunch of plastic flowers behind. I wonder if some other passenger took them. Even now they may be standing in a vase. Let him remember Guo Puyun then. He and the unknown stranger are also brothers. I left the station of Xiaweidian, and followed a path that glowed ghostly white in the dark toward the suspension bridge. Far below was the dried bed of a creek. If I wanted to kill myself this is the place I would do it. But the thought was appalling. The muscles in my calves tightened. I trembled. Something was rocking the bridge. Was it Guo Puyun or the devil? The stars seemed closer than the lights of the village. They glowed like eyes of men or beasts. I muttered to myself, a dying man is afraid of nothing!

Once I reached the branch line of the railway tracks I breathed easier. I picked up stones from the road bed, bounced them in my hand, and threw them away as I went. The only sound was the dull thud of stones hitting the hill side; sounds I made. I could control them. I could control the world. I was not afraid of it, nor was it afraid of me. We need each other. The night and the looming sihouette of the mountain was friendly. The poetic inspiration that touched Guo Puyun touched me. I was happy. I smoked a cigarette on top of Colt Mountain. Perhaps Guo Puyun had done the same. If smoking was banned the world over, the tops of mountains, rugged or flat, warm or cold, ought to be places reserved for smokers.

What a feeling to look down and have the whole world spread out at one's feet! The shriek of the train whistle, and the clatter of its wheels echoed through the valley. There were sounds of life everywhere. Voices, laughter, weeping, scolding, all held in the gentle embrace of the pale moon and the stars. Thoughts and feelings flowed in all directions with infinite freedom. The bitter and the sweet, laughter and tears, fantasy and reality, life and death. Nothing mattered. Did Guo Puyun have the same experience?

I can't understand you.

I groped my way down Colt Mountain to the reservoir. I was still clutching two rocks I had picked up along the railway track. The surface of the water was flat, and the moon of Qingming was reflected in it. The silvery sheen on the water looked infinitely clean. I gazed at it mesmerised. If I did not tear myself away I might walk into it. Guo Puyun did not intend to die. He only wanted to wash himself to make himself more beautiful and perfect. But he was intoxicated by the idea. He fell asleep, and so slipped into the quiet world he dreamed of.

I think I understand you now, my friend.

I threw a stone far into the reservoir. The reflection of the moon disintegrated, the fragments trembled sending off tiny sparks of light. I threw the other stone farther still. The shadow of the moon exploded again. I had destroyed a planet. If I wished I could throw myself into the water too, and the moon, shattered or whole, would be my companion always. Whether I live or die the moon would be there, through eternity. I grasped all that.

I knew when to throw something away; the time, the place, the way and the result. Now all I wanted to throw were two dumb rocks, to play a prank on the moon. I wanted to find a dry spot to sit a while and smoke, and eat the breakfast I brought in my bag. I did not dislike the water that Guo Puyun drowned in. One day I will go in it myself. But I will not go fully clothed. I will wear swim trunks. The water would be the right temperature, so that it would not raise goose flesh on my body, and give me a chill. I need a healthy body to work, to breathe, to eat. I need water to expend my energy, to maintain a clean appearance, for recreation. I will not let it harm me.

In the cold wind of the small hours of Qingming, I waited for the dawn. Never have I waited so impatiently for day-break. When I struck more than ten matches and still could not light a cigarette the disheartening thought occurred to me that trying to analyse Guo Puyun had been a mistake, as grave as stumbling blindly into leftist opportunism. From another vantage, I was a fool. I had wielded a scalpel and all I accomplished was sound and fury, and a semblance of serious thought. The conclusion was glaringly fragile. Suicide is a reality, and not imagination. One who takes his own life is at once the cowardly deserter who flees in the face of the enemy, and the lone warrior who fights on alone. It is impossible to settle this conflict, except by taking on one of the roles. If one is not too subjective one could place the suicide on a pedestal as a reminder of the infinite possibilities of life. ·

I forgot my mission. My clumsy imitation of Guo Puyun was a failure. The thought stuck in my mind, and I could not get rid of it. My breathing quickened. I was excited and happy. My brain was churning. I cared about nothing.

At about three o'clock a fisherman appeared at the edge of the water, wrapped in a raincoat. He spread some plastic sheeting and we sat chatting like long-lost friends.

"Doesn't your wife resent you fishing at night?"

"I'd slap her if she did!"

He was a rough fellow. When he asked my business, I told him quite frankly. He listened without a word, the ends of his whiskers gleaming in the light of his burning cigarette.

"Fool! Should've left him where he was!"

"Have pity. He was a good man."

"I've never met a good man in my life!"

He was world-weary. Finally I curled up and went to sleep. When I woke the sun had risen. The reservoir glowed red, and the disk of the sun swam in its green depths. The fisherman stood legs apart at the water's edge, in the brilliant light, emptying his bladder into the waters that buried Guo Puyun. He tossed off a raucous snatch of song as though it was not urine but the sticky stuff of life that he poured in the lake.

I left the contented fisherman. Guo Puyun's grave lay in the sunlight. I did not want to think anymore, nor did I have any deep thoughts for the dead. I was hungry, and tired. My own physical needs changed my outlook. I stayed only five minutes. I looked back at the shabby stone, that mark of sadness. How would I write about this journey to Wu Yan? The letter about this pilgrimage would be no different from the thousands of lying letters that flew across the ocean everyday. But it would be a white lie.

I stopped in the only presentable restaurant at Xiaweidian and downed a few beers. It was amazing that one could find good beer in such a place. A sad looking young miner sat across from me. I could have hugged him. I love you, you bastard. Drink up!

They started getting busy outside in the sunlight.

伏曦伏曦

刘 恒

熊猫丛书

*

中国文学出版社出版

（中国北京百万庄路 24 号）

中国国际图书贸易总公司发行

（中国北京车公庄西路 21 号）

北京邮政信箱第 399 号　　邮政编码 100044

1991 第 1 版（英）

1994 第 2 次印刷

ISBN 7-5071-0072-3/I. 66（外）

01500

10 — E — 2516P